ROYALLY ARRANGED

ALSO BY NORA FLITE

Bad Boy Royals

Royally Bad
Royally Ruined
Royally Arranged

Big City Billionaires

Billion Dollar Bad Boy

Other Books

Never Kiss a Bad Boy
The Bad Boy Arrangement
My Secret Master
Last of the Bad Boys

NORA FLITE

Montlake
Romance

Published by Montlake Romance, Seattle

www.apub.com

Amazon, the Amazon logo, and Montlake Romance are trademarks of Amazon.com, Inc., or its affiliates.

ISBN-13: 9781503904620
ISBN-10: 1503904628

Cover design by Tammy Seidick

Cover photo credit: Wander Aguiar Photography

Printed in the United States of America

This story is for the middle children.

All the second bests. Never first at anything, never last. Never indulged for being the baby or truly trusted as the oldest.

Only you will understand the pain that comes with this role. It's not so much of a burden that it feels worth discussing at length. Even so, it digs at us from the day our little siblings come into the world. Because just as we looked up to our elders, they do the same, skipping us entirely in the process. And we can tell ourselves it's all right. It never mattered.

But it does.

There's a reason they named a syndrome after us.

While we grimace and grow sick of being stuck in the center of every family photo, every family road trip, think of this comfort unique to our position— something that being in the middle brings that first and last have no claim over: there is always a loving heart on either side of us.

- CHAPTER ONE -

NOVA

Six months ago I met a beautiful man who said ugly things.

Not to me, of course. Hawthorne Badd didn't speak a single word to me for the entire hour I sat across from him. But to others there, he was quick to let a sarcastic remark bleed from his tongue at every opportunity. He was especially crisp toward my father.

Secretly I loved that.

I'd never liked the way Dad did things. I'd also never say that to his face; I was a good daughter where it counted. I bowed my head and went wherever I was told to go. But I still hated it.

My father's personal life had long ago mixed with his corrupt business, and there was no way to pull the two apart. It was like mangling a wad of gum into your scalp and then trying to clean every individual strand of hair. He was tangled in sin, and we, as his children, were tangled up, too.

Not that my brothers cared. Both Larchmont and Richard had been eager to come to this meeting between our family and the Badds. They were reveling in having the upper hand, an advantage brought on by gruesome violence and the fear of more to come.

I was different. I'd hoped to go on forever keeping my distance. Neither Mom nor Dad had asked me to dirty my hands. Not yet. The reality is that you can't separate yourself from family just by wishing. And you definitely can't walk away once blood has been spilled.

So I sat at the table in the middle of the Badd family's ballroom, breaking bread with our enemies and waiting for Maverick—the patriarch—and his two other sons to show up. We'd been sitting in near silence for fifteen minutes already.

Like the ballroom we were in, their whole estate was gorgeous. I was especially jealous of all the land they had. My parents were more interested in the clean lines of modern architecture than in greenery and dirt. I'd grown up crawling across cement and marble. I'd wandered nervously down dark halls past the array of warped statues that my mother fancied. They'd watched me with their dead eyes, their arms wound tight over their chests, unable to hold or hug or touch.

Maybe that was why Mom liked them so much.

My attention kept zipping to the door, to the security guards—theirs and ours. If I wasn't so afraid of the consequences I could walk out of here, get in my car, and be back in Boston within the hour. Even accounting for the time needed to get some Dunkin' coffee, I'd be snuggled in my bed with a sketch pad before dinner. It'd be heaven.

"What's wrong?" a feathery voice asked in my right ear. Darla, my younger sister.

"I don't want to be here," I mumbled. I wanted nothing to do with any of this. And I was ignorant enough to think that if I just sat there and stared at my chocolate strawberries, I could walk away from this meeting unchanged.

Then he entered the room.

He was shorter than his father and his older brother, Costello, who had entered with him. But somehow he defied reality, his presence looming, filling every crack in the ballroom. Thorne wore long sleeves and a high-necked shirt the color of fresh wheat, things that only hinted at the shape of his body. But I could tell his shoulders were broad, his torso lean and powerful.

Maverick scanned the room with his piercingly icy eyes. Thorne's were starkly different. They were like those of his mother—who hadn't stopped watching us from the head of the table—black as a galaxy. He moved with ease, comfortable in a roomful of people who would have loved to see him dead. This was a battlefield seconds before someone began the charge, and he didn't care.

His strong chin cut the air, his gaze sweeping across the table, ultimately falling on me. I wasn't ready for that. I don't think anybody could be. It was like jumping into a swirling storm when you'd been promised a sunny day.

Instantly I ducked my head. In my ears I heard Darla's muffled giggle, then the warm, heart-pulling sound of Thorne's chuckle. I glanced up in time to see him whisper something to Costello as they sat down. He didn't look at me again after that.

I prayed he would, but . . . it never happened. It drove me mad.

I couldn't explain what had created such a yearning inside me. Why was I so focused on getting this man to notice me? Maybe it was because I'd heard so much about him. It was no secret under my roof that my family was obsessed with his. I'd seen photos and videos and even had intel recited to me about the Badds.

I'd always thought Thorne was interesting. Unquestionably handsome, no doubt. But a picture can't compare to flesh and blood. Hearing his gritty, low voice as it purred casual insults that were hard to counter . . . seeing him relax in his seat and swirl his glass and not care at all about what his family *or* mine thought of his behavior . . .

It was fascinating.

But Thorne Badd didn't find me nearly as interesting. Through all the back-and-forth discussion between his family and mine, he acted like I didn't exist. And I began to feel like I didn't. Selfishly, I wished that something would happen. Something that would make him look at me, *see me.*

My father was speaking—things were heating up. I saw how Costello hunkered in place, his frown severe. His knitted eyebrows pulled the long scar across his face tighter. "We're not at war," Dad said carefully. "Because if we were, none of you would be here. Not one." He lifted his glass. "You're all part of a grand family . . . a grander heritage. Though it's funny you'd choose a name like *the Badds.*" He winked. "What was wrong with Fredricson?"

A ripple moved through the other side of the table. Thorne didn't flinch, but he did glance at Maverick. This was a bomb my father had been waiting to drop: that we knew exactly who the Badds used to be before Maverick changed his last name.

People didn't change their surnames without good reason when it gave them access to the advantages of a royal lineage. I knew the reason. But did they know why we knew? Covertly I watched Thorne—he was facing away, showing me his sharp profile. He was gorgeous from every angle.

With a soft sigh, my father said, "We're a simple family that profits greatly from all of you remembering your place." His dimples deepened with his wide smile. "This peace was almost broken by one man's simple mistake."

He was talking about my brother Darien. He was the reason we were all here.

My dad kept talking. "In the future there will be *no more* mistakes of such magnitude. If none of you chase the power your father abandoned . . . we'll all live long, *happy* lives."

He was promising them a truce. I was sure that deep down he didn't mean it; my father had always spoken out of one side of his mouth while lying out of the other. I didn't get the feeling that any of these people believed him. But I wasn't focusing. I was distracted beyond reason in the middle of this political tension. All I wanted was to catch *his* eye one more time. I had no clue how to make it happen.

Darla was the one who made guys' heads spin. She fought off their advances with a tilted smile and perfectly timed hair flips. I didn't have her skills—I was too shy, too afraid of making some sort of mistake. The boys I'd grown up with wanted their girls to be bold.

I was not bold.

I had never been bold.

But I wished I could be. Because I had the sense that my whole world would open up if I could be less afraid. People would look at me and *see* me. I'd be capable of slouching as comfortably in my own skin as Hawthorne was. And men like him wouldn't forget I was sitting within arm's length.

I wanted that so much that my very being ached like a pulled muscle. So I sat there and silently made my pathetic wish. I couldn't have known then that I was curling a finger on the proverbial monkey's paw. My parents had told me many times that for every gain there must be a sacrifice. Nothing in life comes free. Not money, not power, and certainly not love.

I assumed that, to become who I wanted to be, I'd have to suffer.

I didn't know I'd have to die as well.

- CHAPTER TWO -

HAWTHORNE

Was it wrong to mourn the death of a strip club?

Staring at the yellow tape crisscrossing the black, locked door of the building, I experienced mixed emotions. It was too easy to imagine the neon sign, shaped like a girl in a martini glass, never lighting up again.

No more dancers.

No more late-night rounds of tequila.

No more girls trying to charm me so they could get away with skipping stage sets or being late.

For the past eight years, I'd helped run the Dirty Dolls. I've never been known as the responsible one in my family, so I should have been relieved that the chore was off my shoulders.

I wasn't.

Don't get all psychoanalytical, I quickly told myself. *I'm only bummed because I hoped to kill a few more years stretched out on that VIP couch.*

Thanks to Darien Valentine, it wasn't going to happen. Seven months ago I'd nearly lost more than a strip club because of that psycho. I'd thought he was just another suit-wearing asshole getting handsy with whatever pair of legs got too close.

I couldn't have guessed he was dangerous . . . or that he'd hurt Gina. She'd been dancing at the Dirty Dolls long enough for it to be her career. People asked for her because she wielded a healthy pair of tits. But me? I'd loved her no-nonsense attitude. She didn't take shit from anyone.

Unfortunately, that included our lawyers.

My father had confided to me weeks ago that the club would be running once we settled out of court with Gina. Except she was dragging her feet, asking for more security, more rules, more everything. And she was right. If we'd done our jobs she wouldn't have gotten hurt.

And *I* wouldn't be missing my cotton-candy-and-cocoa-butter-smelling VIP couch.

Sighing, I adjusted my jacket and turned away from the building. Without the Dirty Dolls, I didn't know how to spend my days and nights. I didn't even have my siblings around to mess with. Each of them was busy with their own shit.

Life was quiet.

Life was . . . boring.

After climbing into my Escalade, I floored it down the street. A ribbon of blue peeked above, sometimes hidden by the tall buildings. The humidity was oppressive, and it had only just rolled over into June. *Another reason I miss the club,* I mused bitterly. *The low lights and air-conditioning were hard to beat.* I'd spent many a summer wasting away in glorious slothfulness on my beloved couch.

Determined to break free of my poor mood, I sped up until I exited onto the highway. Here I could drive faster than the tight city streets allowed. But my freedom was short; without any traffic, it didn't take long to make it into Newport, where my family's home was.

Gliding up to the huge twisted-metal gates, I tapped a button near my steering wheel. The gates split apart like a giant raven's wings. The sun lit up the slate driveway that curved down toward the sprawling estate.

When I was small, I used to run around the corridors of our mansion with wild abandon. It drove my father into a furious state. But I didn't care—I was too busy searching for the inevitable doorway to some secret world. A place full of magic and adventure. Somewhere I could feel like I had a purpose.

I never found it.

Home sweet home. Red lights blinked at me from different positions in the yard. You see, Darien Valentine had been just the tip of all the drama this past year. His whole family was a bunch of psychos who, for reasons I'm still not sure of, would prefer me and the rest of the Badds buried in the cold ground.

My father had ultimately arranged a sit-down with their whole crew. I'd been there, too—we were all expected to attend. It had been strange to eat finger sandwiches with the people who'd caused everyone so much damn trouble.

Kurtis Valentine—the dad of the filthy bunch—had offered us a truce that felt like a warning. Like he knew everything about all of us, about my father and his history, and he'd be more than pleased to use it against us if he could.

But here we were now, all boring bliss and nothing gained but security cameras. Oh, and guard dogs. Lots of those. Francesca, my little sister, loathed them. She was sure the German shepherds would eat her little terrier, Mic.

It didn't help that I'd made one . . . or five . . . jokes about it. It was too easy to ruffle her feathers. I hadn't meant to drive her away on some "vacation" to Miami. Fran hadn't *said* it was my fault, but I knew.

After parking my car in the massive garage, I stepped out and scanned the vehicles. We owned everything from yellow Mustangs to violet-and-gold motorcycles. That wasn't my sort of thing. Kain—Fran's twin brother—was Mr. Bad Boy Extreme. I preferred walls of metal surrounding me as I floored it at ninety-five miles an hour. Most noninsane people would agree with me.

I considered the shiny cars. *Maybe I'll drive a different one tomorrow.* It would be a change in my routine. A minor change, but these days I'd take what I could get.

Entering the mudroom attached to the garage, I draped my thin jacket over a brass hook on the wall. "I'm home," I said, wending my way toward the kitchen. The second I passed through the front room with its curving staircases, a young woman in a dark gray dress and crisp apron spotted me. Sucey was one of our many maids. "Sir," she said, bobbing her head so her chin-length red hair swayed.

"You know I hate when you call me that." Sighing, I scratched at the back of my neck. "Is anyone else home?"

She pointed upward. "Lulabelle is in her room." Her finger changed direction. "Your father is in his study. Mrs. Badd was with him, last I saw." Without turning she gestured over her shoulder to the back of the mansion. "And your mother's guests are eating in the garden."

Mom had hated how empty our house was. She'd gone and invited several relatives to stay with us. I didn't know most of these random aunts, uncles, and cousins who'd come to live with us for the summer. I didn't care to. But it was nice for Mom; she had people to entertain. I liked seeing her happy.

"Thanks," I said, starting to walk down the hallway toward the parlor.

"Of course, sir," Sucey said, ignoring my request that she *not* call me that.

My shoes glided over the maroon rug. As loud as I tended to speak, I naturally walked with a silent ease. I'd startled many enemies—and delighted many women—when I'd appeared behind them without notice. I'd been told it was a skill people were jealous of.

Would they be so envious if they knew I'd gained it by spending my childhood tiptoeing around my father?

Maverick Badd had always been a pillar of intense anger and not much else. You could probably set him in front of a movie about a dozen cute puppies dying in a plane crash and he still wouldn't shed a tear.

That was why, when I walked into his study and saw him hunched forward in his wing-backed chair, I instantly knew something was wrong. His head was low enough that I could see the faint thinning of his dark hair on his scalp. His wide legs looked unstable, as if he couldn't have stood up if he tried.

In his fingers he clutched his phone. He rubbed the edge of it over and over. The blue-blooded bastard who'd scowled at me since I'd been able to form memories—judging me, berating me to be a better man—now looked like a strong wind could knock him over. He'd never seemed old, but here, in the orange glow of the lamps studding the wide room, Maverick was frail beyond his years.

What the hell had happened?

I started forward, my shoes brushing over the expensive carpet. My approach stirred him; his blue eyes locked on me, the edges red. Had he been crying? That set my mind spinning.

My father scanned my face; he saw my open concern. Reaching up, he drew a wide palm over his features. It reset him somewhat, enough that when he looked at me again, I didn't think he was on the verge of falling apart. "Thorne," he said, tucking his phone away. "Come in. We need to talk."

"What is it?" I asked, letting a nervous laugh break free. "You look like someone just died."

He didn't correct me.

"Shit," I whispered.

My father sighed. "I received a phone call an hour ago."

He's been sitting here like this for an hour?

His eyes drifted away, then back to me. Some of the fierceness I knew too well was back in his stare. "The call was about Torino."

It was a name I'd heard so rarely I could count the times on one hand. Torino was the country my father had grown up in. The place he would have ruled as king—and my brothers and I as princes—if he hadn't abandoned the crown and come to the States before any of us were even born.

I'd never been to Torino. I knew very little about the place. Dad spoke grandly of our heritage, but when it came down to the details, he seemed fine with leaving it all in the past.

"Okay," I said, sitting on the chaise across from him. "You have my full attention."

His fingers twitched, like he was imagining he was still holding his phone. "I don't know how much this will mean to you, Hawthorne. Even your mother doesn't seem to know how to react to this news." He studied the mantel over the cold fireplace. I wondered what he was seeing. "I'll skip to the important bit," he said, not meeting my curious eyes. "The king of Torino has passed away. My brother is dead." I didn't know how much that should mean to me, either. I'd never met my uncle. Never seen a photo of him. If I was wondering anything, it was how someone had known how to reach Maverick from across the ocean. Was I wrong, was he still in touch with his home country?

Maverick's eyes darted to me. I swear he was reading my mind. "I haven't talked to anyone from Torino since the day I boarded that plane and left. One of my men has been keeping tabs online for any mention of the place. When news broke about my brother's death . . . he called me."

Agitation controlled my limbs. I rubbed the velvety chaise, then, once I noticed I was doing it, forced myself to hold still. "I'm sorry." I didn't know what else to say. How did I even try to comfort my father over this?

Air slid loudly through his nose. "I'm flying out to attend the funeral. I want you to come with me."

"Me?" I asked, startled. "Why?"

Grunting, he pushed himself to his feet; I watched him circle around to stand over me. The weakness was gone. *This* was the lion of a father I'd grown up with. "Because I said so."

I crinkled my nose. "I feel like I'd be your last choice. Did you already ask Kain, or Frannie? Is everyone you'd rather take too busy to drop their lives and go with you?"

He narrowed his eyes. "Are you going to come or do you have something more important to attend to?"

Of course he knew I had nothing going on. Biting back a sarcastic response, I caught motion from the corner of my eye. My mother was hovering in the doorway. She was wearing a flowing dress crafted from lilac silk, and her expression was built from sorrow. She didn't need to speak for me to know her thoughts; I'd always been close with her. *She wants me to go with him.*

"All right," I sighed, shrugging sharply. "When do we fly out?"

Satisfied—and like he'd expected to win this debate—he slid his phone into the open once more. "Pack your things right now. We're leaving in the morning."

- CHAPTER THREE -

HAWTHORNE

Dad had already reserved the seats. He'd been positive I'd go with him; I should have been more sour about that. It was hard to be pissed off, though, when I came face-to-face with my mother the next day. The cool blue of the morning turned her tan skin lifeless. Disturbingly, she reminded me of why I was flying to Torino. "Be patient with him," she said, pulling me into a hug. Her nose rubbed in my hair the way it always did when she held me close. "He's lost his brother, Thorne."

"A brother he hasn't seen since before he met you."

Her arms tightened around me. "Would you feel nothing if one of your siblings died?"

I started to answer. Then I breathed out, returning her hug. "You don't have to convince me, I'm going with him. Even if it's just to be the shoulder he needs to rub his tears and snot into." She pulled away, trying to whack me in the arm, but I just hugged her again so she couldn't. "Relax, Ma. It'll be fine. Are you sure you don't want to come along?"

She chanced a look over her shoulder at the car, where my father and our driver were waiting for me. "Maverick wants me to continue to entertain my family. We were hoping to strengthen our connections with them. We really need their help, especially with all the extra security we've had to hire, and, oh, don't get me started on how many of our business partners have abandoned us to go work with the Valentines!"

It made sense. We'd lost most of our hold over this city. New faces were rolling into our territory every day. Our enemies—even the smaller ones—were happy to take advantage of our weak spots. If my mother's father, the head of the Cassava family, could help us out, it would be a great relief. Never let anyone tell you it doesn't pay to marry into the local Mafia.

I lifted my suitcase. "I'll see you soon."

"Take lots of photos," she said, following me out the door.

"Aren't you going to say bye to Dad?"

"I already did. If I do it again, I'll just start bawling." She clutched her hands to her bosom. "Remember the pictures. And no getting into trouble, okay?"

"Mom—"

"Promise me!"

Laughing, I tossed my bags into the trunk of the parked black Mercedes. "I promise I won't get into any trouble that isn't worth it."

With my phone loaded with music, I was able to relax through the first hour of the flight. Dad sat next to me in relative silence. He flipped through the movie screen on his chair, never settling on any one video. He left each half-finished.

We should talk. It was obvious and that made it painful. I'd never talked for long stretches with Maverick, not unless it was about money. Business talk. Nothing deeper. *What if he gives me the cold shoulder when I try to make conversation?* But even as I wondered this, I was already sliding my earbuds aside.

We were as alone as possible in first class. The white noise of the engines and air filling the cabin ensured us privacy. Shifting, I stretched a bit, doing my best with my body language to tell him, *If you want to talk, now is the time.* I yawned once—twice. He didn't bite.

Drumming my fingers on my thighs, I took a long breath to steady myself. *Just ask him!* I glanced askew; he met my gaze. "Uh, hey," I said. "I'll just come right out and say it. Are you all right?"

His thick eyebrows inched lower. "I'm fine."

"Sure. But, well, come on." Laughing uneasily, I sat deeper in my chair. The ceiling was suddenly very interesting. "Don't make this hard for me."

"You think this is hard *for you?*" he whispered.

Cold, then heat, slid up my spine. I knew that tone the way I knew the fit of an old pair of jeans. He'd done a spectacular job searing fear into my neurons since before I could walk. As much as I didn't want to feel nervous, as much as I mentally knew I was a full-grown man and not a child he could bully, there was an automatic response in my psyche I could never shake.

"Listen," I said warily.

Maverick hesitated, purple tinting around his eyes, like the blood vessels there were doing all they could to keep his anger at bay. Amazingly, he deflated back into his seat. It was so fast I felt whiplash. "This isn't easy. I'm still trying to figure out how to handle this. But you sitting there, pretending you want to help, isn't going to fix my mood. All right?"

My nod was curt. "Loud and clear."

We sat in a long, suffocating quiet. The pressure in my skull was immense; I knew it wasn't just from being thousands of feet in the air. This thick, suffering silence was familiar for us both. I'd been ridiculous to think I could talk to him about his feelings.

I heard his seat belt's buckle clink. He was turning toward me, and with the window outside showing an endless blue world, his irises leached the color from the sky. "I do have something I want to talk about."

My pulse climbed. "Okay. I'm all ears."

"Hester and I didn't part on good terms."

The laughter that exploded from me was born from startled relief. I'd predicted something worse; it was good to be wrong. "I could have guessed that. You've never mentioned his name before."

He faltered, like he was checking his own memory. "No. I guess I never told you."

Never told YOU. As in he'd told someone else, and forgotten it wasn't me. *Probably Costello, then.* He'd been our father's perfect pet for a very long time. After their relationship had soured, Maverick hadn't played favorites any longer. We were all equal fuckups.

"You've never explained *why* you left Torino. Just that it wasn't safe there for you any longer."

Sinking deeper into the airline seat, my father shut his eyes. I noticed all the fine lines that crept toward his temples. "I was twenty when the king—when my father fell ill. As the oldest, everyone expected me to be crowned once he passed. It was how it was done."

How it would be done if we all lived there, I thought. I imagined my older brother; he was stiff, humorless, and often frightening. He'd have made a perfect king. Even Kain, my younger brother, had a sort of air to him that felt regal. Either of them would have been fit to rule. Far better than I could have hoped to be—not that I'd have ever wanted such a job on my shoulders.

Maverick sighed through tight lips. "Hester came to me in private. He'd always had a jealous streak, but I didn't expect him to bluntly lay out his threat. The boy I'd taught marksmanship, or slipped away with to hunt deer in the forest . . . That same boy told me what he would do if I dared to accept my rightful claim to the throne. Can you guess?"

I'd been holding my breath; I let it out, clearing my throat. "Let him have the crown, or he'd kill you."

My father's chuckle held no joy. "That's right."

"I know this story ends with you running off to cozy little Rhode Island, meeting Mom, making a bunch of babies, and all that jazz . . . but I have to know. Why didn't you stand up to your brother?" I'd never known my father to back down from a bully.

He looked at me with such disdain that I leaned backward. "His threat was treason, Thorne. If I'd told anyone, they'd have killed him. How could I choose the crown over my own kin?"

Greed makes people do all sorts of awful things. But I didn't say it.

"What happened between my brother and me," he said, "it's not something siblings should ever suffer. Family is worth more than wealth or power." After a moment he said very softly, "I never wanted him to die. But now it's happened anyway, and I don't have a damn idea how."

"Your inside man, he has no details?"

He shook his head. "None." Hesitating, he fixed me with a hard look. "Thorne, I have no clue what we're about to walk into. It's been almost forty years since I was last in Torino. My country and its people will be different. I don't know who will remember me—or if I should want them to. You have to be cautious."

My smile tugged upward at an angle. "Come on, I'm always careful."

He looked out the small window at the empty sky and didn't reply.

As we descended the escalator toward the luggage area, I spotted a man holding a sign with the name **MAVERICK B** on it. My father waved, then the mustached stranger helped us gather our things and cart them into the trunk of a massive black town car.

When we were inside, the doors slamming shut, I said under my breath, "Are we not going by *either* of our surnames here?"

His jaw tensed. "Don't be stupid, son. I'm not announcing to the world that we're here. Not until I know more about the situation."

"Okay, and who's going to give us all the details?"

He pulled out his phone and started to type. "An old friend. Hopefully they're still a friend, anyway. It's possible he won't even take the message I sent ahead of us and want to meet me. Or he will, and he'll plan an ambush."

Lolling my head back, I spread my knees. "I sure feel comfortable about all our weapons being dismantled in cases in the trunk right now."

"Relax. Rush and Donnie are armed and waiting at our hotel."

That made my head snap forward. "They're here? Are you planning to keep all the details of our little trip to yourself?"

"It wasn't an important detail."

"I want my gun back in my hands as soon as we get to our rooms."

He turned off his phone. "Fine. Anything else?"

"If you're taking requests, I'd also like a stiff drink after that flight."

"It's nine in the morning, Thorne."

"Sure, *here*. I'm still on East Coast time."

"Is everything a damn joke to you?" he growled, facing me in the suddenly small car.

Our driver had closed the partition between him and us. I glanced at it, then back to my dad. "I'm just trying to ease the tension."

"Maybe you should try to take this more seriously instead." Shoving his phone into his pants, he draped a thick arm over the back of the seat next to him. "After everything that went down last winter with the Valentines, I was starting to think you could be trusted with more responsibility. You're proving me wrong with your little games."

"Yeah?" I laughed. "It's like you forgot you were the one who asked me to come on this trip. I never asked to be a part of your reunion."

The car slowed to a halt, we'd arrived at the hotel. "You forget your place, son."

"My place is back home with two girls in my lap and some whiskey in my stomach." I shoved my way out of the car, slamming the door behind me. Why the hell had I agreed to torture myself by spending so much time alone with my dad? In my sympathy over his loss of his brother, I'd forgotten how good he was at getting under my skin.

Seconds after we checked into the Rizenburgh, Donnie—our longest-employed bodyguard—hustled to my father's side. "Upstairs," he whispered, handing us a key card. "He's waiting for you in my room."

"He?" Maverick asked. "You don't mean he came alone?"

Donnie shrugged. "I was surprised, too. He said he didn't need anyone to protect him from you, though."

A rare smile spread on my dad's lips. "Of course he said that. Crazy asshole." Glancing at me, he motioned to follow him to the elevator. Quick enough, the doors parted back open with a crystal clear ring of a bell, depositing us on the fourth floor.

The hallway was long, the rugs green and yellow, the doors solid metal. The Rizenburgh Hotel was a mix of contemporary and old school, like they'd made upgrades on top of the fading pieces but never actually replaced them. New polish was apparently good enough.

I could see, at the end of the hall, a door with two men standing outside. Both watched us approach. I knew these men—they were all ours. Dad had brought plenty of backup. Maybe too much, if there was only one man inside the room waiting for us.

Using Donnie's card, my father opened the door. It was a small room—harder to hide people. A smart precaution. Big windows faced the city of Maurine below, the sun turning all the wallpaper a washed-out white.

Standing beside the queen bed, making it look like a twin in comparison, was a huge man with a reddish beard. It faded into hair darker by a shade or two, the thick pieces cropped tight by his ears.

He was dressed in tan pants, heavy boots, and a dark blue shirt with the top three buttons clasped shut. It covered his arms, straining to hold his muscles in. He came close, sizing me up. "I'll be damned. He looks just like you, Mav."

I knotted my eyebrows. "Usually people say compliments when they first meet. Helps them get along."

He stared, then his huge chest swelled as he laughed. "No doubt about it, same sharp tongue as you, too." He thrust his hand at me. "I'm Glen Finbar, head of the royal guard. Your dad and I grew up together."

Maverick leaned out into the hall, said something to the men, then shut us inside. "It's good to see you, Glen."

He faced my father, his green eyes flashing. "Damn near forty years, Mav. I didn't know if you were dead or if you'd abandoned the throne like Hester claimed. You know how hard it was guarding over him, staring at the back of his vulnerable neck, wondering every day if he'd killed you and—"

"No," Maverick said, cutting him off. "He never harmed a hair on my head. I won't have his memory tarnished."

It was a chore not to speak up. Was my father still covering for Hester, even when it no longer mattered? Glen had a doubtful squint crunching his forehead into deep grooves. He sighed, looking around at the men in the hotel suite. "We'll need to prepare an entourage. The people closest to the former king and current queen will want to be informed that Maverick Fredricson has returned."

"I don't want everyone to know," my father said. "Not yet."

Glen lifted an eyebrow. "Fine. But those involved with the funeral will need this info. Otherwise you won't be allowed in to see his body."

His body. That phrase made me swallow. I saw my father tense, his fingers curling at his hips. Maverick gathered himself, standing to his full height. "How did he die?"

"Of course," Glen mumbled, "you wouldn't know. He grew ill around three years ago. But last year was when his health rapidly declined."

"He was only fifty-six," my father said solemnly.

Glen tossed a fleeting look at me. "Youth doesn't protect us from death. Hester had bone cancer. It's amazing he made it this long."

"He was a fighter," Maverick said. He lifted his chin high, his tone clean and clear, and I recognized it as his way of signaling that the subject was changed. "Give me a rundown of the country on the whole. Maurine looked busy when we arrived, how are the farther, more rural areas?"

"It's not good," Glen said flatly. "Hester and Austere have been bleeding Torino dry between high taxes and personal loans. The farmers are furious, food is far too expensive to grow, and almost no one can afford to purchase it."

They talked with their heads together. If forty years had passed, it wasn't obvious. These two conversed as comfortably as any friends. The longer they spoke intensely about Torino and the pieces of it I didn't know, the more I sensed that I didn't belong here. They weren't including me because I had nothing to contribute.

"If you're going to discuss corn and cows," I said, backing toward the door, "I think I'll get the CliffsNotes later."

Glen folded his arms over his massive chest. "Not interested in the place your ancestors lived and breathed?"

My father's scowl pulled his jaw tight. "It's fine. Hawthorne was never one for political lessons. Or lessons of any kind, honestly."

His dig pricked at my pride. But I'd been down this road over and over before. Dad didn't care if I learned anything about Torino; he just wanted to make me listen to him talk. That was his way. He needed to be the voice of knowledge . . . of authority. That was how we'd spent my youth: him dictating, and me enduring. As a child I'd been perfect at zipping my mouth and tuning in to his every syllable. I was convinced that if I gave him the ear he wanted, he would reward me with love.

Back then, I was too naive to know the most important lesson he'd eventually teach me.

How replaceable I was.

- CHAPTER FOUR -

HAWTHORNE

Everything smelled like clean salt.

Torino was a very beautiful coastal country. Our hotel was situated in the center of the main city, and still it didn't take much walking before I saw the white tips of boats on the horizon. When I followed the natural slope of the streets toward the water, I turned onto an area that was open enough for me to glimpse the castle in the distance.

It spiraled up toward the clouds like it had every right to be part of the sky. The tiles were a rich blue, the stone polished and white. *That's where Dad grew up. Where I would have, too, if he'd stayed here.* Picturing myself running around the city . . . swimming in the sparkling ocean below the statues carved into the cliffside . . . it was appealing. Who wouldn't want to grow up in such a place?

As lovely as it all was, the people didn't seem so happy.

Many grim faces eyed me as I walked down the streets. I was astounded by the amount of homeless people crouched in the shadows of buildings. There were whispers about whether the country would get better or worse with the king dead.

"Not like the queen will do anything," a wrinkled man confided to another as they leaned on a stone wall I was following. "Haven't even seen her face in a year."

I wanted to listen more, but I couldn't do it without being obvious. *If I find a spot to sit by a busy corner, I'll overhear things for sure.* Plus I was getting hungry after exploring for so long, the day was getting away from me. And everything around here smelled amazing.

The predominant language of Torino was English; however, I caught a bit of French here and there. The first café I spotted was called Gull's Boulangerie. This whole area was saturated by a Parisian feel. It made me like it even more.

"Help! Stop him! Someone, stop him!"

The beat of my heart went erratic. Twisting, I watched as an older lady pointed after a man who was rushing away in broad daylight. He had a very purple purse clutched in his grip. "Help!" she screamed again. "Thief!"

Say what you will about my lax attitude; I'd never stand idly by while someone literally screamed for help in my face. My shoes pounded on the cobblestones as I closed in on the purse snatcher. I didn't see the young woman who caught up with him first, not until she slammed into his shoulder, sending him sprawling to the ground. She straddled his back, one hand in his hair, the other squeezing at the wrist that clutched the stolen purse.

Her shoulder-length hair covered her face as she leaned in to brace herself and hold the man down. It created a cinnamon curtain, allowing only a hint of her soft features. Through her creamy-looking tight blouse, I could see lean muscles in her arms flexing. Her breasts swelled up and down with her rapid breathing. Her poise screamed *Don't mess with me.*

I can't lie. It was crazy sexy.

"Police!" she shouted, whiskey-colored eyes darting around at the crowd. "Get the police!"

Everyone acted at once. It shook me out of my daze; jumping forward, I helped grapple with the struggling man just as two officers in dark gray uniforms stormed onto the scene. "What happened here?" The one who asked was portly, too much stubble frosting his flabby neck.

The young woman stepped away, letting the police take over. "He stole her purse," she said, pointing at the older lady, who had finally caught up to us. Breathing heavily, the other woman nodded to the cops.

Together the police scooped the man up. I folded my arms, amazed at how quickly it was all resolved. But then, my attention was really on the woman who'd tackled the thief in the first place. Now that we were standing, I could see that she was shorter than I—and shorter than the other men who'd stood around and done nothing while someone yelled for help.

She faced me. It made me stand more upright, like my heart had pumped a wave of air that inflated my limbs. I already liked her for her bravery, but I was startled by her simple, clean prettiness. Not a sexpot, and not girly pink, but with a comfortable-in-her-own-skin kind of style.

I was liking Torino better by the second.

"Ah," she hissed, bending down to inspect the scrape on her left leg.

"Here," I said, helping her sit in a chair at one of the Gull's outdoor tables. "I'll be right back. Get a coffee or an espresso or whatever you like."

She started to argue; I was already hurrying across the street. I'd noticed the small chemist's shop earlier. It was, as I'd hoped, much like a pharmacy in the States. I worked quickly to buy what I needed, grateful that the store took my credit card. I'd traveled abroad before, but I was usually more prepared—I'd have grabbed some local currency from the hotel if I hadn't been so eager to get away from my dad.

The woman watched me as I jogged back to where she was sitting. "Hi again," I chuckled. I'd only bought one thing; I pulled it from my back pocket. Peeling off the plastic backing, I pressed the adhesive bandage onto her knee. My fingertips connected with her skin; it was smooth as buttercream. Touching her sent a spark down to my lower belly.

Blinking, she wiggled her leg and bent to look closer. "Is that the Hulk?"

I grinned wide. "One superhero deserves another."

She was fixated on the blue-and-green bandage. But it was like she wasn't really seeing it. It went on like that for a bit: her staring quietly, me kneeling by her shoes. I didn't mind being so close to her. Finally her pink lips curled into a soft smile. "Thank you."

"It's nothing."

"You're wrong," she whispered, meeting my eyes. I froze under her seriousness. "You helped me when you didn't have to. That's no small thing."

Tiny piano keys tapped one by one through my chest. I knew this tune—I was no stranger to desire. Standing, I dusted my jeans off. "I'm Thorne, by the way."

"Nova," she said, watching me like she was paranoid about something.

I flashed my most winning smile. "Nova. Nice name." I scanned the bare table. "You didn't get that coffee, huh?"

She was still studying me, as if I were the most interesting creature on the planet. Then she crossed her legs, a hint of her smile coming back to roost. "You were so quick I had no time."

"Guess we'll have to fix that."

"Guess we will." She laughed without a flicker of self-consciousness. "After all that action, I could use a stiffer drink."

"I think they only serve coffee and tea here," I said, pointing at the chalkboard sign by the door. "Know a good place with some hard alcohol, where a cute guy and a cuter girl can get to know each other better?"

I expected her to blush, but instead she looked down the road. "I . . . do."

"Lead on." I gestured at her knee. "Or I can carry you, if you like." *I'd certainly like it.*

That time she *did* flush pink. Her teeth bit down on her bottom lip softly, and the sight made my jeans painfully tight. "I'm fine. I can walk."

Her injury didn't slow her down. Together we strolled the cobbled lane, heading up a steep slope until we came to a little building with an outdoor balcony. "What a view," I murmured, shading my eyes and staring out at the blue waves.

"Right?" She sat down at the tiny table. It was so small that when I joined her, our legs accidentally touched. Nova didn't pull away. Smiling, she played with the saltshaker. "I've always loved Torino."

"Do you live here?"

"Oh no." She set the saltshaker down and pulled her hands into her lap. "I just travel here most summers."

"It's my first time," I said. "It's nicer than I imagined."

"What did you imagine?"

Stretching my arm over the back of my chair, I regarded the ocean. The boats rocking gently in the docks resembled white flower petals in a puddle. It was picturesque. Quiet. Nothing like the tragedy my father's cautionary words had conjured up over the years.

He'd told me little about Torino, or about his bad blood with his brother. But I'd known that our heritage was dangerous . . . that I was meant to keep my royalty a secret. I'd also known he used his history as a way to leverage power and favors. He'd certainly used it to help my mother's family agree to give him whatever he needed so he could grow his own empire.

All the whispers I'd picked up while he confided in my older brother, like I wasn't able to hear, like I wasn't even *there*—they'd made being royalty sound like a curse.

"Thorne?"

Blinking, I realized I'd been stewing in my thoughts too long. "Sorry," I chuckled. "Think I'm still adjusting to the time zone change."

Nova was staring at me with her eyes wide and glassy. I knew that look. I hated that look.

"I'm fine," I said quickly, motioning for the waiter to come over. "Let's get those drinks we talked about."

Taking the little paper menu, I ordered myself a grilled cheese—and marveled at the price, even if it was easy for me to afford—as well as a stiff whiskey on ice. Nova didn't even read the menu, she handed it back and asked for a glass of Moscato and their soup of the day. The drinks came quickly. "Here," I said, lifting my glass up. "Cheers to strangers becoming friends." She grimaced, confusing me. "Uh, you okay?"

Nova shook herself, sending her hair tumbling so it caught the light. The strands glowed like molten gold with the sun behind her. "I'm fine, really." Her glass went up, every hint that she'd been shocked going away. "To new friends."

Clinking my glass against hers, I took a quick sip. It burned perfectly going down. As I placed my drink on the table, I spotted something in the street nearby: a police car, different from the ones in the States, but universally recognizable. It wasn't the same cops as earlier, but it made me think about the altercation. "What will happen to him?" I asked.

"The pickpocket?" Her chin tucked lower. "Torino has severe laws. He'll be charged a fine, then locked up for five years."

I clutched my glass tighter. "All that because he snatched a purse?"

"It's the law."

"Still seems extreme to me."

Nova tipped her glass up, sipping. "All right, how would you do it?"

"Excuse me?"

Her eyes twinkled. "You talk like you know how to run this country. So what would the punishment be for the man that was arrested today?"

"I'm not the kind of person who knows how to run anything, believe me."

"I don't. Believe you, I mean." She twirled her glass and finished it off. Her cheeks looked like candy apples. "You give off this . . . natural authority."

My grin hurt my face. "Go on."

She held my wicked stare for a heartbeat. I was shooting mental pictures at Nova that were quite dirty and *very* authoritative. She sat up like she'd been pricked in the ass with a fork. Had my filthy thoughts penetrated her imagination? "Just tell me how you'd punish him," she insisted.

Under the table, I slid my shoe against her ankle. I loved how her breath quickened at my touch. "Nova," I said thickly, feeling the alcohol . . . and our chemistry, "you're really hung up on punishments. If all you want is for me to spank you, we can go somewhere and take care of that."

The candy apples in her cheeks melted until her whole throat was glowing. "That—" she started to sputter. "I'm asking you a serious question, Thorne."

"I'd rather drink more and take it easy. This is the kind of conversation I was trying to avoid when I went out this morning." Her head tilted, sending her reddish hair tumbling beautifully over her shoulder. I knew she was going to ask what I was referring to. And I didn't want to explain because, so far, I'd avoided all talk about the funeral, or who I was, or why I was really here. "Fine," I said hurriedly. "Okay. Give me a second and I'll answer."

Nova seemed pleased. The waiter arrived with her soup, and she plucked a piece of bread out of the basket, then dipped and chewed patiently.

I stared at my sandwich as it was set down. How unfair it was that I couldn't will it to transform into an entire bottle of whiskey, then I'd be drunk and not answering deep questions about morality. *Life would be simpler if you could wish away your problems.* Furrowing my brow, I lifted my eyes. "It would depend on why he stole the purse."

"How do you mean?"

Hefting the sandwich in my hands, I said, "If he had a family to feed. If he himself was starving. A man who steals for greed should be punished, but . . . a man stealing to help others shouldn't be thrown in a cell to rot."

Nova was half smiling. "How noble of you. You'd be the Robin Hood of kings if you made the laws here."

Heat rocketed up my neck. "Well, I don't. And I wouldn't want to. Someone else can handle all that work."

She made a small, soft sound. The kind I wanted to hear in private . . . and over and over again. Her hands crossed under her chin. In her tight white top, she melded with the clouds behind her. She could have been a figurehead on a ship, inspiring men to adventure, or leading them home to their warm beds.

We stayed like that for a while. I ate quietly, enjoying the fresh air, and perhaps the first silence in my life that didn't feel uncomfortable. Nova made this too easy. I didn't mind, it was refreshing . . . different.

"See that?" she said, pointing at one of the boats. "That's the *Sandpiper*, one of the oldest ships around. It doesn't go out anymore, but it's full of really great artifacts, maps, preserved history. You'll have to check it out."

I chuckled. "I've seen boats. I live by the ocean back home."

"Yes," she said defensively. "But not *that* boat. So you will."

My chuckle became a helpless laugh. "And what else will I see while I'm here?"

Nova cupped her own cheeks. "The castle rose gardens are famous! Oh, and then there's this set of statues on the far side of town, been there for a hundred years!"

There were stars in her eyes. Her energy was contagious. "You really do love this place," I whispered. "Well, I hope you'll show me everything you can before we part ways."

She froze, like she realized where we were and who we were: people who'd only met an hour ago. People who knew nothing of each other; I didn't even know where she lived. Just that it wasn't here.

Nova considered me long and hard. The stars in her eyes had been replaced by something that burned hotter, brighter—impossibly so—as she said, "Come with me."

We slid carefully along a rough path that curled around the cliffs on the far edge of the city. The sharp wall of the cliff on our right rose, then lowered. I could glimpse the purple crest of the waves where they brushed the lowering sun. Every minute with Nova blew by faster than seemed fair.

She'd clearly been this way many times; her glittering flats dodged holes and patches of sand. In her confidence she moved too fast. "Watch it!" I said, catching her by her elbow when her heel went out from under her.

Bracing herself in my arms, Nova gaped up at me. "Sorry. I lost my balance."

Gently, lingering with my fingers wrapped around her upper arms, I steadied her. The narrow path pushed our bodies ever closer. "Don't be sorry. I'll take any chance to catch a pretty girl that I can get."

Her laugh echoed, bouncing off the rocks. "Come on, we're almost there."

"You still haven't said where *there* is, or what it . . ." Trailing off, I rounded the last corner. The path spilled out onto a flat section of beach that was white as bleached bone. It was surrounded by glassy, polished rocks that curved up in layered pieces—like a giant hand was cupping us. "What's this?" I asked, marveling at the beauty of the land. It had been eroded by the waves over what must have been millennia.

"I wanted you to see my favorite spot. I thought maybe you'd understand my feelings about Torino if you did."

She reached for my hand. Smiling, I let her take it, enjoying the tight warmth of her grip. Nova guided me down to the soft sand, then farther, until we were perched on the rock edge and able to see the waves foaming only a few feet below. We were sheltered, but the salty spray sometimes flicked up into our faces when a particularly huge wave rolled into place.

"It's beautiful," I said, and though we'd stopped moving, I kept hold of her hand.

"Earlier," she whispered, "I asked you what you imagined this country would be like. You never answered me."

We were standing shoulder to shoulder. The setting sun had fallen low enough that it looked like a giant egg yolk sinking into the water. Crimson light cast Nova in a halo that made her auburn hair into bright embers.

My hand unlinked from hers; she ran her fingertips across my palm as it did. Gently I captured her chin with two of my fingers, turning her toward me. "I thought it would be terrifying here." Her skin was warm. Pulling her closer made it a furnace. "I thought I'd hate it."

Her tongue glided over her plump bottom lip. "And you don't?"

"How could I? This place allowed me to meet you."

In my shadow her eyes were like polished rocks at the bottom of the sea. There were a million puzzles buried in her pupils. Suddenly . . . I thought she looked incredibly sad. Her expression was full of multiple lifetimes that stretched on and on, and the old rocks around us only enhanced this vision.

My chest constricted around the buzzing of my heart. Another second, and I would have crumbled under her stare. Where was all this pain coming from?

Finally her eyes closed.

Finally I brushed my mouth on hers.

"Thorne," she whispered on my vibrating skin. Her tongue moved curiously, testing me—and I let her. Nova was both confident and uncertain. She touched me like she kept expecting me to evaporate into thin air. There was an eagerness to her palms on my shoulders . . . a wonderment in how she experienced me.

Waves crashed in my ears with an insistent rhythm. The heavy noise mixed with my breathing. Mirrored my desire to smash myself on Nova until I left the same impression on her that the water had eroded into the cliffs.

But for everything I gained in this long-lasting kiss . . .

I wondered why I felt like I was missing something.

- CHAPTER FIVE -

HAWTHORNE

The cathedral rose into the pale pink sky. In the distance I could hear the song of sea birds. No matter where you were in this city, the coast wasn't far away.

A long path made from steps cut straight into the rock led toward the cathedral. It wound tighter the closer to the building I got. There was a large crowd gathered around, but all of them were prevented from getting close to the funeral by the many guards.

Each step was staffed by a man who openly displayed a rifle. Some of these guys were ours, but the rest, as far as I could tell, were all members of the royal guard. Who else could they be with their stiff-shouldered blue shirts, their embellished golden buttons down the front?

At the sight of my fast approach one of them frowned. "Hold up," he said, blocking my way.

"It's fine." Glen stepped into view higher on the steps. He waved me forward. "He's got clearance."

The unnamed guard's frown shifted into a confused, openmouthed gape. I felt him eyeing me with curiosity. "You heard him," I said, pushing by. "Let me through."

Glen's shadow slid over me. Behind his ear the early sun had begun to show its face. "My condolences," he said gravely.

His pity didn't sit right with me. "I didn't know my uncle," I said quickly, like I wanted it to be clear no one had to feel sorry for me. I wasn't suffering. Even the strangers surrounding the cathedral, even these nameless guards, all of them had more right to feel sad than I did.

My father's friend hesitated—then looked away.

After that no one stopped me.

At the top of the stairs I smoothed my black suit. The huge door was partly open; I nudged my way inside. The entry was stuffed with so many flowers that the floral smell burned my nostrils. Through a second set of arches was a welcoming glow.

The interior of the church took my breath away.

Tall candelabras had been arranged beyond the threshold, lighting up the long black banners draped from ceiling to floor on the walls. Each of them was embroidered with a simple design. When I saw it, I placed a hand on the right side of my ribs. On the banners was the same symbol that had been etched into my flesh the day I'd turned eighteen; the crown was a rich crimson, the edges sharp, knifelike tips pointing toward the sky.

Stained glass curved overhead in a gorgeous display of skill and piety. The pews that flowed toward the front of the room were carved from burnished oak.

There were a number of people lining the walls and seats; everyone was dressed in stark black as a sign of respect.

Searching the wide room for my father, I saw another familiar face first. She would have been easy to miss but for the fact that she was staring right at me. Nova's hair was wrapped in a netlike veil pinned to her tightly wound bun. The long-sleeved dress hid her curves and most of her wringing hands. But nothing hid her wide eyes.

What the hell was she doing here?

The people around her swayed; more eyes were on me now. I knew them, too. After all, I'd sat down with the Valentines just six months back in an attempt at flimsy peace. Now they were here. And Nova was with them.

In a gut punch that made me ill, I remembered who she was. It was strange that I'd forgotten . . . but the woman I'd met yesterday was nothing like the shy, mousy girl who'd sat with her family as we talked about how to go forward without trying to murder each other.

That Nova Valentine hadn't left an impression on me. This one had.

What had changed her so much in such a short time?

"Thorne," a feminine voice said. Twisting, I stared at my mother in her thick swirls of dark lace.

"Mom?" I asked, coming forward and taking her hands. "What are you doing here?"

She embraced me; her cheeks were wet from tears. "I'm weak. I flew out soon after you and your father. Lulabelle offered to stay behind and help, though I'm not sure she'll even *try* to work out any new deals, you know how she is, but . . . Screw the business, I couldn't handle the idea of him facing this without me." She placed her hand on the middle of my back, guiding me deeper into the church. "I should have stopped by your hotel room, but I arrived after midnight and hated to wake you. I knew I'd see you this morning, here."

I was barely listening. It took everything I had to stop staring at Nova. I felt her eyes on me as I approached the lower pews. My mind was jammed—I kept playing that meeting on repeat. I'd met Nova before . . . Even if I'd forgotten, I doubted she had. Why hadn't she reminded me about it?

The anxious threads of paranoia were abruptly chopped when I lifted my head to see what was at the front of the church. Sitting on a low platform was a shiny coffin covered in gold filigree. It was so saturated in color that my father was easier to spot than normal.

He, too, was all in black. It made him seem like a shapeless shadow from behind. I watched him as he gazed down on his brother. It hit me then. The last time they'd seen each other, Hester had been alive. He'd been so much more than this emaciated corpse.

Ice traveled the length of my spine. A bomb had been rolling in my chest since I walked into the cathedral; it exploded until I thought it would fill up every crevice in my body.

Two siblings forced apart by greed.

This was a tragedy . . . This was beyond cruel.

I felt grateful to my father. Even if he'd fled into exile to save his own skin, he'd prevented his children from enduring the same game of royal chess that he'd grown up with.

On the sidelines I caught motion; Nova was leaning forward from the straight-backed row of her family. Her perceptive eyes were stuck on me—like she was waiting for me to cry. Like she expected me to. My nose burned as I sucked in air. On stiff legs I headed over to my father. My mother grabbed my elbow, pulling me into a seat beside her. "Leave him," she pleaded.

I didn't resist her firm grip. But her command broke me out of my stupor. "Why the *fuck* are the Valentines here?" I hissed into her ear.

She looked straight ahead. "We'll talk about it after. This isn't the time."

I burned with a wild need to confront them. To stalk over there and stare down Kurtis Valentine and his whole brood. To ask them what their connection was to Hester . . . to Torino.

To ask *her* what she was up to.

Nova, I thought, my hands tightening into fists in my lap. *Were you playing with me yesterday? Did you kiss me as part of some trap?* I hated not knowing. I prided myself on staying ahead of the game. But I hadn't just stumbled, I'd fallen flat on my face.

My father approached us. He dropped bonelessly on the opposite side of my mother. The priest approached the casket; Maverick was

36

staring that way, his eyes dry, his skin ashen. I saw my mother take his hand. He clutched it.

As the priest went on about life, death, and the power of heaven, the small crowd made quiet sniffling sounds. A high keening cry soon started from a corner. There was a woman covered head to toe in black silk and a nearly opaque veil. She was sobbing, hugging herself; my eyes narrowed when Kurtis Valentine's wife, Valencia, hurried over to talk to her.

"Austere Fredricson," my mother whispered in my ear. "The king's widow."

I felt a tickle of suspicion seeing Valencia holding Austere close, talking to her in a soothing way. Their behavior was too familiar. How did they know each other? How did the Valentines know *anyone* in this country? They were a Boston Mafia family. Dangerous, powerful, rich like mine . . . but clearly that wasn't all. There was more happening here.

I was determined to understand everything.

- CHAPTER SIX -

HAWTHORNE

"They're snakes," my father said. He leveled his glare on me—and even knowing his anger wasn't for me but the Valentines, I stepped back. "Everything they've been up to makes sense now."

"Tell me." I bit the words in two, narrowing my eyes in Nova's direction. She had the grace to turn away.

My father led me and my mother farther into the cathedral. He didn't want anyone else to hear. "Glen brought me up to speed yesterday. It seems that my brother fell in love with the queen around thirty years ago. She was visiting with her family . . . with her sister, Valencia."

That information made me dizzy. "Austere is Valencia Valentine's sister?"

Crinkling her lace-gloved hands into a ball, my mother scowled. "They've been involved with Torino since the start. That's how they knew who you were, Maverick," she said, looking at her husband.

Back in the States, my father had changed his surname from Fredricson to Badd, so our royal blood would remain a secret. Not many knew who we really were—though telling a girl that you're a prince in hiding is easy-mode for a good time. If you like things easy, anyway.

Maverick's nod was ponderous. "The real issue is that, ten years ago, it became clear that Austere wasn't going to produce an heir." He studied me closely. "How much did you listen to what I told you about the rule of succession to the throne?"

"Let's not make this about me. Get to what matters." *I want to talk to Nova.*

His forehead tightened with new stress lines. "Hester has no children. His death means that the next in line would be me or Costello, in that order."

The stomping in my veins grew into a parade. My mother covered her mouth. "That's why they threatened us . . . why they kept interfering with our lives. The Valentines were benefiting greatly from Valencia's sister being the queen. They knew she'd be removed from the throne if someone with a better claim appeared."

My mind was working through the details. I felt a bony hand clutch my heart. "All this time they've been worried we'd come back to Torino and take the crown?"

Maverick was looking over my head. I followed his eyes; the entire Valentine family was watching us from the same wall they'd been lined up against at the start of the funeral. "Yes," he said grimly. "They've been in the shadows, observing us, knowing this moment was coming. Without an heir, the Valentines have no claim to this kingdom."

"Unless all of us are dead and out of the way," I said. "This was what their bullshit 'truce' was all about. They wanted us to stay far away from Torino, they probably thought Dad was aware of the situation and was just biding his time until he could return. And here we are. Just like they were afraid of."

I was suddenly counting the number of guards in the room. I didn't think the Valentines would do something so rash as to try to kill us in front of an audience, but after learning how long they'd been watching us, I wasn't sure of anything anymore.

Nova.

Why had she spent so much time with me? What was her part in all of this?

A firm hand clasped my shoulder. I looked up at Maverick curiously. "Come on," he said. "It's time for us to find out what they want."

"We know what they want. They want us dead."

My mother gave me a somber look. "They had this whole time to attack us again, and they didn't."

"They knew we were on edge," I said, chasing reasons. "It'd be suicide to attack us so soon after the mess with Darien and Gina."

She reached for me with that familiar pity that I was so sick of. "Thorne . . ."

All at once I had to get out of the room. I couldn't stomach a conversation with the Valentines. I was resistant to the idea that talking could solve anything with these people.

But mostly . . .

I couldn't face the woman who'd looked into my eyes, held me close, and kissed me while knowing how stupid I was.

"Hawthorne!" My father kept calling to me as I walked away. Ignoring him, I strode through a side door of the cathedral. I didn't know where it led, just that it would take me away from that stuffy room with its grand art and two-faced people.

A small set of steps—weathered by the salty air and coated with moss—took me into a tree-shaded graveyard. The monuments were all huge, many of them decorated with swords or life-size men in crowns. This was the cemetery that Hester would be buried in. *The place my corpse will be laid to rest if Maverick takes the crown.* The idea made me shiver.

I sucked in the clean air like it could heal me. I was too many things at once. I couldn't settle on feeling angry, or betrayed, or dejected. Pressing a hand to my ribs, I looked up at the foliage spreading over me. A few small birds chirped, darting around and back again, free of the weight of family affairs. Leaning against the cool stone of the cathedral,

I shut my eyes and listened to my heart. It sounded like the ocean waves I'd heard last night.

When I'd first kissed Nova.

She'd been so welcoming . . . her mouth hungry, pliant, and silken. I'd wanted to kiss her until the stars rose above, then beyond that, until they sank into the sea for the last time in eternity. Ocean spray had made her taste like a wonderful secret from the abyss. A treasure discovered by me and *only* me.

"Hawthorne?" a voice called gently. As if it had escaped my daydream.

When I opened my eyes, I saw it wasn't my imagination.

Nova was standing in front of me.

- CHAPTER SEVEN -

HAWTHORNE

The shadow of the church made her look muted and gray. It reminded me of how my mother had appeared the other morning as I'd left our home. That same vibe of empathy . . . of a sadness that wasn't entirely about me.

I didn't move off the wall. "Why didn't you tell me who you were?"

Nova's eyebrows crept higher. "That's not fair. I *did* tell you, you're the one who didn't recognize me."

My mouth fell open.

"I was positive you did at first," she went on, staring me down. "The longer you spent with me, the more I realized you had no clue. I was kind of offended."

I shook off her mild jab. "I'm bad with faces." It was a lame excuse, I grabbed for another because I desperately needed to make sense of *how* I had forgotten. "We weren't properly introduced at that meeting. You were sitting at a table with a bunch of your family under pretty tense terms."

Her smile grew. It was as tempting as if she'd inched her dress up to expose her thigh. "There were a lot of distractions that day." She pulled in some air, let it out. "It felt awkward to say anything once I knew you didn't recognize me."

Dammit, her honesty was disarming me. I wasn't ready to let go of my distrust yet. But talking was so effortless with her. "Sorry I didn't recognize you. In my defense, you don't act at *all* like you did months ago."

That froze her smile in its tracks. "How do you mean?"

My memory ran back that day to me. "You were quiet. Shy, even." I traced her body with a pointed look. "You weren't shy yesterday."

She shifted under my scrutiny. "What we did—the way I acted with you—it was something I'd always wanted to do." She clamped her mouth shut, looking at me with her eyes stretched wide, daring me to smother her bluntness with my usual sarcasm.

Whatever armor I'd put on had already rusted and fallen away. I softened my tone, wondering if she'd hear my heart thudding. "Are you trying to tell me you've been crushing on me for months?"

Nova's fists curled against her dress. Magnetic jolts flew between us as we held each other's stare. It was as if she knew saying more than she had would be dangerous, that it would give me too much power. And she was right—it would.

My lower belly was already flaring, my tongue tingling, as I considered that this beautiful girl had been carrying a torch for me. There's nothing sexier than knowing someone wants you.

Nothing.

"What's going on out here?" A tall figure stepped through the archway. He was wearing a jacket that fell all the way to his thighs, black as tar and spread open to show off his slim, hard-muscled body. He flicked his honey-colored eyes at me.

Larchmont Valentine. Nova's brother. I knew little else about him.

His smirk was jagged as he said, "Looks like a party we weren't invited to, Richard."

A second man followed Larchmont out of the church. He was beefier, his bronze skin almost the same shade as his closely shaved hair. This guy would have fit right in at a military boot camp.

Nova spoke to them without any kindness in her tone. "Why are you here, is everyone done talking inside?"

"Talking," Larchmont scoffed. He lifted his head so he could stare down his nose at me. I was slouching, which made it easier for him. "What bullshit. I'm tired of all the talk. It's not like anyone gives a shit what I want, anyway."

"Weird," I said, smiling at him. "You'd think someone with your pleasant manners would be really convincing in a discussion."

Richard's wide body moved so he could block me in against the stone wall, partially hiding my view of Nova. He was keeping me from accessing the steps that led down into the grassy cemetery. Larchmont's position cut me off from dodging back inside the cathedral.

I was trapped.

Larch barely cocked his head. His movements were precise as those of a spider perched on a web, waiting for its prey to land. "Oh," he whispered, "I just remembered that you're the funny one in your family."

"Yeah," I grunted, pushing forward until I was standing nose to nose with the gold-eyed man. "That's me, Mr. Funny." I wished I had my damn gun. My decision to be respectful and not bring a weapon to the funeral had been a mistake.

"Tell me a joke, Funny Man," he said. His sneer was so much like his father's.

Nova lifted her hands. "Larch. Don't."

I glanced at Richard, noting how he was tense but unmoving. "I don't tell jokes," I said patiently. "I make clever commentary. Why don't you just cut right to what you want from me?" It was obvious something was pissing Larchmont off. What had they been talking about inside?

He skimmed his thumb over his chin. "Impatient little shit. Why did they ever choose someone like you?"

My muscles went slack in confusion. "Choose me for what?"

Richard slammed me against the stone wall. Nova shouted in surprise, but after that I couldn't hear her. I couldn't hear anything but the blood thrumming in my ears, my attention focusing on the big man who'd assaulted me.

People assume a lot about my family. When talking about which of my brothers is the most deadly, Costello is the one they usually bet on. And if they don't bet on my older brother, they throw in for Kain. They liked to call him *passionate*. A nicer word for irrational.

No one ever remembers that I've had the same teachers as them. The exact same lessons in weapons, self-defense, even some light MMA. The only difference between us was that I'd always done my best to *stay out of trouble*. That didn't mean I was weak or lazy. It meant I was smart.

Smart people know how to win when the odds are against them.

Richard's grip fell away the second I jabbed my knee into his balls. Catching his jacket, I clawed it tight and ducked low. With a great heave, I leveraged him up into the air. I wished I could see how that looked—me balancing this huge ox of a man on my back.

He rolled down the steps that led to the grass below, staring at the sky in surprise as he fought to draw in air. I'd knocked the wind out of him.

"Look out!" Nova screamed.

I spun just in time to take Larchmont's knuckles to my mouth. It was a solid hit that filled my taste buds with the flavor of warm copper. He was leering like he was fucking proud he'd sucker punched me, like he couldn't *wait* to do it again.

Adrenaline cascaded through my body. It numbed any pain or sense of danger. Larch saw the fury in my face, but he wasn't quick enough to decide what to do about it. I had an idea that he was used to hitting men who couldn't fight back.

"Come on!" I laughed. "Let's fucking go!" I snatched the collar of his shirt before he could backpedal out of reach. Stitches ripped; the sound was gratifying. My fist crunching into his nose was even better.

He went spinning away from me, half bent over as he clutched at his face. I stayed where I was so I could catch my breath. And because I needed to keep an eye on Richard. Glancing back, I saw the big man was standing now, his hands at his sides like he was a linebacker ready to make a tackle. He'd have to ascend the steps, which would at least give me time to react.

"You think you're better than me," Larchmont said, wheezing.

I turned enough to eyeball him in disbelief. "Excuse me?"

He wiped his nose and stared at the red stains. His glare was full of accusations I didn't understand. "You're not special, you just got lucky. You didn't have to work for anything. Not you, not your dad. You're all just fucking lucky your moms banged the right men."

"Stand up," I spit. Blood came out with my saliva. The sight of it made me laugh—a hard bark that turned Larchmont's scowl into an uncertain frown. He didn't know what I would do next. I wasn't sure I knew, either. "I'm ready for another round. I didn't quite break your nose, huh? Another solid hit should do it, let's see if I'm as *lucky* as you say." My foot slid forward; Larch backed up on shaky legs. "Fight me!" I shouted. "Come the fuck on, let's keep going!"

"Thorne!" my father roared. He was standing in the archway of the side door, his lips pulled back over his snarl. Now *that* was an expression I was familiar with. Dad's disappointment tasted like undiluted nostalgia. "What the hell is going on here?"

"He's insane," Larch said, retreating to my father's side.

"Insane?" I laughed. "I thought I was the 'funny one.' Sounds like you're sore you couldn't hold your own against me." I shot a look at Richard. "Neither of you could. Attack me together, might increase your chances."

46

Larchmont sniffed loudly, drawing attention to his bloody nose. "You better get your kid under control, old man."

Rage swelled hotly in my guts. "He doesn't fucking control me."

"Hawthorne," Maverick said. "You aren't behaving appropriately. It's embarrassing."

That pulled me up short. "These two chuckle-fucks come out here and throw some cheap punches, and you're worried that I'm *embarrassing you?*"

Richard had made it up the steps, but he was staying at a distance. His expression was only slightly more neutral than Dad's. As for Larchmont, his smugness could have been scraped off his face and served up on toast. "People will think you're a violent fool," Maverick said.

"I don't care what anyone thinks about me." I wished my words would make him flinch. But my father showed no sign of being affected.

Someone else did, though.

Nova's frown spread over her face like a warning. It left me cold and unbalanced. That wasn't the reaction I'd been looking for.

"Maybe you should tell him that his actions matter to his future subjects," Larchmont scoffed, his red-tinted teeth showing.

There—I spotted guilt in my father's eyes. "What the hell is he talking about?" I asked.

"If you'd stayed inside to talk, like I told you to, you'd know," he said.

"I'm listening now. Ears wide open." Was it possible to feel more adrenaline than I had while fighting for my life?

The guilt was replaced by stoniness. "This country won't accept you sitting on the throne if you act like a wild animal," Maverick said coolly.

Blazing heat traveled over my skin. My adrenaline was washed away by panic, Larchmont's words from earlier echoing in my head: *Why did they ever choose someone like you?*

"And why the hell," I asked cautiously, "would I ever want to sit on the throne?"

"Because it's the only choice you've got." It was the first time Richard had spoken out loud—and I wished he'd remained a damn mute. "It's what was decided," he said firmly.

To my horror, my father hung his head. "You're joking," I whispered. "Where the hell is this coming from?"

"No one else can do this," Maverick said quickly. "Costello has his woman. Kain is already married, like me."

Rules of succession. "Wait, slow the hell down." I was dizzy, and when I pressed my palm to my temple, everything resonated viciously. "'Already married'? You expect me to *marry* someone?"

"It's the path to peace with the Valentines," my father said. "A way to bring hope to this country. The only one eligible to wear the crown . . . is you, son."

He's asking me to become the king. I eyeballed him, then the others. Richard looked somber; Larchmont had gone back to scowling. *That's why Larch was so pissed at me.* I glanced at the church. *He's jealous he can't take the crown. He thinks I'm lucky this is happening to me. They were all discussing this behind my back.*

Nova was wide-eyed but not surprised.

Everyone knew.

Her hands were clasped over her lips.

Lips I'd kissed.

She knew.

I wiped the blood off my mouth and stormed off.

- CHAPTER EIGHT -

HAWTHORNE

I walked through the church, ignoring my mother as she called out to me. Aware of all the eyes but not giving them the satisfaction of my attention.

How could this happen?

I asked myself that a hundred times as I exited the building, marching down the long stairs out front. More eyes burned on me in the open and I zoned those out, too. I wasn't paying attention to where I was going. I didn't care.

In minutes they planned my life out behind my damn back, I thought angrily. *They did it without asking my input.*

"Thorne! Wait!" I felt Nova's presence as she drew closer.

I continued walking, my strides getting faster.

"I'm not going to stop following you," she said. "Please, just slow down and talk to me."

Cars zoomed by on the busy street, forcing me to stop if I didn't want to take several tons of metal to my organs. The knuckles on my right hand were throbbing, reminding me of the fight. My jaw ached as well—I could still taste my own blood.

"Thorne," she said, softer that time.

I looked at her over my shoulder. "You should leave. Why would you want to hang out with a *violent fool* like me?"

"I don't think of you like that," she said.

"You shouldn't think of me at all." That made her step back—a small movement, but I saw it. Behind her I spotted two people perched on the top step of the church. Even at a distance I could make out the severe, angular silhouettes of her parents. I gestured at them. "You've got people waiting for you. Go do some more talking about me with them. Plan more of my life."

The wind tugged at the veil pinned in her hair; she grabbed it, clutching it fiercely, like she needed to hold *something*. "For the record, I didn't realize you had no idea this was going to happen. When you said yesterday that you didn't make the laws and had no plan to, I thought you were being coy." With a wishful, sympathetic look at me, she reached out to brush her fingers over my forearm. I felt her nails through the fabric. "And I can't help but think about you. It's just like you said earlier. You've been in my head since we first met."

The thick, curdled anger in my blood smoothed away. Even after I'd been picturing her hiding in the shadows, plotting with her family and mine about setting me on the throne, her admission was so damn enticing.

Before I could respond, Nova turned and hurried back to the church. When she reached her parents, her mother put a possessive arm around her slim shoulders.

I couldn't see Valencia's face well, but Kurtis's lips were stretched in a frown. I held his stare for a second. Had he expected me to relish becoming the king? Was he, like his sons, jealous that I'd been born with the right blood through no effort on my part?

I twisted so I could keep walking to the Rizenburgh. It wasn't far, the needle tip rising into view as I traveled the few blocks toward it. The doorman did a double take at me as I passed through the automatic glass doors. *What's his problem?*

When I approached my room in the hallway, I noticed a figure standing outside it. He was a broad man, arms crossed like a pretzel over his chest. Rush hadn't been working for my family for very long, but he'd proven to be a good-hearted man.

Months back, he'd been a member of a gang called the Deep Shots. We'd put them on our payroll, happy to increase our hold on the city streets of Providence, where most of our less savory businesses were.

Except the tension between us and the Valentines had caused dissension in the ranks. Many of the Deep Shots felt they would be better off with another employer—one who would reward them, even encourage them, for getting their hands bloody. They thought no one was off-limits . . . not even innocent young women.

But Rush didn't agree.

He'd shown his loyalty to my family, risking his life to protect Costello and his girl, Scotch, when letting them die would have been easier. He'd quickly climbed the ranks and ended up as one of our most trusted bodyguards.

"Hey," he said, nodding at me as I approached.

"How much is he paying you to spy on me?" I asked, sliding out my key card.

Rush laughed self-consciously, his nails chafing the side of his thick neck. "Not enough." When I stared at him seriously he straightened up and cleared his throat. "Kidding. I'm not spying on you, Maverick didn't ask me to. My job, as always, is to keep you safe."

"Right now I don't need safety, I need to saturate myself in whiskey." Grabbing my hotel door handle, I unlocked it, the green light flashing. "Alcohol: the cure to all ailments."

Rush chuckled, and when I didn't shut the door immediately, he got the hint and followed me inside. I headed to the minibar and yanked out the bottle of Seagram's and a can of ginger ale. After filling one of the glasses that had been left by the staff, I filled a second and offered it to Rush.

He took it, but he didn't drink. "How was the funeral?"

It was a complicated thing to answer. In my pissed-off state I was tempted to say, *Oh, you know, got the news I'm expected to become the king of a country I just visited for the first time yesterday!*

I went the easy route instead. "Grim. Depressing. There was a dead body in a casket, how do you think it went?"

He sighed and took a deep drink from the glass in his hands. I lifted my glass high in a quick salute before downing the contents in one gulp.

"So nothing else happened?" he asked.

Disbelief rocketed through me. "Do *you* know about the plans for the crown?" If everyone had been told before me, I was going to lose it.

Rush knotted up his forehead. "What? I just assumed something must've happened because you've got dried blood on your mouth, man."

Touching my jaw, I chuckled dryly. "I forgot about that." Now I knew why the doorman had looked so surprised. "Yeah, the funeral was a little wild." I refilled my glass, eager to let the warm buzz smother my poor mood. Of course Rush didn't know, why would anyone have told him what was going on? This political intrigue was meant for the inner circles of my family and the Valentines. But Rush *would* learn about the plan . . . as soon as I told everyone a very flat no.

I wouldn't agree to this insanity. Did anyone seriously expect me to?

Pushing down the part of me that wanted to dissect the dangers of not complying with something so paramount that *both* my father and Kurtis had agreed to it, I opened a second can of ginger ale to mix with the Seagram's.

Marriage. Please. What a thought. And to whom? *It doesn't matter.*

"You planning to get shitfaced?" he asked me as I worked on my new drink.

Forcing on one of the big smirks I was known for, I swallowed audibly. "I don't get shitfaced, I just have a good time."

"What's on the good-time agenda?"

"First, I need to get out of these depressing clothes." Abandoning my empty glass, I headed over to my suitcase, digging through it for something clean. Under some folded denim I saw the tip of my pistol.

It reminded me of when I'd stumbled back to the hotel last night. How much I'd been floating on a high over kissing Nova. Rush had been outside my room then, too, but he'd just given me a knowing smile and told me he'd left my weapon in my suitcase under some jeans. My father had, amazingly, relayed the message to him about how I wanted my gun at some point after I'd gone wandering off.

If only dear old Dad could relay important messages to me directly. I grabbed the gun and took it into the bathroom with the new clothes hooked over my arm. The room was huge—only the best on the family dime—and I was able to drape my outfit on the counter and still have an entire second sink to myself. Leaving the door cracked so I could keep talking to Rush, I ran the water, splashing my face multiple times.

It felt disjointedly good to half drown myself. Gasping, I hung my head, watching the droplets spatter rhythmically into the drain. My head came back up; I studied my mouth, noting it was only a little tender. Larchmont hadn't hit me as hard as I'd thought, or maybe I was tougher than either of us guessed.

I tugged at the skin under my eyes. There were little red lines snaking through the whites around my irises. I was so damn exhausted.

"You alive in there?" I grabbed a towel and dried my skin vigorously. "Just cleaning up." There were drops of dried blood on my shirt. I yanked it over my head and threw it to the floor in a crumpled heap. "Tonight I want to explore what this country has to offer."

He chuckled thickly. "You mean see what the girls are like."

The instant he said it, a worm of guilt started to eat through my heart. Thinking about girls made me think about Nova. "Sure," I said, trying to sound chipper. "Don't know how much longer we'll be here, should get while the getting is good."

"Yeah, your father hasn't told me when we're flying home." I heard him pacing the room. Again, I wondered if he was spying on me. But I decided it didn't matter. Let him spy, let him tell my dad what I was up to. It wasn't like anyone was going to stop me from going out. Though if I lingered, there was a chance my mom or dad would show up and try to corner me.

After sliding on some gray jeans that sat low on my hips, I stretched my arms upward with a grunt. My reflection showed off the fit muscles that had remained even with my "easy" club job. Tattoos ran from my throat down to my wrists, and all the way across my torso and stomach. They were on me back to front. I was pretty much wearing a bodysuit made from ink. The only free spots were above my neck, my hands, and my feet.

Oh, and my cock. I hadn't gone *that* far yet.

Tattoos were something I'd always been obsessed with. You're never more of a focus to a person than when they're stabbing your skin with needles. I loved the precise pain . . . the carefulness that tattoos demanded.

The art was smooth and dark. I preferred black and gray; the only pop of color was on the right side of my ribs. There the red-and-black crown stood out sharply.

I touched it, exploring the ridges of muscle where the crown sat. I'd probably pressed my fingers to that small piece of art a million times since I'd gotten it when I was eighteen. It was customary in my family, a tradition—one of the few that my father had brought back with him from Torino. It made me think, again, about the situation I was in.

"How is your dad holding up?" Rush asked.

I paused in strapping on my gun's holster over my clean white shirt. "He's about as fine as can be expected," I said slowly.

"Must be hard for him, losing a brother and all."

I yanked the last strap tighter than I'd meant to. "Yeah."

"Did you get to see her? I mean, I imagine you did."

"Who?" I asked, straightening my collar.

"The widow, the queen." Rush stopped walking over the rug. "I got a look at her in the papers, but it was a photo from a year ago. People say she hasn't left the castle in that long."

"Didn't take you for much of a gossip reader," I said smoothly.

He laughed. "I'm not some meat-headed ox. I do read. Occasionally."

Studying myself in the mirror, I brushed my fingers through my hair. "So what did the paper say about our widowed queen?"

"A lot of things. I don't get the idea that many people like her. Seems to be some talk about a conspiracy, guess a lot of people think she might've been the one to kill the king herself."

"She didn't seem the type," I said softly. "She just seemed . . . sad." No one was to blame for cancer. I didn't want to tell Rush that I'd already heard the details of how my uncle had died, though, in case it was supposed to be classified.

When I came out of the bathroom adjusting my shirt, Rush looked me up and down. "Was she hot?" he asked bluntly.

Caught off guard, I gave an uneasy laugh. "I don't know, she's like twice my age. Plus most of her was covered in black lace, didn't exactly get a good look at her face."

Rush nodded slowly. "I feel pretty bad for the next guy in line that ends up with her."

I stopped midgrab for my jacket. It took me a few seconds to breathe again. "What?"

He checked under his fingernails, but made no indication that he knew he'd set my nerves on edge. "That's how it works, right? The king is dead so the queen's gotta marry another guy and make him the new king. I don't know much about this whole royalty thing, and your dad hasn't really given me any lessons on this system. I just assumed."

Picturing myself marrying Austere Valentine, a woman I knew nothing about, a woman who was certainly my enemy and my uncle's widow, left me icy. Was Rush right? Was this *also* part of the plan no one had let me in on?

"I don't know how it works, either," I mumbled. "I do feel for the poor bastard, though." I grabbed my dark gray jacket off the back of the chair and slid it into place over my gun. After being attacked by Larchmont and Richard, I wasn't going to walk around without protection. Torino also seemed to be in turmoil. A lot of that was probably from the king's death, but I was getting a good, strong idea that these people didn't like Austere.

The woman I'd just learned I was expected to marry.

"I'm going," I said, opening the door.

Rush followed me out into the hallway, returning to his station next to my room. "Have fun tonight. Don't get into too much trouble."

His advice echoed my mother's from the other day.

But this time I didn't have a charming response.

Tonight, if it meant some relief from the pressure that had been put upon my shoulders, I'd seek out all the trouble that I could.

- CHAPTER NINE -

HAWTHORNE

Evening fell quickly. I killed a lot of time by simply wandering around the city. I strolled along the water, I kept pace with people heading to work, or back to their homes. I had no direction, and I was happy to float, seeing where I would land.

But when the sun began to set, and a darkness brought the lights out across the overhangs on the buildings, I let instinct lead me toward a more sinister path. I'd worked in my family's strip club for a very long time. I knew where to find the seedy sort of fun that I was chasing. I had a sixth sense for it.

Long, skinny alleys threaded through the town, pushing me toward the red-light district. This section of the city was nothing like the rest of it. There were no sweet-smelling cafés, no children jumping across aged wood as they chased each other on the docks. It was a whole new dimension.

Flickering lights hung above doorways; GIRLS GIRLS GIRLS declared one in pink. Another just had a gigantic red blinking X above the door. And God, the women *themselves*. They posed in the windows or strolled along the sidewalks in lingerie that left their best features on display. They were impervious to the cool evening air.

There was no pretense here. That was good.

I was done dealing with dishonesty for the day.

Outside one of the clubs, I slowed to get a better look. There was a trio of women gathered by the entrance. On the other side of the door was a huge man wearing sunglasses even though the sun was long gone. He said nothing, acting like some sort of stone gargoyle.

One of the woman, a redhead with her hair hanging loose and wild, turned to face me. She threw her hips sideways, exaggerating the dip of her waist. "Hey there, honey," she purred. "Looking for something even sweeter?"

I inhaled the scent of the air, the familiar energy that reminded me of the Dirty Dolls and the dent I'd left permanently in the VIP couch. I knew it would be so *easy* to reach out, take this woman's hand, and let her lead me into the club. I was under no illusion that this would be anything but a transaction. I didn't mind. I liked things to be straightforward.

The woman smiled at me, and I found myself thinking so oddly, so out of the blue, of another woman's smile.

Nova.

I shook myself, trying to clear the clinging memories of that girl, of her connections to my enemies. And how plush and *effortless* our first kiss had been.

"Come on, big boy," she said, taking a step my way. She even looked a bit like Nova. Her tall heels clicked on the cobblestones. When she reached for me, I saw her nails wore a glossy, chipped pink polish. Her hand brushed down my shoulder, across my chest. She must have felt the shape of my gun, because she stopped with her palm right on top. "You seem like a *dangerous* man. I like them with some bite."

"I don't know if I'm dangerous," I said dryly. Swallowing, I tried to dig deep and find the natural, flirty sarcasm that had long been my defining feature. "Just stressed out."

She puckered her mouth, cooing at me. "Poor baby." She brushed my sleeve up, revealing my tattoos. "I can definitely help relax you. But it might involve getting you a little more tense first, if you get my drift."

Picturing myself—how this evening was about to go—made me feel wooden. And not in a good way. Everything I'd set out to do tonight was abruptly pointless. The idea of hooking up with a stranger didn't appeal . . . it actually unnerved me.

Stepping backward, away from the woman, I caught the flash of disappointment in her eyes. "Sorry," I said. "I didn't mean to waste your time." I turned, nearly running back up the street. I power walked away until the flashing lights of the clubs stopped bouncing off the street under my feet. *What the hell is wrong with me?*

I didn't owe Nova anything, but I couldn't stop feeling like a piece of shit for considering paying for some play tonight. It didn't make any sense! And besides, even if I did feel guilty, even if I would rather have been around Nova, it didn't matter. She was a Valentine . . . part of a plot to get me to marry her damn aunt. I didn't have all the information, but I was smart enough to know I was a fucking pawn.

Rush had helped me realize the full truth: The Valentines needed me to marry Austere. If I did, they could keep their control of this country. Having the queen in their pocket would give them access to enormous wealth, I was sure of it. They'd do whatever was necessary to maintain the status quo. That included working with my father to arrange a marriage between the royal blood—my blood—and Austere.

And if I refused . . . I knew they weren't above killing my whole family.

I'd been called lazy in the past. Unambitious. And it was probably all correct.

But I'd never risk the lives of the people I cared about.

Wearing the crown and marrying Austere is my only option.

Fuck.

Frustrated, I walked with my head down low. The constant, low roar of the ocean on my left pulled me along. I hadn't gone far before I saw the yellow hue through the windows of a large ship moored at the docks.

The *Sandpiper*, I thought, remembering the ship that Nova had pointed out to me. Again my mind was attacked by the memory of her eager kiss. *She wanted me to see that ship.* Not knowing what else to do to distract myself, I stepped over the old wood until I was standing in front of the huge vessel.

Frayed ropes held the ship in place. A long plank was set into the open door in the side. It was dark, but with the spotlights attached to the hull, I could tell the white paint needed a fresh coat—badly.

"Hello?" a gravelly man's voice said. The speaker leaned around the doorway; he was stocky, dressed in a plum-colored jacket that hid his knees and made him seem even shorter. "We're closing up, son. Sorry about that."

"It's all right. I was just passing by." From my angle on the ramp I could see inside the *Sandpiper*. A heavy net was looped beside a shellacked, motorcycle-size swordfish. There were framed pictures bolted to every surface.

The man considered me. I felt his curious stare as he retreated into the ship. "Still time to take a look, if you don't mind not getting the full tour."

I was close to saying no thanks, but one of the photos caught my eye. "What's this?" I asked, stepping up the plank into the wooden belly of the ship. The picture was faded in its frame, but someone had stamped an official-looking wax seal to the top corner. Imprinted in it was the telltale crown I had tattooed on my ribs.

In the photo were several sailors gathered around a young man who stood beside a shark so big it could have eaten him twice over in one bite. "That would be Hansel Fredricson, father of our recently departed King Hester, may they both rest in peace." He pulled his flat brown hat off his head in reverence. Beneath, his hair was thinned to oblivion. "Name's Mikel, by the way."

Squinting at the photo, I said, "Hawthorne." *This is Maverick's dad?* The young boy looked so damn happy. I wondered if my father had ever looked so cheerful. "Did you know them?" I asked, helplessly intrigued by the history.

"What, the royal family? Yes and no." Putting his hat back on, Mikel waved me deeper into the ship. He took me over to a huge book strapped down to a long table. "When I was small I met the king. Hester was a nice enough boy. Shame what happened to him." Flipping the pages, he pointed. "It was his older brother, though, that came here the most. He signed . . . right there, day he caught that swordfish."

Glancing at the big fish attached to its plaque, I nodded slowly. When I was younger, I did recall going out on the ocean a few times with my father. But I'd thought he'd done it to entertain and win over powerful men with big wallets. Not because he actually liked fishing.

Mikel sighed into his thin beard. "Terrible what that family has gone through. First Hansel's wife passes away when the boys were just teens, then their father goes a year later. Don't think Hansel was able to hang on without Luca around."

Luca? My lungs seized up. I'd been given that as my middle name, but I'd never known it was to honor my father's mom.

He eyed me suddenly. "You go to the funeral?"

He has no idea who I am. Why would he? Looking at Maverick's name scrawled in the book, I said, "Yes. I stopped in."

He nodded like he approved. "Me too. Once it opened to the public, I went and said my piece. Can't more be done than that by us common folk. Whatever happens after this is out of our hands."

My fingers fell away from the book. "Thanks for showing me this."

"Ah, my pleasure." He winked. "Showing people a slice of history is good for my soul. Doing my part and all."

Backing up, I glanced once more at the photo of Hansel. Then the giant swordfish. My father seemed to have had some of the same tastes as his own dad. I wondered how similar they'd been.

Leaving the *Sandpiper* left me plagued with new, but just as heavy, thoughts. Nova had wanted me to see the ship—she'd wanted me to see as much of Torino as possible before I left.

I'd thought I would try, because I'd expected the trip to be short.

I didn't know if I had to be in such a hurry now.

- CHAPTER TEN -

HAWTHORNE

On the air floated a floral scent. Searching the street, I saw that I'd absently wandered back toward the cathedral where the funeral had been. Like I was possessed, I climbed the steps.

The flowers were all still packed in the entry. There were more of them than before. Thanks to Mikel, I knew the residents had been allowed to pay their respects once those closest to the king had cleared out.

Candles lit up the inside of the church. There were no people, and no casket. *Right, they buried him.* It was obvious, and I felt odd for forgetting they would do that. Had my father watched in silence? I pictured my mother holding his hand like she had earlier. As terrible a dad as he'd been, it left me raw to think about him seeing his younger brother put in the cold earth.

On impulse I wandered out toward the cemetery. I was compelled to find the fresh grave. I'd gone this far; attending the funeral without seeing the headstone of my uncle made it feel like a half measure.

It was dark outside, the only light coming from the street beyond the metal fence and the two small sconces on the wall of the side door. It was enough for me to descend the steps to the cemetery grass . . . and enough for me to see what was waiting for me among the graves.

Nova was leaning up against a tree, staring at one of the huge marble squares carved with names and dates of people long forgotten. The wind was tossing her hair, looping it around her ears and her delicate throat.

My mind ran back over everything that had happened today. How she'd seen me fight her brothers . . . how she'd chased me down, desperate to talk to me, and I'd just shrugged her off. I'd been so on edge I was acting like more of an ass than usual.

Steeling myself, I approached her across the soft grass. "You planning to rob some graves?"

She jolted upright. The moon reflected in her open eyes; they were dark as molasses at that hour. "Hawthorne?"

"Listen," I started to say, lifting my foot, closing the gap between us. "About earlier . . ."

"Stop!" she cried.

Stunned, I held up my hands with my fingers spread. "I'm not going to hurt you."

She pointed down as her whole face went red. "Sorry, I know. It's just that you were about to step over a king's grave. It's bad luck."

Running my fingers through my hair, I laughed without any humor. "Do you know what can give me good luck? I'm topped off on bad." Carefully I walked around the grave. Doing so brought me close to her, closer than I'd intended. The trees around us were shedding flower petals like red confetti.

Nova inhaled as she noted our proximity. But with the big monument on one side and a tree on the other, there wasn't any way to create more distance. When her gentle cinnamon scent invaded my nose, I was happy for our predicament.

She ended the silence first. "He's over there."

I followed her slim finger. On the opposite side of the cemetery was a large block of granite. Marigolds and roses had been arranged around it. *Hester's grave.*

"I can give you some privacy," she said gently.

My attention flew back to her. "What?"

"That's why you're here, right? For your uncle?"

"No. I . . . no." Palming my neck, I felt my pulse pounding. "I just wanted to see where he was buried. I wasn't planning to talk to a bunch of dirt."

A hairline of a wrinkle wrapped over her brow. Then it was smoothed away. "How's your jaw?"

Rubbing my chin, I shrugged. "Fine. It's my hand that hurts, your brother is all mouth. It was like punching a wall."

"I'm sorry he and Richard went after you. They aren't happy about you being appointed the new king."

"Yeah, well, I'm not exactly happy, either."

She pulled her light blue jacket closer. It flared like an hourglass, drawing attention to her gorgeous curves in a way I didn't think she intended. "Having them all decide this without you must have felt like sabotage."

"It's an awful joke. I'm sure *he's* got to hate that I'm his only option."

Her thin fingers clutched tighter. "Your father, you mean?"

"Who else?" I asked, drawing in a huge breath. Everything in me felt too tight, my lungs unable to get me enough air. Having Nova here to listen to me was working me up all over again. "He never trusted me with any responsibilities before. He's always thought I was goofing off. And that's fine—it suited me well to not have to be under his damn scrutiny the way everyone else was. He was probably relieved to shove me into that dark hole of a strip club and forget about me."

Nova rocked from side to side uneasily. "Oh."

"You shouldn't be shocked," I said, "your family has been spying on mine forever. You probably have a notebook full of notes about me and all the messed-up stuff I've done, at that club and elsewhere." I looked up at the sky. "I wonder if that miserable queen knows what she's getting into."

"What do you mean?" she asked.

I let my eyes drift back to her. "I'm marrying Austere. You *know* all of this, there's no reason to play dumb."

Nova squinted at me, and for a long while she didn't blink. "I can't believe no one explained this to you. You're not marrying my aunt. My parents expect you to marry me or my sister."

She said it so bluntly. Like it was a fact as simple as water being wet. Even so, I searched her expression for some hint that this wasn't true. Nova remained serene, waiting for me to respond. "You're not kidding," I finally said.

"Of course not." Her laugh was brief and sweet. "What good would marrying my aunt do?"

I had no answer. Dammit, Rush's speculation had depressed me while being ultimately useless.

Her smile went all coy. "How does this info change things, hm?"

Leaning toward her, I watched closely for her reactions. I was hooked on them. "I see through your mysterious mask. You think that I'll happily accept this forced marriage . . . because I could end up with a beautiful woman like you? You're impossibly shameless." She blushed furiously. It changed her lips to a richer red. One of the flower petals landed in her hair; carefully I reached out and plucked it free. My voice was a smoky whisper. "You seem too nice to belong to the Valentines."

The way she angled her chin reminded me temptingly of last night, when we'd kissed. "Maybe I am." She extended her slim hand, and I thought she was going to remove a flower petal from me as I had for her. Many of them had settled on my shoulders and hair. Nova's fingers rested on my collarbone and didn't move. "I hope I'm not too nice for you."

In my gut, I knew I should be wary of this woman. But the shivers she caused erased the pain in my bruised knuckles. No one had ever soothed me so easily. It justified my eagerness to ignore the internal voice that warned me again and again who she was. "You could be nicer."

Her teeth glinted, bright in the moonlight. Her hand on my chest dug in, scraping lightly through my shirt. "I'm open to feedback."

Fucking hell. I groaned at how she was teasing me. "Walking over a grave," I whispered, sliding my hand to cup behind her ear. "You said it was bad luck."

Nova swallowed loudly. "Yes."

"And having sex in the royal family's cemetery? Is that bad luck, too?"

"It is," she said, her eyes dark, drawing me in. "Very bad."

"It's great that I'm not superstitious." Gripping her tight, I captured her mouth with mine. Her other hand joined her first, balling in my shirt to keep her on her feet. She bent into my body, her breasts pushing on my solid chest. My gun pressed between us painfully, but it was nothing compared to my massive hard-on in my jeans.

"It's also illegal," she blurted, gasping for air. Her arms circled my neck, nails digging into my hair. "If anyone catches us . . ."

"I don't care." Kissing her again, I rubbed my nose on hers. "I don't fucking care. Let the ghosts of these old kings rise up and drag me to jail themselves. I don't. Fucking. Care. This is happening."

Her lashes lowered, lines easing across her forehead. In that sacred place surrounded by monuments to the dead, I imagined she was praying; her hands linked together behind my neck, her chin bowed to her chest.

There was a serenity in how she waited for me.

I'd never fucked an angel before, but I thought this would be close.

"Off," I said, tugging at her long jacket. Nova slid her arms free as I helped with the buttons. The heavy material dropped to the grass at our feet—beneath, she was wearing a long dress with pleats. It was the same dark blue as the night sky.

"Your turn," she breathed, and her words created a hot vapor in the cool air. Her fingers trailed over my ash-gray coat, finding the zipper, not waiting for my permission as she slid the metal teeth apart.

There was a tightness in my throat. "Yes, ma'am," I chuckled huskily. I loved a woman who made it clear what she wanted. I was also too eager to bother stripping myself down. I didn't need to be naked to make this happen.

Spinning her around, I pressed her body into the bark of the tree. "Thorne," she said, my name electric from her lips. It drove me further; I found the hem of her dress, scraping it up over her hips.

Her ass was a perfect heart, and it swayed more than the one in my chest. "You want this?" I whispered, hooking a thumb in the elastic of her panties. Tugging them up, I pulled them into her crease. "Been thinking about getting stuffed by royalty, hm?"

"God, yes," she moaned. Her hips ground into my erection. I saw spots of color, working to get my pants undone.

"Good. Because I've been thinking about you since yesterday." The instant I said it, I regretted it. I didn't want to remind her that I'd forgotten her face.

Nova kept whimpering, either too wrapped up in her heat to care, or not thinking about it at all. I was still stunned that I'd forgotten this woman. It seemed impossible now.

I outlined her lower lips, creating a V with two fingers. I traced her lightly, over and over, learning the shape of her pussy and inscribing it on my memory. With the tip of one finger I glided between her legs, gently nudging her hard clit through her panties. It was the barest of touches. Nova cried out in delighted shock.

Her excitement had my dick raging hard. "You sing so damn pretty," I whispered.

She leaned into me, legs crushing my forearm. Her body was responding as if it wanted more but was afraid to take it. Again I rubbed her clit, making insistent, but slow, circles. The cloth acted like a barrier so the sensation was never too much. In fact, it was decidedly *not enough.*

"Want me to finger you?" I asked her coyly.

Her knees seesawed my wrist. "Yes, please, fuck yes."

"Your mouth gets dirty when you get horny," I said, blowing out a puff of hot air. My insides were on fire, steam wafting from my skin. Peeling her panties aside, I rolled my digits across her soaking-wet pussy. *Fucking hell.*

Wetting my fingers, I crossed them like I was making a promise. Then I penetrated her up to my knuckles. "Ah!" she gasped. I struggled to fit my fingers in. Each inch I fought for made her hotter, wetter, wilder.

"They're inside," I said, nuzzling the back of her neck. I kissed her sweating skin. "Feel them? How is it, and don't try lying."

Whimpering, her pussy twitched on my hand. "It's amazing. I've never felt . . . I've never . . ."

"You're not making any sense. Are you asking me to make you come?" Curling my fingers, I caressed the roof of her pussy in consistent waves. My other hand came around her thigh, where she couldn't trap it. I flicked her clitoris and gave it a light squeeze. As I did, I wriggled my fingers again.

"Oh, oh, I . . ." She trailed off in an obscene moan. Nova's inner walls squeezed my fingers, rippling as her orgasm stole her ability to talk. She came shamelessly, mouth open wide, head thrown back.

I tensed all over, my balls heavy, aching for release. "There we go," I said sweetly. "That's it. Fuck, you come beautifully. And quickly, guess you did want me as badly as it sounded." I pulled my fingers out and slid them over my tongue. I was drunk on the taste of her.

Groggy with lust, I undid my pants. I slid them down just enough to heft my engorged dick free. Running the fat head of my cock over the ruined material of her panties between her spread thighs, I shivered. "Listen to that. Your pussy is speaking to me, *begging* me to fuck it."

"Thorne . . . please, hurry. I don't want to wait any longer. I need to feel you, all of you!"

"What if I said too bad?" Leaning low, I nipped her ear. "What if I teased you until your cunt was melting. Made you beg so loud the whole city could hear?"

She trembled, shoving herself back at my throbbing shaft. I was dizzy with my urge, my balls flexing over and over, but I held back. I *loved* the way she was panting like an animal in heat. I could have listened to her breathing while the searing flames between her legs licked at my cock for hours.

Reaching back, she circled the base of my prick with her hand. She couldn't make a full fist; my cock appeared gigantic, and it swelled more from the visual. "Fuck me," she said, looking over her shoulder. "Now."

A wave of arousal tensed all my muscles. "Oh, sugar, you've got it. Remember that you asked for this." Yanking her sopping-wet panties to one side, I spread her swollen lips with my thumbs. Seeing my angry red cock head push against her pussy was glorious.

"Jesus," she gasped. "That's—Oh, ah, it's huge. Can it fit? Fuck, it's sliding in," she babbled, reciting everything that happened like an announcer watching a porno. Her face turned away, her arms folding to brace her against the tree.

"It'll fit," I promised. Gritting my teeth, I grunted as her inner walls smothered my dick. The veins pulsed under my grip while I guided myself inside.

My neck prickled, as if someone was watching us. But when I swiveled my head I saw no one in the cemetery. Just tall stones, taller fence posts blocking us from the street. I threw my head back and became lost in the vastness of the universe. *Of course, the stars.* That was what we were being watched by; a million burning fires that looked on as I buried myself with abandon inside Nova.

"Ah!" she squeaked. My balls hit her ass cheeks; I was all the way in.

"You're so damn tight," I said, shaking my head in wonder.

Instead of responding with her voice, her pussy performed perfect sign language. It stole away some of my control. Squeezing her waist, I bent across her back, my nose in her sweet-smelling hair. "If this is how good you feel all the time, how can I *not* marry you and lock this down?" I growled.

She wriggled under me. "More, just . . . more, please. It feels amazing!"

"I know it does," I managed, my chuckle strained. "Your pussy is applauding me, that's how happy it is." I pulled out a few inches and slammed back inside. Our skin made loud sounds from the impact. Her dress slipped lower, hiding what we were doing. Not that it mattered. Neither of us could pretend we were doing anything but fucking ourselves silly.

Sucking in sweet air through my clenched teeth, I stared down at the back of her head. Her hair was swept to one side. It exposed her caramel neck and the strangely seductive spiral of her ear. Nova embodied *sex*. It consumed me to the brink of bursting.

In a desperate attempt to keep my composure, I closed my eyes. But this just enhanced the smell of her sweat and the deep, earthy musk of our fucking. She was in my nose and in my brain and there was no escape.

Under me she tightened from toe to tip. She squeezed so hard that my eyes opened wide, but I still couldn't see. "Holy hell," I gasped, shaking with the ripples of pleasure her orgasm sent through me.

Nova came violently in my arms. Control was pointless—I gave in, pumping my hips like a beast as I drove toward my own climax. At the last second, I thought, *Don't come inside her!* I'd always used a condom. How the hell had I forgotten one this time?

Her throaty groan tickled my brain stem. Yanking backward, I watched as thick strings of semen exploded onto her inner thighs, some of it getting on the hem of her dress. I wasn't positive I'd pulled out in time. I couldn't tell from just looking.

As I studied the soft gap between her legs, I noticed something else sticking to her skin. Something darker—red. A rush of guilt made my tongue dry out. "Did I hurt you?" I asked, my voice straining from concern.

"No," she said quickly. She didn't move from the tree. Her hands were spread over the bark, it was all that kept her on her feet. I watched her shoulder blades as they rose; I was transfixed by every little pinpoint of her existence.

"You're sure?"

"I think I'd know," she said, facing me with a half smile. "Everything you did was the opposite of *hurt*. That was . . . just wow." When she reached up to fix her hair I noticed there was bark under her fingernails. There was nothing shy about the flushed red dusting her cheeks. Nova was comfortable, maybe even proud of herself.

I moved before I thought it over, kissing her where she stood. When I leaned away to look at her again, she was staring at me. I wasn't sure she'd shut her eyes during the kiss.

Aware of my naked cock arching stiffly from my fly, I tucked it inside my underwear and closed my zipper. "That was amazing," I said, laughing as I heard myself. Fuck, I sounded like a teenager. "I really needed that."

"Me too," she said, her fingers wringing in her dress. A breeze swirled around us in the cemetery. Nova shuddered, working to keep her hair from her face as she hugged herself.

Overcome by a compelling need to shelter her, I grabbed my jacket from the grass and swept it around her shoulders. "Here, use this."

She tugged at the sleeves of my jacket. "Thanks." We both glanced at our feet—at her own coat in easy reach—but didn't mention it. She accepted my chivalry with her flawless smile.

Together we sat on the ground, our hips touching, my arm around her shoulders. The world was quiet, the way the bottom of the ocean was—nothing but infinite blackness and a crushing pressure on the top of your head. It should have felt lonely.

With Nova at my side, it didn't.

"Will you do it?" she whispered. "Take the crown, I mean." *She had to go dragging us back to reality. What a fucking shame.* Lifting my arm, I spread my fingers and stared through the gaps at the starry sky. "Between you and me . . . I don't know what choice I have. Your family has tried to hurt us before. If I back out, they'll do it again." I made a fist, imagining I was crushing a handful of constellations. "The only way I get any sort of happy ending is by suffering for it. Farewell, freedom."

"Would marrying me be so bad?"

The light plea in her voice drew my attention to her. We were inches apart, the flecks in her irises glowing more than the moon over our heads. "As amazing as I certainly am," I teased, "why would *you* agree to this? Why marry me just because they say so?"

Her gaze fell to the side. A cold flare in my gut told me she was thinking of how to lie to me. "I never said I was doing anything because of them."

Startled, I touched her shoulder until she looked at me again. "You didn't say it, but it's the only thing that makes sense."

Pain rippled through her face. It darkened her eyes. Then it was gone, hidden behind her shuttered lashes and a placid frown. "You're not the only one who has had to suffer to earn their happy ending."

"Do you like being cryptic?" I asked. "You told me nothing that would help me understand you."

She stood up, dropping my jacket onto the grass. Nova stepped backward, and for a second I almost reached for her. She sensed my urge and hesitated in place, giving me a chance. I didn't take it in time.

Moving away, she tugged her own jacket on. "You might not get me," she said, "but I'm starting to understand you."

"Am I that easy to figure out?" I scoffed playfully.

Nova watched me zip my jacket, studying my movements and thinking things I couldn't possibly guess. I ached to ask her what she'd learned about me. To beg her for even a hint of what she'd gleaned. Because after all these years, I wasn't sure I understood myself.

- CHAPTER ELEVEN -

Nova

The streets were mostly empty as I ran through them toward my hotel. It was doubtful I'd have noticed anyone if they were there, though. My brain was full of one thing.

Hawthorne Badd.

When I'd run into him yesterday, it had been an accident. I hadn't thought twice about leaping in to help the poor woman who'd been robbed. But then I'd looked up, and my heart had tangled in my ribs. Hawthorne was right there. Right in front of me.

Even though I'd changed drastically in the six months since we'd seen each other . . .

He hadn't.

He was still painfully beautiful, the same haunting hurt buried in his eyes and behind his ever-present smile. I'd actually thought I'd messed everything up, that he'd recognize me and wonder what was going on, why my family was here. It was better for my situation that he didn't know. It still stung. Worse, he'd thought I'd misled him all along.

I didn't get it—how could his father not have prepared him? I *knew* my father had talked to the man about wanting to arrange this marriage. Just last night he'd sent a message to Maverick's hotel room, laying out the general offer.

Why had Thorne's own father not warned him?

Because he didn't have a chance, I realized abruptly. Frosty shame slowed my running. *Thorne was with me all night, he didn't go back to his hotel until after we separated.* That had been close to midnight.

Thinking it over, I wondered if a warning would have made much difference. *He really doesn't want to be the king.* I'd expected him to be excited about the news. Most people would jump for joy over such a blessing. I'd listened to my brothers seethe over being told they couldn't claim the throne by force, that it didn't work that way. If you didn't have blue blood, Torino wouldn't accept you as a ruler.

Thorne was entitled to the position.

But he still resisted. When I remembered his cold shoulder as he'd run away from me outside the church, it turned my stomach inside out. I'd been shocked when he'd confronted me in the cemetery tonight. I'd gone there to get some privacy . . . tired of all the manipulation my family couldn't resist taking part in.

After Thorne appeared, plucking flowers from my hair, I hadn't wanted to be alone.

Thinking about it made my skin sizzle.

How was it possible for me to come away from what we'd done and remain so unchanged? Was it because I'd already transformed so much? Remembering the hard edges of his teeth where they'd explored my softest spots, I clutched a hand to my chest. Did he have any guess what it meant for me? Could he sense the sheer magnitude of it?

I almost ran straight into my brothers as I pushed through the doors of the hotel we were staying at. They were standing in the lobby, talking in hushed tones. Larchmont spotted me, his skin oddly shiny, like he'd been out for a jog. His face still swollen.

Thorne hadn't managed to break my brother's nose—and even if it was awful, I wished he had. It might have washed off some of

Larch's self-righteous elitism. Seeing them fight had been a shock for me. I was so used to my brothers having the upper hand in everything. But Thorne had held his own, he'd fought back like he was angry at something much bigger than any of them.

Larchmont nudged Richard, who turned, scanning my face.

"Why do you two look so guilty?" I asked, eyeing them up and down as I tried to get to the stairs.

Larch snorted, blocking my path. "Us? You're the one who was gone all night. What were you doing?"

"Getting some air. Out of my way."

Richard moved aside, but my other brother didn't. "Slow down." He grabbed my upper arm, squeezing me tight, keeping me from going anywhere. "Remember who you're talking to." He dug in until I winced in pain. The men at the front desk busied themselves, avoiding getting involved. "Don't forget whose side you're on, sis."

He released me, I gingerly rubbed my skin. "I know what side I'm on."

"Sure you do," he said quietly, something dangerous putting an edge to his tone. "You were only crying out for Thorne, warning him in the fight, because you were trying to help *me*."

I held his stare. "Attacking him was your choice, not mine. I wasn't going to stand there while you and Richard ruined everything." When I slid my glare to Richard, he had the grace to turn away and stare at the floor. "It's like you didn't even listen to Dad."

"I listened. I was just seeing what made that shithead so worthy of the crown."

My eyes danced to his facial bruises. "Did you find out?"

That made his smug smile crumble. Quickly, I hurried up the stairs. He didn't follow, and I was grateful. It was stupid to egg Larch on, but his violent urges made my skin crawl.

Behind me in the hallway came footsteps. I whirled around, ready to face off with Larchmont again. But it wasn't him following me. "Richard?" I asked, knotting my eyebrows.

The biggest of my brothers approached. He filled the hallway, his size known to intimidate everyone. Not me, though. As awfully as I'd been treated by my family, Richard had never wielded the same cruelty.

He put his hands in his pockets. Casting a shifty glance over his shoulder, he came to stand over me. "Nova, listen. I don't think you should be starting fights with Larch."

My eyes narrowed. "Is that what you really wanted to talk to me about?"

His head shifted down. When he finally met my stare, his pupils were wide, his frown gentle. "I'm not oblivious. I saw the way you chased Hawthorne down the street after the funeral."

Heat flowed up my neck. *He saw that?* "If Larchmont sent you to hammer the point home—"

"He didn't." Richard fidgeted, his large shoulders rising. "I'm here because I'm worried about you. Nova, don't get too close to Hawthorne. Even if you might end up marrying him, we're your family. Not him." His features twisted. "I hate the idea of you being alone with that guy."

The anger melted from my body. It happened too fast for me to grab it, and with it went my armor. "Richard, I get that you're concerned. But please don't treat me like I'm weak."

He flinched, like he realized he was talking down to me the way my parents always did. "You're not weak," he started, carefully picking his words. "But after what you've been through . . ."

"What I went through is what *made* me strong," I said flatly. I glanced toward the wall, still speaking to him. "If you think I'm being manipulated by Thorne, you're wrong."

He went silent. Finally I heard him start to leave. "Regardless, I've got your back." His words flowed over his shoulder just before he vanished around the corner.

It took me a while to gather myself. I was tempted to run after Richard and thank him for his concern. He'd always been quiet. If he was telling me he was worried, then he really meant it. I appreciated that—but his concern was misplaced.

I reached my room on the third floor without taking the elevator. I didn't mind the effort—I was buzzing with too much energy and needed to burn it off. Richard had left my mind swirling. I made myself focus on something better.

Hawthorne.

Talking to that man was one thing, but kissing him . . . having sex with him . . . it had taken my brain and stretched it out to dry in the sun. I'd been flayed open and I *loved* it.

The memory of his hard muscles made me shiver deliciously. I opened my door and stopped on the threshold. Sitting on my bed were two women: my mother, Valencia, and my younger sister, Darla. She was a carbon copy of my mom. Slender, with the same golden-red hair, except she kept hers curled into big, bouncy ringlets, the kind a little girl's doll would have. Even though she was twenty-two, she loved to wear a mix of childish ribbons, stockings, and Mary Janes, all while her hems were too high, or her necklines too deep. It was oddly perverse. Darla appeared half-asleep, the way a lazy cat that always got what it wanted did. "Look who's finally back," she said, kicking her feet at the edge of the bed.

By my large window I saw a third figure. Austere was still wearing the same black lace she'd worn at the funeral. "Auntie," I said, acknowledging her. The older woman glanced once at me, her smile sad, before she stared out at the city again. Watching my mother, I popped the buttons open on my coat. "Were you all waiting for me?"

When she swayed onto her feet, my mother reminded me of a willow switch blowing in a light breeze. Those beautiful, slim branches could be used to burn cuts into sensitive skin. "Where did you go after dinner?" she asked.

"For a walk. I told Darla I was going out." She'd caught me in the hallway outside my room after I'd slipped into my jacket. Now she was watching me with the kind of glee unique to those who enjoyed their siblings getting in trouble.

My mother didn't even look at Darla on the bed. She kept her burned-maple eyes firmly on me. "You're saying you've been wandering around for the last three hours?"

Heat started to swim up my body. I did my best to keep it from showing in my face; I willed myself to remain neutral. "It was lovely by the ocean. I lost track of time."

She judged me, and I knew she was trying to see where my lies began and ended. Finally she sighed, giving me some relief when she turned away to fix her hair in the dresser mirror. "You should have called me. You could have gotten lost, and then where would we be?"

I tensed up, hearing what was being said between the lines about my capabilities. "I wouldn't get lost. I've been to this city a number of times. I'm not scatterbrained."

My mother studied me as she spoke. "Perhaps. But you're clearly not aware enough to have noticed that this city is full of unseemly types these days."

"I *know*," Darla gushed, wrinkling her nose. "Did you see all the dirty people sleeping next to our hotel? Disgusting."

Clenching my fists was all I could do to keep myself from shouting *It's our fault they're homeless!* My parents had been siphoning money from the royal vault for some time, and the effect on the country got worse every year.

"Anyway," Darla said, leaning eagerly toward me off the bed. Her lips were pulled back in an excited grin. "I heard you were there earlier when Larch and Rich got their butts kicked by Hawthorne. Tell me all the gritty details."

"Don't gossip about your brothers getting injured," my mother huffed.

Darla rolled her eyes. "Mom, maybe you and Auntie should go to bed. Leave us two girls alone, hm?"

"Watch it, young lady."

"That's soon-to-be young *queen*," my sister chuckled. Her words made my tongue stick to the roof of my mouth. "And when I'm married to that *violent fool*, as I heard him described, you'll be the ones who have to watch out." She winked.

Off to the side, Austere angled her body, scrutinizing my sister. I wondered what she was thinking about all this—did it hurt to have us casually discuss that we'd be replacing her?

Drawing to her full height, my mother stared down at Darla. Quickly my sister threw up her hands, laughing. "Kidding! I'm kidding. I'm not going to try and push you around, Mom."

Hanging my coat up by the door, I fingered the cuff, speaking more to it than them. "You think he'll choose you?"

"Of course he will," Darla said. She'd jumped to her feet and was adjusting her dress. "Look at me. I'm his dream girl."

"Why would you want to marry someone you just met?" I asked, mirroring Thorne's question to me in the cemetery.

Darla squinted, as if I'd started spinning on my head. "That's a stupid question. Who would turn down a chance at being a queen?" Studying her nails, she picked at one. "Besides, he's kind of hot." Her eyes shot back to me, her smile faltering. "Wait. Wait wait wait. Don't tell me *you* want to marry him?"

Before I could respond, my mother came to stand beside me. Her hand was solid on my shoulder. Her affection was a recent thing. I was still adjusting to it. A greedy part of me was hungry for any kindness she'd offer, after going so long without it. "It doesn't matter what either of you want. Darla, you're the obvious choice, and if he picks you, I'm sure you'll know what to do. But Nova . . ." She trailed off, then tightened her grip. "I expect you'll accept your duty all the same."

I touched her hand, then walked over to sit on the bed and pull off my shoes. "I knew what I was getting into when you and Dad told us the plan." I'd had to control myself from smiling too much at the time. The idea of marrying Hawthorne Badd . . . It was wild. More than I'd ever thought would happen. But any uncertainty I'd had, any doubt, had vanished after our first kiss.

"Darla?" Mom pried.

"Yes, yes, I know." She flipped her hair over her shoulders. "But an arranged marriage is *still* a marriage, and we all know that I'm the one the guys chase. Unless . . . have men been chasing you that I don't know about, Nova?"

Her jab was meant to be cruel. She wanted to nail me on how I'd never dated anyone before. But I was busy smiling at something on my leg. Touching the bandage Thorne had pressed to my scrape yesterday, I shrugged. "Who knows."

I felt Darla's stare. Giving her a side-eye, I held my silent smile. I knew she was trying to read my face. I also knew she couldn't.

Black lace swept into my vision on the floor. Austere had come to stand before me. She'd tossed her veil back, letting me see her benevolent smile. Unlike my mother's, her eyes were green. Austere had always seemed older than she was, the way adults are when you've known them since you were small, but the last few years had turned her soft skin into hardened, wiry grooves.

"You know," she said, her hands glued together in front of her waist, like she was afraid to touch anything around her, "I was nervous about marrying Hester originally. But your mother encouraged me to go for it. In the end, I did love him very much. The same could happen between you and Thorne."

She'd misread my defensiveness as fear. I didn't correct her. "Auntie . . . will you really leave this place after living here for so long?"

Her stare drifted away, seeing something other than the hotel room. "Yes. This country never welcomed me. All I want is to return to the States so I can mourn Hester in peace."

As much as I loathed what she had helped my parents do to Torino, it struck me as incredibly sad to realize Austere had loved a man who was now gone forever.

When she walked around me toward the door, I whispered, "I hope you find that peace you want. I mean it."

Her eyes widened in shock, her smile hesitant but genuine.

"Come on," my mother said. "Let's get to bed, Darla. We'll see you in the morning. Remember to wear something nice for the luncheon. The black dress I hung up for you is the one I'd prefer."

She doesn't even trust me enough to dress myself. That stung almost as much as the fact that she didn't know I hated the color black. She'd had one of our staff back home go shopping for me for this trip, giving them a list of her own preferences, never once asking my input.

When I was alone I finished stripping down. In front of the bathroom mirror, I turned from side to side, checking myself for . . . any hint that there was a difference in me after I'd had sex with Thorne. If I didn't feel it internally, perhaps it would show on the outside. Hadn't Larchmont said I looked guilty when I ran into him?

But there was nothing I could see. Just my smooth skin, free of tattoos, nothing at all like that man's stunning form. Even if I wasn't as flawless as he, I wasn't ashamed of my soft shape. Once I had been. Not any longer.

I traced a finger up my hip, then around, finally rolling over the raised scar tissue on my lower stomach. He hadn't seen it because we hadn't undressed. Would I tell him about it if he asked? Part of me thought I'd spill my soul to him. My secrets were by omission, I didn't intend to lie. It was just . . . it didn't matter. Nothing about who I'd been or how I'd found my way to metamorphosis was important.

The only thing I cared about was *now*.

Turning off the light, I fumbled for my bed in my blindness. I welcomed the pressure of the thick, heavy covers. They made me feel solid. Like I wasn't about to vanish into thin air.

Lying there, I gazed at the ceiling I couldn't see in the dark. My mind was racing too much for me to sleep. But I was used to staying awake. I didn't sleep much these days—I spent my quiet time reading or drawing. Whatever struck my mood. Every minute I wasn't doing *something* was a waste.

Tomorrow he'll decide who he'll marry. Darla was oblivious to the connection I had with Thorne. I'd clung to it since the start . . . since long before I'd ever spoken to the man. Even before seeing him in person, I'd been eager to know more about him. It had arisen from the pages of data my father had his spies collect. He'd handed them out to us, drilled us on the knowledge so that we were always aware of what the Badds were up to.

It was my father's game that I had to be a part of. I did as he asked, and he left me alone. I'd thought that was enough. I was sure that life consisted of looking at my feet while never standing up to men like my father.

Meeting Hawthorne really had changed everything.

Shutting my eyes, I stared at an inkiness no different from the lightless room. I was filled with a glorious, relaxed soreness I'd never experienced before. The insides of my thighs were tender. Parts of me were raw when I rocked this way or that. Life was *so good.*

Remembering my wish, I placed my palm gently on my scar. I didn't wonder if my suffering had been worth it. Not when I thought about the way Thorne had flirted with me . . . courted me . . . kissed me.

Fucked me.

Karma made me confident that it wasn't possible for life to throw any more tragedy at my feet. I fell asleep not realizing how naive I was. How wrong I was.

But I would learn.

- CHAPTER TWELVE -

HAWTHORNE

Lifting the newspaper, I offered it to my father when he opened the door to his hotel room. "Happy Back from the Dead Day," I said with a smile.

His grim frown didn't budge. "Get in here."

"I'm guessing you already saw the paper," I said, following him inside. My mother was sitting at a table in the morning sunlight. She'd pulled her hair up on her head. It showed off her long neck where her velvety pale purple robe didn't hide it. There were pockets under her tired eyes.

Looking at me, she offered a croissant from the basket she had. They must have ordered room service. "Morning, Thorne," she said. "Here. Eat up, you're going to need your energy today."

"As opposed to every other day." I dropped the paper on the table. I took the croissant, bit off a hunk, and chewed. My father was sitting on the huge bed, gripping his own copy of the newspaper and staring at it. I knew what he was reading; I'd read it multiple times, too, when I'd picked it up off my hallway floor.

"Long-Lost Prince Returns. Will He Take the Crown?"

Swallowing the bread, I flapped the paper I'd brought and read it aloud. "'Maverick Fredricson comes back from the dead. Multiple authorities have confirmed his identity after an official statement from Glen Finbar of the royal guard, but no one can confirm why our lost prince has come home. Does he want to take his late brother's place?'" I squinted at my dad. "Well, does he?"

My mother's hand rested on mine. "Sit," she said. "Please." Hesitating, I settled across from her at the table. She didn't let go of me. "I know this isn't what you wanted when you came to Torino."

"It's not what I wanted *ever*," I corrected. "I'm not Kain or Costello. I don't want a wife to stroke my ego all day—though now that I say it . . ."

"Stop playing around," Maverick snapped. I glanced at him as he rose from the bed. "You're always making damn jokes. There's nothing to laugh at here."

"Laughter is the only thing keeping me from swinging my fists." I chuckled sourly; my mother squeezed my hand, drawing my attention again. "Ma, it's nice that you're trying to calm me down, but nothing you say is going to make this easier."

"I know that." Her eyes fell away, over to the window. "Thorne . . . you don't have to become king."

"What?" I asked, stunned.

"What?" my father growled.

She looked at each of us in turn. "No one will force you. Especially not us." My father moved our way; he stopped when she glared at him and lifted her hand in the air. "Especially not us," she repeated.

"Carmina . . . ," Maverick said warily.

Her dark eyes flashed. She was the only person I knew who could challenge my father and win. When he remained standing, she looked back at me with a small, gentle smile. "This is your choice. I'm going to give you all the information you need so you can decide what you want to do."

I held her eyes. "I want to know what happens if I say no." I had a strong suspicion but needed to hear her say it.

"The Valentines will fight to keep the throne. They'll kill everyone who dares to threaten their claim."

"Our whole family," I said, frowning.

"Yes. But not just us. The people of Torino will reject them, too. They believe strongly in the royal succession. It'll be a bloodbath before they give the crown to a family that has no claim."

A void formed in my belly. I tasted bile instead of the sweet pastry from before. "Can't we just tell them we won't take the throne or whatever?" I pointed at Maverick. "You ran once. Let's tell them we'll run again and never come back."

He made bulging fists at his sides. "It's not that easy."

"Sure it is! We shake Kurtis's hand, tell them good luck, and off we go."

"No," he said, looking at the floor. "I can't."

Confused, I judged his expression—how flustered he suddenly seemed. A cold tingle swam through the creases of my brain. "You don't *want* to give the crown up, do you?"

He managed to look at me. I think, if I'd been in his shoes, I would have been too ashamed to do the same. "This country is a mess. My brother left it in shambles. I can't turn my back on everyone a second time."

His honesty shocked me enough that some of my anger dissipated. "What's stopping you from becoming the king again?"

"Weren't you listening yesterday?" he sighed. "They want to put one of their own up there next to you. That's the agreement, and I'm not getting a divorce to make that happen."

My mom clicked her tongue. "Of course not."

"And me trying to take the crown by force is as good as going to war with the Valentines," he said. "I won't put so many people in danger."

I wanted to ask if saving this place was worth sacrificing me. Instead I turned back to my mother. "Tell me what happens if I say yes."

My parents shared a quick look. "I think," she said slowly, "that depends on you. They've got two girls, Darla and Nova. Both have agreed to the marriage."

"So I do get *some* say in this," I said, chuckling. I didn't tell them Nova had already explained this part to me. It felt good to have one secret when they had so many. "Is this how they did it when you were younger, Dad? Arranged marriages?"

He shook his head and folded his arms. "No. Though many families would try to get their daughters close to my brother and me, vying for attention. The things they'd do to win us over . . ." My mother tightened her lips; he cleared his throat. "Anyway, it sounds like you're considering this offer now."

I leaned my chair back on its rear legs, balancing. "You staked Rush at my room yesterday. Did you have him there to give you a heads-up in case I ran away after what went down at the funeral?"

Maverick considered me for a minute. "I always expect the best from my children."

"You must be disappointed constantly, then," I said, standing. "I want to talk this over with the Valentines more. I need to know what everyone is getting out of this, *beyond* us keeping our heads."

Some tension left my father's face. "It's already been set."

"What has?"

My mother rose and headed to the bathroom. "The meeting," she said, vanishing around the corner. "They're expecting us for lunch today."

Of course they are. "When I become king, everyone has to start telling me the plans. I hate being out of the loop."

"When you become king," my dad said, clapping me on the shoulder, "you'll have a lot more to worry about than lunch meetings."

It was an interesting experience leaving the hotel.

I knew word had gotten out about my father returning to the country, but I wasn't quite ready for the amount of attention that would bring us. Rush warned us before we left our rooms.

He and the other guards made sure there was a path for us so we could get from the lobby to the car that was waiting on the street. I tried to tell how my father felt about the rows of cameras waiting to take pictures of us as we hovered just inside the hotel's front doors. His emotionless expression made it too hard.

My mother, at least, was enjoying the attention. Back home, she was very aware that the local news might snap a photo or two of her while she was out on the town or having lunch with a friend. She seemed quite comfortable with her dark glasses hiding her eyes and her lips shining deep pink as they held a perfect smile.

She'd even changed the outfit she was going to wear when Rush came to our room with the news about the paparazzi outside. Instead of the lovely but simple green sundress that she'd been wearing, she'd quickly changed into something more luxurious and expensive. It looked like a white power suit, except that the middle was a corset in glittery gold, a skirtlike flare sticking out at her hips.

"It's a peplum," she told me when she saw my baffled look. I had no clue what that was, but I nodded.

Following my father down the front steps, we braced for the explosive questions and flashing lights of the cameras. "Maverick!" someone shouted. "What do you think about your brother's death?"

"Maverick, Maverick!" someone else demanded. "Is it true you've been running this country from the shadows all this time?"

"Are you here to take the crown?"

"Will you move into the castle?"

"Is it true you changed your last name?"

The reporters got too close, screaming questions at my parents. I was partially blinded by all the flashes, and I wished that I'd worn sunglasses like my mother. "Hey!" one of the paparazzi shouted. "Hey, Maverick, why don't you get the fuck out of here, huh?"

I turned, squinting to see who was saying such bold things to my father. Didn't they know who he was? *Of course they do, that's why they're so angry.*

"What did you do, run away? Abandon your country, hightail it out of here when your daddy got sick because you couldn't handle the pressure? Hester ruined Torino, do you get that? Your brother was a piece of shit. And you're a piece of shit, too!"

I saw the man now; he was wearing a badge like all the other paparazzi, so he wasn't just some crazy rando in the street. People were videotaping the encounter. My father faced the car with stiff shoulders. He seemed frozen with inaction. I'd never seen him take such abuse so quietly.

My mother put a hand out, comforting him. I couldn't hear what she said over the murmur of the crowd. But I did hear what the reporter yelled.

"Is that who you left us for, some piece of ass?"

Anger turned my blood hot.

"Was she worth it? Was the bitch worth making the rest of us suffer thanks to you being a goddamn coward?"

"Hey!" I shouted, stomping toward the man. He'd pushed forward so much that he was leaning over the arm of one of the security guards.

"Hawthorne, no," my mom hissed.

Ignoring her, I went nose to nose with the reporter. I saw Rush nearby, his eyebrows arched with panic. They'd been ready to stop the paparazzi, but not ready to stop me. "I don't know who you are," I said, looming over him, "but you need to back off. Now."

The man gave a haphazard grin. His eyes flashed toward my mother, then back to me. "Who are you? Huh? Her personal bodyguard? Sleeping with her and Maverick in some twisted little ménage?"

A tornado of fury made my vision swim. "Stop saying sick shit about my mom, or you're going to be finding out what your camera tastes like."

His eyes narrowed. "Your *mom*? That makes you Maverick's son?"

My mother grabbed my wrist, taking me toward the car. I couldn't rip my eyes away from that asshole, I stared at him until I was in the vehicle and behind the tinted windows.

"Fuck, that pisses me off," I said softly. My mother gave my wrist a pat. Turning, I looked at my dad. "Why didn't you say anything?"

He stared straight ahead. "What could I say? They're not wrong. I did run away."

Thrown off, I bent around my mom, yelling at him. My voice was louder than it needed to be in the car but I didn't care. "Not about that! That guy was insulting your *wife*."

Maverick blinked. He turned, looking at me, then to my mother. Firmly, he took her hands, cupping them in his. "You're right. I'm sorry, Carmina. I was . . . distracted." He winced, and I thought, if I wasn't there, he would have told her more.

Instead he went quiet, aided by her head falling on his shoulder. "It's all right. Those bastards out there are small potatoes. You ever listen to the gossip rags in Providence? They've said way worse things about me than these schmucks."

She brushed it off so casually. I actually believed that the words thrown at her hadn't hurt her at all. But they'd sliced right through me. I loved my mother with all I had, and I wasn't sure I could control myself if the paparazzi went off on her in front of me again.

Picturing that man's face whenever I shut my eyes, I instead stared out the window at the busy streets for the entire trip. None of us spoke, though my dad did field a few text messages. Business never stopped for him.

The Valentines were waiting for us in a beautiful garden patio that was hidden at the back of the Tin Whistle Grill. It was quiet, I was sure the servers had arranged to keep our sequestered table more private than usual. The sky could be glimpsed through the wooden beams overhead. Vines hung with trumpet-shaped flowers draped the beams from end to end. Tiny hummingbirds the color of overripe grapes darted through the air, helping themselves to the nectar.

It was a fantastical sight, but my interest lay in something even more attractive.

Nova sat at the table with her hands folded in her lap. She was wearing a layered dress the color of cream soda. It made her cinnamon eyes look extra vibrant. Her hair was braided in a design that kept her neck exposed.

Kurtis and Valencia were sitting to her left. On her right was a young woman I'd seen with them at the funeral. I assumed this was her sister, Darla. The green top she had on was clinging to her breasts like a pair of angry hands. If her long ringlets hadn't been draped over her shoulders to hide most of her cleavage, the outfit would have been too obscene to wear in public.

I was relieved that none of Nova's brothers were around. I'd be happy to never see them again. Approaching the table, I placed myself directly in front of Nova. "Hey there," I said with a smile.

"Hey," she responded. When I rested my hands on the table, she looked at them. I wondered if she was remembering how they had felt on her body. How they had felt inside her. With a slight grin, I flexed my two fingers, like I was scratching at the tabletop.

Nova swallowed, shifting from side to side. Yes, she definitely remembered how my fingers had felt inside her tight pussy last night.

"Kurtis," my father said as he sat down beside me. My mother joined him, nodding politely at the others.

"I hope you didn't wait long," she said. "This is a lovely place."

"It is," Valencia agreed. "And I've heard that the crab bisque they serve is divine."

Their empty back-and-forth instantly got under my skin. "All right," I said, leaning back in my chair. "Are we all just going to pretend that this is a normal lunch we're having here? Because I'm not that great at playing pretend."

The girl I didn't know giggled. It was a sharp sound, too loud, too enthusiastic to be real. "You *are* funny," she said, folding her hands under her chin and leaning my way over the table.

The way she called me funny reminded me disturbingly of Larchmont.

"I'm Darla, by the way." She extended her arm toward me. Her hands looked smooth, with the same healthy tan that the rest of the Valentines had. While Nova kept her nails clean and bare, her sister wore glittery purple polish.

I gripped her hand. "I'm Hawthorne, but I'm guessing you knew that. We've met before, haven't we?"

She held my hand like she didn't want me to pull away. When I did, her smile twitched but stayed on her face. "So you do remember me. I got to visit your lovely estate a while back."

I'd recognized Darla easier than I had Nova, which filled me with shame. But Darla was just the type of girl who drew attention to herself. Even if it wasn't the best kind of attention, even if it didn't endear me to her, she knew how to draw you in. It leaked out of her every movement.

The air around her seemed to attract and confuse the hummingbirds. Her perfume made her smell sweet, but there was no nourishment here for the birds. Everything about this girl was a lie within a lie, and she definitely fit in with her family more than Nova did.

Kurtis rocked forward, his elbows on the table and his fingers woven together. "I don't mind getting to the point. I assume your mother and father laid out our offer?"

"Is that what you're calling it, *your offer*?" I snorted. "Say it for what it is: a threat so that I'll marry Nova. This isn't much different than the offer you made to me and my family months ago. How did you put it back then? Something about no danger coming to us as long as we didn't try to rise above our stations?"

Every eye was on me. Kurtis's lips were thin from being pressed together. I wondered what my father's expression was, but I didn't break from my stare-down. I wanted Kurtis to know he didn't scare me. None of them did.

Valencia breathed in, gathering herself and shattering the tension with a little clap. "All I heard in that little rant of yours is that you've chosen Nova. Which is good, that's a step in the right direction."

I stiffened at her observation. I'd been angry, but I hadn't meant to reveal something that they could use against me. I looked over at Nova. She was chewing on her bottom lip, pulling it back and forth over her bottom row of teeth. I wondered what she was thinking. She was much harder to read than her sister, who was turning pink and openly scowling at me. I guessed she'd stop wasting her time flirting with me now.

Maverick motioned for a waiter. "The vibe is a bit aggressive," he said. "Let's order some drinks, and then we can continue with the details."

"Fine." I leaned over my mother so that I could speak to the waiter first. "Do you know how to make a brown derby?" The waiter blinked stupidly. "It's not complicated. Tell your bartender to just mix some bourbon with some honey and grapefruit juice."

Everyone else ordered wine. In silence we sat, and even after the drinks came, we still tiptoed around the elephant in the room. It was driving me mad. I started to count the hummingbirds to stay sane.

Under the table, something nudged me. Lifting my eyes, I caught Nova smiling. It was a tiny twist of her lips, like she was silently apologizing for the situation her family had put us in. I wanted to tell her she didn't have to be sorry. I knew the helplessness that came along with being the child of a power-hungry father.

Setting her goblet down, Valencia went, "*Ahem.*" It drew everyone's attention. "Let me start by saying this. My sister has lived a very comfortable life here for many, many years."

My mother *hmm*'d under her breath. "Amazing that she's willing to just walk away from all that comfort. I see she didn't deign to join us, either."

The other woman's smile was plastic beneath her vibrant peach-colored lipstick. "Let me finish. She lived comfortably, but the people here never embraced her. She's quite relieved to exit and return to the States. Austere won't interfere with you taking the crown," she finished while turning her hooded eyes to me.

"Of course she won't," I said, shrugging lazily. "She's got a sister who'll keep feeding her money, money probably supplied by this kingdom. All the reward, none of the work."

"Thorne . . . ," my mother sighed. Then she pursed her lips and said flatly, "Well. He's not wrong." She glanced over at Kurtis and his wife. "Both of you clearly benefited from her being the queen. I expect you'll give her anything she needs to support her lavish lifestyle elsewhere."

Her directness had me and my father grinning into our drinks.

Kurtis pushed his shoulder blades back, cracking his joints. "There's more than enough wealth in the royal vaults to go around. A little to my sister-in-law won't hurt anyone."

Nova squirmed, suddenly interested in the basket of bread on the table. She took a piece, but she didn't eat it, just looked at it from multiple angles.

"So break it down for me," I said. "How exactly would you like this to go?"

Kurtis eyed his two daughters as he spoke to me. "You would marry one of them. Nova sounds like your preference." He tossed me a quick look and a quicker smile. "We would then stage an engagement photo session to announce to Torino and the world that the crown prince in line for the throne is marrying Nova Valentine. That would lead some positive buzz into the coronation dinner. After that, it would be a simple matter to arrange the wedding, making it official."

"You really do have our lives planned out," I mused. Why was my glass empty already? I didn't recall inhaling my drink, but I must have.

"There is more." Kurtis turned his attention to my parents. "We all know that this marriage would only protect my family for so long. If something happened to Hawthorne, well, we'd be back to square one."

"How considerate of you to worry about my health." I didn't hide the poison in my voice. "What would keep this union from just being a waste of time?" And as I asked, I knew the answer.

"A baby," Nova said, finally lifting her eyes from the torn-up bread. "My parents expect us to create the heir that Austere couldn't."

Sweat began to sprout along my throat.

"Yes," her father said. "That's exactly it. A child is the only thing that would truly protect my family from being tossed aside in the long run. It secures our future claim to the crown by blood."

"Thorne?" my mother asked gently. "You're hearing this?"

"Oh, I'm hearing it. Loud and clear." I tilted my glass, squinting into it. It was empty, it didn't matter. No amount of alcohol could wipe clean the sensation of unease growing inside me.

I was going to become not just the king, but a father. My whole life was laid out in front of me. But it wasn't *my* fate. It wasn't ever supposed to be. If it belonged to anyone, it was Costello. That thought made me realize how little my father had said in this whole meeting.

How could he sit there, silently letting this happen?

I pivoted so I could level my glare at him. He was hunched forward, all hard planes and emotionless rock. "I guess you shouldn't have wasted all that time preparing Costello for this kind of life, huh?" I laughed, and I was sure they could all hear my disgust. "It's just crazy."

"I know it's a lot," Nova said gently. "And if you don't want to do it, I understand."

Her mother whipped her head around so fast it sent her hair rippling down her bare shoulders. She was watching her daughter like she was prepared to smack a palm over her mouth to shut her up.

Nova ignored her. She only had eyes for me. "I really, *really* would understand if you didn't want to do this. When I sat in that meeting at your estate, I was terrified." Her frown fluttered into place. I wanted to kiss it away. "You didn't know me, I didn't know you. I'm sure you thought I was as awful as my brothers. And I know you didn't like the tentative peace treaty we all agreed on.

"You have no reason to want to be with me, not a single one." She made fists on the table, and a wave of determination moved through the line of her jaw, making it harder. "If you give me a chance, I think we can make this work. And if it means that everyone you love, and everyone I love, can go on and live for years and years without looking over their shoulders in fear, isn't it worth a shot?"

The entire table was silent. My heart was throbbing and I didn't know whether it was from appreciation for her honesty or panic over the fact that I felt myself agreeing with her. If she was tricking me, she was doing a damn good job of it.

I was compelled to back down from the growing disgust inside me. "I want everyone to know that I'm not a fan of this kind of ambush," I said carefully. "But I'm even less of a fan of my family or myself having our throats slit." I looked at Nova, studying how still she was. How brave was this woman? Or was I just an idiot to believe her speech?

"I'll do it," I said. "I mean, you probably guessed that I would, since you aren't really giving me many options. I'd planned to make a *much* bigger deal about this and be much more difficult, but Nova . . . let's just say she's more charming than I was ready for."

Darla rolled her eyes. "Why am I even here?" she asked. "I could've avoided being embarrassed like this if Nova had just said that she had this guy wrapped around her little finger."

"Darla," Valencia warned.

Her daughter folded her arms. "Just let me know when I can bring my things over to the castle, I'm sick of that hotel room. And I should at least get something nice out of this trip for all my troubles."

If I hadn't been turned off by Darla before, I definitely was now.

"About that," my father said. "I, too, would like to move into the castle. I expect that won't be a problem?"

"Your son is about to become king." Kurtis chuckled. "I don't see anyone trying to bar you from entering the castle. It belongs to all of us. We're all going to be one big, happy family now, aren't we?"

His words turned my stomach. Under the table I gave Nova's foot a slight kick, just to get her attention. It worked, and she rewarded me with a questioning smile. "You're really sure about this?" I asked, as quietly as I could. It was for her ears alone.

She glanced around, then back to me. "Of course. I wouldn't be here if I wasn't sure."

Her confidence made my pulse throb. It drove me crazy wondering how much of her wanted this marriage with me, and how much of her was after something else. There were a lot of unknowns.

I waved my empty glass at the waiter. "Then I guess we should toast our inevitable engagement. Did you buy the ring already, too?" I asked, arching my eyebrows at Kurtis and his wife. "Write our vows while you were at it?"

Nova flinched. But my mother, her eyes lit up. "We might as well have some fun with this," she said. "I'll meet with the engagement photographer. And I definitely want to help with the wedding. Oh, gosh, we'll need to invite everyone we can with such short notice. Your siblings would kill me if they missed this."

The rest of the meal went by mostly in silence. No one really had anything to discuss, and it was obvious we were still on shaky ground. None of us were friends. All of us wanted something from each other.

And as I finished off the new drink the waiter brought me, I wondered if any of us would get what we were after.

- CHAPTER THIRTEEN -

HAWTHORNE

I'd seen the castle from a distance. It had felt like a painting, something that you never expected to come into full focus. The closer we got, the more magnificent the structure became. It was set back from the center of the city. I wondered why, until I noticed the right side faced the ocean. *That makes it more secure from attack.* There'd be no way for enemies to scale the cliff walls without the castle having an advantage.

I'd learned that in one of the many war-room-style meetings my father had had me sit through. It was strange to have something from a history lesson be so relevant now.

My car lifted dust as it maneuvered toward the long stretch of spike-topped gates. They were open for us. Waiting. People standing at roadside fruit stands, buying or selling, stared at my window as I passed. They couldn't see through the tint, but they didn't need to in order to know our caravan of fancy cars was important.

My town car was in the middle—Rush and more security had gone ahead. Behind me were vans with my luggage, as well as my parents'. They were back there somewhere, too; I'd asked to ride alone.

It might be the last bit of solitude I get for a while, I thought, dreading what was to come. Were the Valentines really going to move into the castle with us? They were taking this "one big happy family" shit too far.

When my driver pulled onto the flat stones in front of the giant arched doors, I sucked in a hard breath. Then another. I still struggled to believe this was happening. It was all so damn fast. Surreal.

The attendants must have thought I was waiting for them to open my door, and not that I was hiding, grasping at every last second I had in the back seat, because I saw a young man hurry over and yank on the handle. "Sir," he said, beaming. "Welcome to Red Crown Palace. Let me help you out of there." He stretched his arm out toward me expectantly.

I stared at him from inside the car. He stared back.

His smile cracked. "Uh, is everything all right?"

My eyes darted pointedly to his half-curled fingers. "I thought so, but now you're making me wonder if my legs are broken or something." His whole face shaded crimson. "I appreciate how badly you want to feel my grip. But didn't you hear? I'm off the market. No more slutty hand-holding for me."

He was still blushing as he moved out of my way so I could step into the sun. Shielding my forehead, I squinted at the cloudless expanse of sky. I'd been in this country for a week now, it amazed me that I hadn't seen a drop of rain.

The young man bowed his head to me. "I'll help get your things and bring them inside. If you need anything, just shout. My name's Drake." He jogged away, his ears still glowing. I almost felt bad for teasing him.

Our motorcade filled up the long driveway. I spotted my parents as they exited their car. My father said something in my mother's ear. She kissed his cheek, leaving him and coming toward me. "Isn't this amazing?" she gushed, giving her light green shawl a toss over her shoulders. "And the view of the ocean!"

"It's fine." *Nova will love it.* I shook myself, hands in the pockets of my slate-blue trousers. "Let's see if it's as nice on the inside."

I'd always imagined castles as purely exteriors. Just pointy towers and stones, maybe a moat. I hadn't spent any time picturing the inside of such a huge structure. My mother and I passed through the giant doors that were partially open. I'd thought the cathedral was magnificent. This, though? This was something else entirely.

Standing where I was, I could see that every exit from the foyer was flanked by shiny statues. They were as bronze as the floors, as old as the walls. Crimson rugs splayed out toward the tall staircases that headed to the second-floor balcony above.

It was all strangely familiar. But I couldn't place why.

My mother was twirling in a circle, gasping as she gazed around the castle. "It's so gorgeous!"

"It seems a little extreme. Do we really need all the space?"

"What, do you want to start renovating things already?" she teased. "You've barely moved in and you're already nitpicking."

"You should want me to feel comfortable." My hands were still in my pockets. My limbs were taut, stiff—as if I was too nervous to touch anything. I was a foreigner here, no matter what people said . . . no matter what preparations had been made.

My father's friend, Glen, had been the ambassador for us. The bearer of the big news. Every inhabitant of the castle now knew exactly who we were. And who I *would* be.

I could feel them watching me as I stood there. The castle guards gave me brief glances, and the maids and butlers pursed their lips in my peripheral vision. They were wondering if I was going to be worse than my uncle. Or maybe they were wondering why someone they'd never met was running their home.

It mirrored my first day at the Dirty Dolls. No one had liked me then, either. They'd just pretended to out of fear. I'd worked hard to gain the trust of all the girls. I'd stayed after hours many nights to get to know the bodyguards and bartenders. It had taken a lot of work before they'd welcomed me. Years, even.

I wasn't looking forward to repeating that here.

"Come on," my mother said. "Let's take a tour."

Looking over my shoulder, I saw that my father was talking to Glen. They had their heads bent together. The tense lines that had haunted my father since we'd arrived hadn't vanished; if anything, they'd increased.

Part of me wanted to be included in their discussion. At the same time, I was relieved that they hadn't tried to involve me. I didn't know what they were talking about, but I was sure it was something stressful.

"All right," I said with a smile, "lead on."

My mother glided through the long hallways, gasping at every single oil painting and elaborate vase and colored window. The castle was much bigger than the home I'd grown up in.

When we walked outside into the gardens and I saw all the white roses, I realized why everything felt so familiar to me. My father had grown up here. He'd used much of his old home as the inspiration for the estate he'd built in Rhode Island. Our gardens back there were very much like these. And the architecture, the color schemes, the rugs I'd taken my first steps on . . . all of it had been influenced by my father's memories.

My feet slowed, then halted, on the grass. *All along, he was still attached to this place. He never actually let it go when he ran.*

My mother must have realized as well, because she was staring out over the greenery with a wistful smile on her face. She turned, catching me watching her. The vulnerability in her expression went up like smoke. "This is where the engagement photos are going to be done," she chirped.

She doesn't want to talk about it. "It's as good a place as any." I spoke with a casual shrug, doing my best to go along with her wish to drop the unspoken subject.

My mother gave me a light tap on the shoulder. "I know this is hard, but try to enjoy it for what it is."

"Do I look like I'm not having a good time?" I asked, making sure my voice was light. "I'd like to think that for someone being forced into early fatherhood, I'm doing a pretty good job on the cheerful front."

She clicked her tongue at me. "Say whatever you want, but I can tell you like her."

I laughed harder than I should have. "Yeah?"

"Don't forget, I'm your mother. I know you better than anyone. And you like that girl."

The urge to argue bubbled up. Her chin was jutting forward—she always did that when she was feeling cocky. She had every reason to be. My mother was right. I did like Nova, and thinking about her genuine laughter as it tickled from her throat . . . of how perfectly her waist dipped into her deliciously round ass . . . it left me distracted.

"The situation could be worse," I admitted. "So when is this photo shoot happening again?"

"Tomorrow. I'll try to find something nice for you to wear."

"Make sure it brings out my eyes."

Swirling on her heel, she sent her shawl gliding through the air. Clutching it back in place, she walked toward the patio doors. "I'm going to go check out the kitchen, are you coming with me?"

"Not yet. I could use a little fresh air."

She left me there. Folding my arms behind my back, I strolled through the hedges. It was like a small maze created from roses and ivy. Not so big that I could get lost, but enough that I could feel like I was alone.

Wandering aimlessly, I gazed up at faded ivory statues of cherubs. An angel with wide wings guarded a waterless fountain. My phone buzzed in my pocket, startling me. I checked it, scowling at the pointless spam email alert. I'd thought it was a message.

Frowning, I ran my thumb on the corner of my phone. Opening my text app, I was halfway to typing a message to . . . well, I didn't even know who. It wasn't like I was really close to my brothers or my sisters. Not enough that I could send them a message telling them what I was feeling. As it was, I wasn't so sure myself.

Sighing, I fingered the screen, making little circles. Leaning against the hedges, I inhaled the heady scent of roses. I hadn't seen Nova since the luncheon four days ago. I didn't know where she was staying, and I hadn't felt like I could ask anyone for her information without looking desperate. If not tonight, I'd see her tomorrow at the engagement shoot. I just had to be patient.

Voices crept into my ears. I leaned away from the hedges, peering through leaves. I caught the telltale profile of my father, then the deep voice of Glen as they moved through the grass nearby. They must have come outside looking for somewhere more private to talk.

"It's bad," Glen said. "I don't know if you understand how much your brother left this country in ruins."

"I got a sense for it just from looking around," my father mumbled. "But tell me what you can. I'm not allowed to touch any official documents or even the ledger until Thorne is crowned."

"Hester spent money greasing the palms of corrupt officials so he could keep even more coin for himself. And the queen, my God! Between her and her brother-in-law, the amount of loans they've taken from the Royal Bank is astronomical. And I call them loans, but there's no intent to pay them back."

They discussed more of the country's struggling condition. I'd heard some of this at the hotel, but at the time I'd felt too awkward to get involved. Now this talk about the country falling apart served to terrify me. I didn't know anything about the laws here . . . the ins and outs. How was I going to rule Torino? *I should step out and just ask them for advice.*

"Fixing this place is going to take everything we have," my father said, sighing. His voice was gravel and sand. "We'll have to arrange multiple meetings daily once the coronation is complete."

There was a pregnant pause. "Do you think your son can handle it?" Glen asked.

All the blood in my body tingled—it swam through my skull. The thorny bushes scraped my cheek as I desperately pressed closer so I could hear my dad's answer.

"Being king requires work ethic, dedication, and passion." The grass crunched under Maverick's heavy heels; he was walking away. "Hawthorne has none of those things."

A blossom of pain grew in my heart. They were still talking, but their voices were fading. If I'd been farther away . . . if they'd left sooner . . . I wouldn't have heard what my father thought about my capabilities. What he thought about *me*.

I'd always suspected it.

That wasn't enough to prepare me for his brutal honesty.

I didn't remember walking back to the castle, but I must have, because all around me were the pale stone walls of the foyer. In my fog I ascended one of the two long staircases that flanked the entryway. Resting my arms on the banister, I observed the porters rushing around with boxes. My suitcases were being unloaded right now, no doubt.

Up here no one noticed me. I was free to watch maids gossip to each other. I saw someone drop a suitcase so hard it *had* to have broken anything fragile inside, look around guiltily, then act like nothing had happened.

Across from me, over the big doors, was a huge oil painting. It spanned most of the wall—ten feet across or more. The colors were hauntingly dark, showing a man with a russet beard and mounds of sideburns. With all that hair, he made me think of a grizzly bear that had stolen a white suit and squeezed itself into it. On his head rested a crown as stiff and severe as his stone-hard expression.

He was standing beside a woman whose brunette curls were piled higher than a twelve-tier cake. In front of them, toy soldiers in red dress shirts and blue slacks, their shoes glistening like obsidian, were two young boys. Probably no more than eight or ten, half the size of the gigantic hunting dogs in the painting with them. Both boys had bright sapphire eyes.

A fingertip of intuition scratched up my brain stem. *That's Dad and his brother, isn't it?* I squinted at the older couple with new appreciation. *Then that must be their father and mother.* Hansel . . . and Luca, the woman my middle name was birthed from.

I could see the resemblance between them and Maverick easily. They all shared the same intense features. Had my father been humorless even as a child? *Well, that's not hard to believe.* Thinking about him made my hackles rise. *He thinks I'm a failure.* He always had. Why did it scald me hotter now than ever before?

Through the open doors below, a long shadow spread on the red carpet. It heralded the swaying skirt and easy grace of Nova Valentine. From where I was, I could see the part in her hair—somehow paler than the rest of her skin. It stood out from her auburn hair, guiding my eyes down like an arrow to her nose, her collarbone, and ultimately the hint of cleavage.

This was a very, *very* good spot I'd picked to stand at.

She glanced around, but it wasn't with the same curiosity I'd had. As if she'd been in many castles and they bored her now. As if she'd been in *this* castle before.

Behind her came Darla, Richard, and their mother. Then Larchmont. He walked with a swagger. I was pleased to see the purplish bruise lingering by the bridge of his nose almost a week after our fight. He, too, gazed around like he didn't care where he was.

He bent low, whispering to Nova. My hands crushed the banister. Nova frowned, moving away from him and vanishing down the east wing. The others followed her, the only audible noise Larchmont's cringe-inducing laughter as it echoed around the wide foyer.

I debated following them. My urge to talk to Nova . . . to be close to her . . . was maddening. *Slow down, Casanova,* I told myself. *You're acting like a lovestruck moron.* While I wanted to trust Nova, I had to remember who she was. Seeing her with her family was one of the few things capable of driving a sharp, solid bolt of ice into my guts. There was no denying the physical pull between us, our sexual chemistry was out of this world. That was dangerous. Even if she had the same motives as me, a desire to avoid a bloody revolution, she was still a part of the Valentines. My enemies.

Stepping off the last stair, I moved toward the front doors. I was hoping to find that kid Drake and learn where the hell my things were. I'd never find my bedroom in this castle without guidance.

"Thorne," Nova said. I froze midstep. She was standing in the hallway where I'd seen her go with her family. Now she was alone. Her expression was a mix of surprise and delight at seeing me. "When did you get here?"

"Around half an hour ago," I said.

She came closer, looking from me to the doors, then back. "Were you going out?"

Say you're leaving. Say goodbye. Remember who she is.

"Want to come with me?" I asked. *Fuck.*

Nova's eyes brightened. "I'd love that."

The way that sounded from her tongue, *love,* created a whirl of excitement in my belly. *What's the point in being suspicious?* I asked myself, reaching for her hand. *I already agreed to the marriage. Might as well go all in and enjoy it.*

"Where are we going?" She beamed as she chased me out the front of the castle.

Scanning the area, I waved when I spotted Drake. "We're going to indulge in something I haven't in far too long." He ran over, letting me whisper in his ear. He blinked, then handed me some keys while pointing at one of the many cars glistening in the gigantic driveway.

"And what's that?" she laughed, still holding my hand, still gripping it tight.

I winked at her. "Retail therapy."

- CHAPTER FOURTEEN -

Nova

I didn't expect to be alone with Thorne again so soon. But here I was, flying down the road, wind from the open windows tossing my hair into a knot.

"Do you mind if I put on some music?" he asked. I shook my head and he cranked the radio. Channels and static crackled through the speakers: pop music, something in French, then the tinkle of instrumental piano.

I figured he'd keep going. He didn't.

"You like classical?" I asked, not able to hide my surprise.

"I do." His black eyes bounced to me, then back to the road. "I know. I don't look like the type, but I actually used to play piano."

His long fingers, gripping the wheel, took on a new meaning. Thorne had been skilled with them, playing me like I was an instrument he knew by heart. "I always wanted to play an instrument."

"Why didn't you?"

Looking at my hands, I smiled solemnly. "Ah. My parents didn't bother to let me try. I think they didn't see much value in it." I noticed him side-eyeing me and cleared my throat. "You probably started when you were really little, right? That's how all the greats begin."

His chuckle was full of grit. "I began playing when I was barely five years old. My parents hired the finest, most expensive teachers to increase my potential. I also sat and practiced beside my older sister, Lulabelle. You know she had her first performance when she was just eight years old? I remember sitting in the audience, dreaming about that being me someday . . . glowing in the spotlight while everyone watches and claps."

The faraway look in his eyes made my heart thrum.

He blinked, clarity returning as he concentrated on the road. "Lula was a natural at any instrument she tried. Gifted, everyone said. I wasn't. I struggled for every gain. Worked my ass off right up until the day my father told me it was a waste of time." Something squeaked in the car; it was the leather of the steering wheel as he constricted it. "He was right. I was never going to be good enough at it to matter."

My heart cracked at how he said that. "I'd love to hear you play."

Again he glanced at me, his eyebrows squirming. It was a feat that they managed to keep from touching. He opened his mouth, then closed it, abandoning whatever he'd wanted to say.

We parked in the lot outside the city's main shopping center. He cut the engine but yanked the keys out so quick that they tumbled from his fingers, landing by my feet. "Shit!" he cursed. Faster than I could react, he leaned toward me, his thick shoulder brushing my arm.

I'd thought I'd been awake before. The sensation of him grinding on my skin set me into hyperawareness. Thorne smelled like a fire on a misty mountain. At this angle, I could catch a glimpse of the ink cresting along the base of his neck through the top of his shirt.

My bottom lip trembled. I was struggling with an urge to kiss him, strip him, fuck him right here in the car. After we'd had sex, I was confused that nothing about me had changed. It had taken a full day before I'd noticed what he'd done; Thorne had woken up an insatiable hunger in me—a beast that was mad for more of what only he could give.

Being near him was both electrifying and frightening. I was scared of what I'd do if he stayed too close. Afraid of another moment spent without him touching me. Each night since the cemetery I'd writhed in my bed, soaking my sheets and clenching around the emptiness between my thighs. I'd never experienced such a massive craving in all my life.

"You all right?" he whispered. He'd gone still next to me. The keys were in his hands, dangling there, showing us both what he'd really been after.

"Yeah." I unstuck my tongue from the roof of my dry mouth. "I'm good. Let's go do this retail therapy stuff."

"Wait."

My breath tangled up in my chest.

Thorne slid his phone out, holding it between us. "Let's exchange numbers. We don't want to get separated in there and not be able to get in touch."

I eased back into my seat. "Right."

"Also," he added as we typed our numbers in, "it's probably a step we should have done before we agreed to marry each other." He grinned in that boyish way of his. His humor calmed me down, and I found myself smiling easily again.

We exited the car and entered the shopping center together. There were a ton of stores, from high-end things like Gucci to three different McDonald's. As we passed one of the latter, Thorne stopped in his tracks. "What in the world is that?" he asked. He was pointing at the gigantic machine that displayed rotating three-dimensional images of different food.

"Have you never seen one of those before?"

"A fast-food ATM?" Laughing, he strolled up to the brightly glowing machine. "No. I have to say I have not." He tapped it with his knuckles. "Do the sandwiches come out of this?"

"No, no." I was smiling so big my face hurt. I pointed farther down, to the small counter space manned by a single employee. "You order here, then pick up there."

"Seems a little redundant."

Backtracking a step, I started to walk, but he didn't follow. "Are you coming?"

Flicking out his wallet, he raised an eyebrow at me. "And miss trying out the fast-food machine of the future? I think not." He poked the screen, scrolling through the options. "This is all in French. Why would they do that to me? Me, the nice man who wants an AI-ordered burger?"

All right, that was too much. Laughing with my head thrown back, I sidled up to him. "You're not ancient enough to not understand technology, Thorne." Two *clicks* and I'd switched the machine to English. Then I ordered myself a vanilla shake. "My payment," I explained.

"You're so greedy," he scoffed. "A *whole* milkshake?" Scanning the menu, he ordered himself some fries, then slid his card into the slot to pay. A little word bubble popped up, telling us to go to the counter to pick up our food.

"I'll get it," I said, jogging over and claiming the small tray. But when I came back to the machine, Thorne was standing there, his wallet still open, his credit card still in his hand. "What's up?" I asked, sucking at the vanilla shake.

He turned his credit card between his fingers. "It occurred to me that you've taken away one of my advantages. I've never bought lunch for a woman who was as rich as me. Spoiling girls is one of my favorite things, but I can't spoil you."

The shake became thicker in my mouth; I struggled to get it down. Hawthorne had on a half smile, as if he was kidding around. I didn't think he was. This actually bothered him.

I handed him his fries. "You can still spoil me."

"How?"

Slipping my hand into his, I tugged, encouraging him to walk. "Like this." I squeezed as hard as I could. Thorne stood straighter, clutching the fries. "I've never been out with . . . well, someone like you," I said as my cheeks went hot. "It's fun to be seen. To feel special."

He looped the crook of his arm around mine firmly, his shoulders pulling back, tugging me into his hip. "You know how to make a guy's ego swell. And other things."

Sparks tortured my core; I nearly tripped. His pupils vanished into his irises so that everything became big pools of black. I was glad for my icy shake, it helped soothe some of the hellfire between my legs.

"But," he added after a minute, "you don't have to lie to me. There's no way a girl like you hasn't been carted around on the arm of someone who, while probably less amazing than me, was still worth counting."

I couldn't correct him without revealing my chaste past. So I didn't, I just shrugged playfully and led us to a table in the food court. The center of the ceiling was all glass, allowing the sun to leak inside. The building was quiet today. We sat alone among a sea of round tables, munching fries and sharing my shake.

"You're good at that," he said, passing my shake back. "Sharing, I mean."

"With four other siblings, you have to be."

"Hah. I know that too well." Putting his chin on a fist, he squinted at me. "Is it rude to ask how old you are?"

"Twenty-six," I said, bending my straw back and forth. *Same as you.*

"Same as me," he said, echoing my thoughts. "I know you're not the oldest, are you the youngest?"

"That would be sweet little Darla." Holding up a hand, I ticked down a finger each time I said a name. "It goes Larchmont, Darien, me, Richard, then her."

He spun his empty fry container. "You're a middler, like me."

"Yes, I'm the middle child." This normal conversation was incredibly refreshing. I sucked at my shake, draining most of the contents. Thorne reached out, silently asking for more. I grinned and slid it out of the way, taking another sip.

Slapping his palms onto the table, he stretched over it, partially climbing across. It was the kind of action I'd expect out of a kid. Not a grown man. The few people walking by us slowed down to stare; I was stunned enough that I didn't fight him as he snatched the drink.

Dropping onto his chair, he bit the straw, winking at me. "My siblings didn't share as well as you. I've pulled that move multiple times, it always works." His cheeks hollowed as he emptied my shake. "Come on," he said, hopping up, throwing our trash into the bin. "Let's get on with my lesson in retail therapy 101."

Over the next hour we shopped in a way I never had. He was right, I had money thanks to my family, but I wasn't prone to spending it. That was Darla's preferred hobby.

He kept encouraging me to try out the newest smartphones, or expensive shoes, or even purses. At one point he handed me off to an employee in a department store, instructing her to "take care" of me while he went off to handle something else. "I'll be back," he assured me, darting out the doors.

"He's cute," the clerk said, watching him go.

More than cute. Blinking, I faced the woman. "I don't even know what you could help me with. I think we've bought more outfits than I could wear every day for the next month."

She laughed, patting my back roughly. "Let's start with what you *need*. Any special celebrations coming up?"

I started to shake my head. Then I stopped. "Actually, there *is* something."

- CHAPTER FIFTEEN -

HAWTHORNE

It took longer to get back to the department store than I'd expected.

Catching my breath, I peered from side to side for Nova. I didn't see her, so I grabbed my phone and typed her a message. **Where are you?**

The little dots popped up—she was typing. I stared without blinking, so eager for her response. For any response from her at all.

The bubble vanished.

It didn't come back.

Confused, I tapped my phone, writing something else. Was she mad I'd run off? I'd had a reason, one I thought would be good enough in the long term. But maybe I should have been quicker . . . maybe I shouldn't have made her wait, when I'd been the one to ask her on this trip, and . . .

"Boo," she said in my ear.

My muscles had years of reflexive instinct drilled into them. The second her breath tickled the hairs on my temple, I whirled around, snatching her wrists, gripping her like she was going to attack me. Nova's eyes flew wide. So did her pink lips.

Instantly I released her, backing up. "Fuck. Sorry, you surprised me."

"I know," she said, squinting. "That was the idea."

"Sorry," I repeated, hot with shame.

Watching me for a few heartbeats, Nova finally closed the distance between us. There was no fear in her face, just innocent curiosity. "You're fast."

"I really didn't mean to freak you out."

"You didn't." She lowered her eyelashes, her smile soft . . . tempting. "I liked it."

What I'd thought was fear morphed into high heat. Her chest rose up and down, tits pushing on the fabric, her nipples hard buds testing the strength of her bra padding.

A throaty groan escaped my clenched molars. "Fuck. Come with me." Grabbing her wrist, I pulled her toward the restrooms I'd seen while I was exploring earlier. Nova had to take two steps for each of mine.

Not bothering to look around for anyone watching, I opened a door, yanked her in, then locked it behind us. I spun to face her in that tiny closet of a room. She was rose-colored everywhere I could see.

"Suck me off," I growled, moving to stand in front of the white sink. "You've got my cock too hard to function until this is taken care of."

Nova crumbled to her knees. Her fingers worked at my belt, removing it eagerly. Her fingers skirted across the button of my pants, slipping it through the hole with an audible pop. She gripped the top of my zipper, inching it down; every time it got lower, the bulge of my erection shoved through the opening until it was pressing the black fabric of my boxers desperately toward her face.

My cock sensed that she was there. When she inhaled at the sight of me, before I was even naked, it sent another pulse of excitement through my shaft. Nova lifted her hands toward the elastic band of my underwear. She moved very slowly, and it struck me as being from anxiousness. But that didn't make sense. There was too much anticipation glowing in her eyes. *Probably has to do with the fact that we're hiding in a public bathroom.*

Her fingers pushed between the fabric of my underwear and the hot skin of my stomach. I watched her lips part as she gasped; she'd made contact with me. Her reaction enhanced my reaction. I had to grab the sink behind me to keep myself from yanking my cock into the open and shoving it into her mouth.

She peeled my underwear down my slim hips. The tip of my prick revealed itself where it lay heavily against my belly. Without my underwear holding it in place it fell forward, arching toward the ceiling in a thick, veined crescent. She licked her lips and I groaned.

My pants came down just enough that she could reveal my balls. On her knees, Nova scooted closer, her mouth hovering next to my swollen, glistening head.

Her right hand circled me, unable to fully close. God, I loved how huge I looked in her grip. "Is this okay?" she asked in a whisper, looking up at me through her eyelashes.

"Sweetheart, it's more than okay. I'm ready to fucking tap dance. I can't handle how sexy you look with my dick in your hand."

She took a shuddering breath. With her other palm resting on my hip, Nova rubbed her cheek along my shaft from base to tip. I left a wet streak on her cheek from my precome. "Fucking Christ," I growled.

Her chest flared, her lungs filling with my male scent. The edge of Nova's tongue slid across the underside of my dick. When it reached the crown of my cock head and she tasted the sticky juices, she groaned louder than I had. She leaned back slightly; I watched my precome connect between us in the air, a thin, silky filament. Before it broke, she dove forward, circling me with her mouth and taking me in halfway.

Nova squeezed me at the root while sucking me off in increasingly excited strokes. She worked me with gusto, as if my dick was covered in sugar, or cocaine, or something that could make her addicted to my taste.

Hot tingles moved in my cells, expanding out and then down, until my balls were drawing up, readying to explode. I put my hands in her scalp, unable to resist touching her any longer. Her hair was so soft, easy to wrap around my fingers. I thought of myself as a patient man, but I couldn't keep myself from thrusting her head down on me, trying to fit all of my length into her throat. She coughed, but she kept working to get the last inches of me past her gag reflex.

"Good fucking girl," I whispered hoarsely. "That's so damn fucking good. Take me, suck me off all the way. I want to feel my come shooting right into your belly. Can you feel me twitching? So damn close, I'm going to come any second."

She whimpered around my cock, her tongue grinding on the sensitive cleft under my cock's head. Then her hands came down, cupping and fondling my balls. I couldn't take it; her touch was magic.

Hunching forward, I broke past her gag reflex and heard her wet, muffled gag. I went blind with pleasure, smelling her hair and feeling the impossible suction of her hot mouth as my cock swelled bigger than ever. My climax obliterated my senses. Come shot fast and hard into her throat.

Nova pulled away at the last second, before I was finished emptying my load. The final spurt spread on her lips, sliding down her chin. She gasped for air and so did I. I held the sink behind me, worried I'd crack the porcelain in my overwhelmed state.

"That was really, really good," I said. "Really," I added, as if it wasn't enough emphasis.

Looking at me with a sly smile, she wiped the last of my seed off her mouth with her finger, then sucked it like it was a lollipop. The vision of that made my cock twitch. I thought that with a few more minutes of watching her do that, I could've gone for another round.

Nova was better than any aphrodisiac.

"Have you really been crushing on me for six months?" I asked, impossibly curious about what I'd done to gain her attention at our original meeting on my estate.

She placed her fingertips to her upper lip, drumming. "That's not the right way to put it. When I met you in person, you left an impression on me. I felt . . ." Her arm dropped down, her eyes went with it. "I felt like I wanted to *be you*."

That was a first. "Why would anyone ever want that?"

I meant to make her smile, but Nova didn't crack. She simply folded her arms to hug herself. Under the halogen lights, her normally vibrant skin looked sickly. "Because you're not afraid. Because you're this bold, funny, amazing person who's more comfortable in being themselves than anyone I've ever met."

Her words were sincere, but they made no sense to me. Gripping her hands, I pushed my fingers into the gaps between hers, locking us together. "You don't need to make me your role model. You're already bold, and strong, and just—Nova, I've never met a woman as easygoing as you. Not a single one."

"Yes," she agreed slowly. "I'm like this now."

I waited for her to finish her thought. Instead she escaped from my grasp. Her palm pressed on the door of the restroom. "I'll go out first. Wait a bit, we don't want to create a big scandal about you and me having sex in public."

I almost made a joke, complaining that it was unfair to say that when we hadn't actually had sex. But I held my tongue. I watched her peek outside, and I stared at where she'd been long after she was gone.

- CHAPTER SIXTEEN -

HAWTHORNE

There was a box on my bed.

Eyeing it, I undid my tie and tossed it over the back of a chair. I'd been up to my new room once since we'd returned to the castle—so I could change for dinner—and this box hadn't been here.

It was rectangular; white, with a slim gold ribbon strung across at an angle. It stuck out on the richly emerald blankets, which matched my curtains . . . the circular floor rug . . . even the backsplash over my bathroom sink.

Sitting on the mattress, I pulled the box into my lap. Who would leave me a gift? Had Mom sent me clothes for tomorrow? Popping the lid off, I paused. Inside the container, wrapped in tissue paper, was a silk dress the same shade of red as the garden roses. Silver lined the open back, and when I lifted it high to see the length, I whistled. *Unless I missed something, I don't think my mother expects me to wear THIS for the photo shoot.*

Digging through the paper, I discovered a small receipt. Venus Fashion. That was the store I'd left Nova at while I'd run off to take care of something. *If this is what she bought* . . . Of course; whoever had unloaded all our shopping bags from the car had mixed things up, leaving this in my room instead of hers.

Pressing the receipt back into the tissue paper, I noticed there were more items in the box. Flaring my nostrils, I strung the lacy lingerie across my fingers. My mind was rapidly forming a mental image of this underwear cupping her perfect ass and pussy.

"Jesus," I breathed out, shifting on the bed. My erection was swollen and hot against my thigh in my boxers. The wrongness of exploring her underwear was a perverse turn-on. *She bought this while I wasn't with her.* Was she hoping to surprise me? After folding everything back into the box, I hoisted it under my arm. I had an excuse to go see Nova; of course I was going to use it.

Leaving my room, I wandered down the long hall. I didn't know where she was staying exactly, but she'd told me, after we'd returned, that her quarters were in the east wing of the castle. Apparently her family was staying in the rooms they usually occupied when they visited Austere and Hester for the summer. That was why none of them had looked curious; they'd spent plenty of time in the castle in the past.

It was another advantage they had over me.

As I walked, I passed a servant here and there. They always nodded, making sure I saw they were acknowledging my presence. The coronation wasn't for another two weeks, but it didn't matter if there wasn't a crown on my head; everyone knew I was the son of their long-lost would-be king, Maverick.

Clutching the box, I walked faster, cutting through the foyer. The front doors were shut. I could hear talking in the direction of the dining room through the doors under the stairs. My parents were catching up with all manner of important people, doing the work I had no desire to.

The east wing was quiet. It looked just like any other hallway with its big paintings and old statues. If you let yourself, you could pretend you were back in the old days when this castle had been constructed.

Which room is hers? I could have sent a text, but I wanted to surprise her. Stopping in front of the first door I saw, I knocked softly. No answer. Moving down, I knocked on the next one. It went like that until I got to lucky door number four—that time, when I rapped my knuckles, I heard movement inside.

Bracing myself with the box in hand, I waited. The handle twitched; my heart copied it. But the person who peered out at me wasn't Nova.

"Thorne?" Darla asked. She was dressed in a pink satin robe with a plunging neckline. Her long hair was damp, tugged into a messy bun. She looked around me, like she'd expected someone else. Her manicured eyebrows went up. "This is a surprise."

"Ah, actually," I started to say.

Her attention dashed to the box I held. "Oh! Did you bring me a gift?" Clasping her hands together like a little girl on Christmas, Darla grabbed my wrist, trying to pull me into the room. "Why are you standing there like that? Get in here."

Digging my heels in was enough to keep her from yanking me through the doorway. Darla let go, her expression downshifting into one of disbelief. "I was looking for Nova."

The bow shape of her mouth unfurled into an ugly frown. "Well, you found someone better. Maybe this is a happy accident." Crossing her arms, she exaggerated the dramatic line of her cleavage. "You sure you don't want to come inside? No one would have to know."

"I'm flattered, but . . . I'd know." My smile was crooked. "Can you point me to your sister's room, please?"

Her honey-colored eyes turned darker. "What is it about Nova that you like so much? I can't figure it out." Her nails were knotting up in the fabric of her robe. I kept expecting the pink material to rip under the pressure.

She's not used to being rejected. "Listen," I said cautiously, "I'd rather not do this."

"I asked because I want to know. I'm a big fucking girl, Hawthorne."

123

The thing was, it didn't matter if she could handle the truth . . . because I didn't know what the damn truth was. How could I lay out in words, so plainly, the things that Nova did to me? She was my enemy—and she also wasn't. That woman was nothing like the rest of the Valentines.

She'd raced to help someone who'd been robbed. She'd been keen on showing me how wonderful this country was. Nova had shared her secret spot with me . . . and she'd graced me with a kiss so explosive it had erased every other pair of lips I'd touched from history.

It was too soon to tell Nova why I was growing obsessed with her. Telling someone like Darla was impossible.

"I really don't know," I said, shrugging absently.

"You don't *know?*" she laughed cruelly. "I'm losing to my sister and you can't even explain why."

"This isn't a competition."

"Yes it is!" In the hallway her loud voice was enhanced. "Tell me her secret. Did she make you feel bad for her? Did she guilt you, going all, 'Woe is me'?"

I went very still. "It sounds like you don't know your sister very well."

"Believe me," she snorted, "I know her better than you do."

"Hey," a voice said behind me. I pivoted, seeing Nova was standing nearby. Her face was puzzled; she looked from me to Darla. "What's going on here?"

Darla rolled her eyes. "Nothing. Good night." She slammed her door, and I clenched my teeth at the awful sound.

Facing Nova, I gave a half shrug. "I think your sister might be— what's the word—kind of a bitch?"

She was still staring at the door. Nova was dressed in a robe as Darla had been, but it was thick cotton, white, and not at all revealing. It *still* made my stomach do a flip. "Thorne, why are you in the east wing?"

"Can I say, 'Because I missed you already'? Or is that too much?"

Nova smiled, tucking her hair behind her ear. "What's the real reason?"

Chuckling warmly, I offered her the box. "This is yours. It was left in my room by accident."

Her eyes opened wide. "Did you look inside?" she asked anxiously.

Remembering the sexy lingerie, I breathed in raggedly. "I didn't mean to peek. I'm not sorry I did, though." Pressing forward, I stood over her. I could smell jasmine soap from her recent shower. "Do you know how hot it is to realize what you'll be wearing under your dress tomorrow?"

I was close enough to see the dip at the base of her throat flutter. "Do you like what I picked?"

"I fucking love it, Nova."

Chewing at the edge of her lip, she took the box from me. "I wanted to surprise you."

My hand cupped her cheek as I backed her against the castle wall. The hallway was dead around us. "You already have," I whispered.

She trembled under my touch. Fuck, she made me feel so *powerful*. Trailing my lips on hers, I leaned back a few centimeters, enough so she couldn't kiss me. Her frustrated groan scraped in my skull, it left me breathless, my cock jumping angrily in my pants.

I nipped the sensitive flesh behind her ear. Nova whimpered— threatening to undo all the control I had left. Gathering myself, I leaned away. Her skin was smooth and free of makeup, free of everything but the little bite mark I'd left on her throat. She seemed so vulnerable.

A flash of something wicked danced through my cells. I peeled open the box and tugged out the panties. Nova was frozen as she watched. "I like surprises," I said, twisting the lace around my fingers. It vanished into my pocket. "But I like having my directions followed, too." I brushed the box over her chest; she gasped, hugging it, taking it from me. "Tomorrow, don't wear anything under your dress."

"That's . . . What if someone sees?"

"Don't let them," I laughed. "In fact, you better not let a single person catch a glimpse of that sweet pussy of yours. It's for *my eyes only*."

Her voice came out high and breathy. "You're impossible." Hugging the box, she half slid against the wall. Then, with one final look at me—a single, arousal-filled glance that made my shaft thicken—Nova entered her room.

She hadn't said she'd follow my directions.

She didn't need to.

The ecstasy in her eyes made me certain she would.

My dreams were filled with visions of rosy nipples and cinnamon eyes.

All impossibly seductive.

All belonging to Nova.

Tap. Tap. Tap.

That irritating noise jammed its way into my dream, prying the soft, sweet images away and leaving me with nothing but an early-morning headache. Cracking my weary lids, I stared around the room. It wasn't familiar; it took me a second to remember I was in the castle.

The tapping came again. *Who the hell is knocking?* I wondered, throwing off my covers. I'd gone to sleep in just my boxers. My little chat with Nova had given me terrible blue balls. Taking care of that had kept me up for an extra hour.

Again, more loud knocking. "Hang on!" I shouted, snatching some pants off the back of a chair. I stumbled into them, barely clasping the top button before I ripped the door open. Standing outside was a young woman in a dark gray dress. Her blonde hair was braided over her shoulder, and a thin pair of glasses perched on her nose. "Morning, sir."

Palming my forehead, I yawned until my jaw creaked. "What is it, what do you want so badly that you had to knock my door down?"

She offered me a slip of paper. It was thick, pale yellow card stock. On it was a scribbled list; I recognized my mother's handwriting. "This is for you. It's your schedule for the coming weeks."

Rubbing my eyeballs, I squinted. "Dinner with the head of infrastructure . . . lunch with the stable master . . . *croquet* with the entire Maurine Symphony?" I read aloud. Not a single day of the month wasn't filled with shit. At the very bottom was an item that made me tense.

The Royal Wedding.

"Sir," she said, hands folded primly in front of her. "Unless you need something else . . ."

"What?" I'd forgotten she was even there. "No. Just—I'm fine." I waved a hand absently. "You can leave."

Bowing her head, the woman whose name I never got left me alone. I crumpled the list into a firm ball and threw it in the corner. This was the same junk I'd rejected years ago and gone out of my way to sidestep. But there was no dark strip club to hide away in here.

I'd nearly shut the door when a new voice stopped me. "Thorne! Good, you're awake," my mother said, swinging her way inside. Even though it couldn't possibly be past breakfast time, she was dressed to the nines in a sky-blue-and-magenta lace gown. Her hair was braided into a crown on her head, the sight of it reminding me of the coronation, of the list.

Swallowing my rising bile, I smiled at her. "You're bright-eyed and bushy-tailed, Ma."

Closing the door, she beamed at me. She held a small box no bigger than a chocolate bar. Her attention went straight to the plastic bags full of merchandise in the corner. "I *was* going to see if you still needed me to have someone rush out and buy you something nice for today, but it looks like you bought an entire department store."

"I'm wounded," I said, putting a hand to my bare chest. "Do you think all of that is for me?" I fished in the bags and grabbed a medium-size box, then passed it to her. "No good son goes shopping without buying his mom something pretty."

Her rouge lips thinned as her smile kept growing. "You didn't!" She yanked the silver Louis Vuitton bracelet out, gasping. "It's perfect. Just perfect."

Stretching, I glanced over the pile, trying to remember which bag held my new clothes. "Anyway, don't bother sending anyone out on some fancy suit quest. I bought an outfit for today, figured I needed something expensive-looking for the photos."

"It's nice to see you taking this seriously." But by the way she squinted at me, I knew she was wondering where my change of heart had come from. "Thanks for this," she said, tucking the jewelry back in the box. "Coincidentally I brought a gift for you, too." She held up the box she'd entered with. Opening it under my nose, my mother winked. "Aren't they pretty?"

There was black velvet inside. Sitting about half an inch apart were several stunning diamond rings. She didn't have to explain. I knew what these were meant for.

"Now," she went on, talking through the pulsing in my skull, "I swiped these from the royal vault with Glen's help. I'm not sure what they're each worth, but looking at them, any one of these will do the trick."

My entire jaw was suddenly heavy. "Any one, huh?" I mumbled with difficulty.

"Yes, they're all suitable. It doesn't really matter which you pick."

"Just like your sons, then." I backed away from the box. "Long as we get the job done, who cares?"

She drew herself up, bristling and snapping the case closed. "What are you saying?"

"I'm saying Dad doesn't care who he throws to the Valentines. If Kain or Costello were free, he'd have picked one of them for this marriage before me. Am I wrong?"

Disgust smoldered in her eyes. I knew mine mirrored hers. "Hawthorne Luca Badd, you need to watch your fucking tone. Your father and I are doing our best with this situation. We're trying to help you."

Her anger soothed some of mine. Lowering my head, I looked at the case in her hands. "*You* are, Ma. I know that. But you're kidding yourself if you think Dad gives a shit about helping me." The memory of what he'd said in the garden cut my soul into ribbons. "I don't think he appreciates that I'm choosing this family over my own desires."

"Ease up on your father."

"Maybe when he eases up on me."

"You've got no idea what he's been through!"

I do have some idea. But everything I learned, I learned from other people, I thought sullenly. Pointing my toes to the side, I walked around her, opening the door wide. "You're right. I don't have a clue because he never talks to me. Go, please. I need to get cleaned up and dressed." I gestured out into the hallway.

Her face fell. Then she lifted her nose high, finding some of her familiar pride as she swept past me. Looking over her shoulder, she waved the box. "What about the rings?"

Those fucking rings. My hand tightened, white knuckled, on the door. "I don't need that secondhand trash." My mother's eyes widened. I almost felt bad; she'd meant to help. I knew that. It was her cavalier attitude that had gotten under my skin. She thought the ring didn't matter.

But I knew it should. Just like I knew *I* should.

- CHAPTER SEVENTEEN -

NOVA

I'd woken up before daybreak, then spent the hour before the sun tickled the sky doing my hair in the mirror. When the servants my mother had arranged to do my makeup and hair arrived, they'd looked at my work and been unsure what was left for them to do. But I couldn't help it—I had to stay busy.

Every minute that I was allowed to think . . . Thorne came spiraling into my mind.

And then everything got harder.

Eating.

Talking.

Walking.

It all was swept behind the rest of my synapses that were eager to gorge themselves on Hawthorne. Squirming in the chair in front of my vanity, I pressed my knees together. Following his directions was incredibly arousing. The old me, if faced with his dominant filthiness, would have fainted.

Just breathe, I reminded myself, touching the stray pieces of hair that had escaped my French updo. *Remember how brave you are now.*

I hesitated. *And going all weak in the knees has nothing to do with fear, anyway. He's too hot for anyone to be unaffected, that includes me.*

With a final press of some gloss on my lips, I left my room. The maids in the hall tipped their chins at me as I passed. "You look beautiful," one of them said politely. "Like a delicate flower."

That was nice—but would she say that if she knew I was naked beneath my dress like some sex-obsessed monster?

Probably not.

My mother spotted me when I crossed the steps from the patio that led to the rose garden path. She was sitting at a gazebo, her head covered in a floppy hat. In front of her was Carmina, Thorne's mother. I didn't know if they'd been talking before I appeared, but they were tight-lipped now. The only thing their mouths opened for was to drink the Bloody Marys that had been arranged for them on the table.

"Nova!" Mom called.

I was tempted to ignore her and just walk into the garden maze. Instead I moved toward her, chiding myself for my wicked thought. I owed so much to my mother. The least I could do was come when she called.

"Hi, Mom," I said, leaning in to kiss her cheek. She traced my arm, then her hand fell away, grabbing for her drink. "Are you two going to sit here while the photos are taken?"

"Yes," Carmina said, smiling my way. She had sharp eyes; under her observation, I was suddenly cut apart. My dress became too thin, my makeup and hair a sham, my grace an act; a frailer woman would have crumbled, begging to be accepted by her. I came close to it.

Reaching out, I spread my fingers. "Mrs. Badd, we never really got a proper introduction. It's nice to meet you, and nice to have you here supporting your husband and son."

Her eyebrows inched down slowly. Then she reached out, shaking my hand. The silver bracelet she wore caught the light and glinted.

"Thank you. I'll say that supporting Thorne hasn't been too hard, he's a good son. Plus he likes you." She winked.

Laughing, I let her go. "Thank you. Love your bracelet, by the way."

"Oh!" Her eyes sparkled with pleasure as she showed it off. "Like I said, Thorne is a good son. He bought this for me yesterday."

"Yesterday?" That was strange, I didn't remember seeing him buying any jewelry.

"Speaking of," Carmina said, rocking her chair to see past me. I twisted around. Hawthorne was striding over the close-cut grass toward me.

My heart floated up, tasting like butter in my mouth.

He was wearing cobalt-blue trousers, a matching jacket buttoned once in the middle by a metallic button. I could see the dress shirt he had on beneath—the color of cream, and probably as soft. His collar was high and drawn tight by a slim silver tie.

Though we'd had sex in the cemetery, I hadn't seen him naked yet. He'd kept his clothes on, only unbuttoning his pants to slide out his—I shivered, hit by a wave of stability-stealing lust as I remembered his thick cock. I'd seen *that* twice now.

But not the rest of him.

What would he look like on full display?

"Morning," he said, dipping to kiss me on the cheek. Champagne bubbles of delight rose up in me. I knew I was blushing. Thorne had shown me again and again that the more time we spent together, the easier it was for him to erase my neutral calmness.

He turned me into a bumbling girl with a schoolyard crush.

The smirk on his face said he knew, and he loved it.

Playing with my dress nervously, I cleared my throat. "Morning. You look very nice."

"I tried." He swept me with his gaze—the stark black centers piercing me. *He's wondering if I did what he told me.* Shifting from side to side, I became far too aware of how vulnerable I was between my legs.

He squinted, trying again to figure me out. Enjoying that he wasn't positive I'd listened, I grabbed hold of that upper hand and pointed out at the gardens. "I see the photographer is waiting for us. Shall we?"

Thorne's smirk pushed out at the corners until it was an amused smile. He curled his elbow around mine, flicking his fingers at our mothers to say goodbye. Together we walked across the grass. He was warm beside me, smelling like oranges with notes of chocolate.

Bending so his breath tickled my ear canal, he whispered, "Keep your secret. I'll find out soon enough." Then, as I was looking flustered, he grinned at the photographer we'd reached. "Hey there! Hawthorne, nice to meet you. Please make me look good today." He laughed, shaking the man's hand with both of his.

He was good at acting relaxed. It let down other people's guards, I was realizing. That could be wonderful for social interactions . . . but it could also be dangerous. Underestimated men were impossible to predict.

Thorne graced me with his intense stare. I thrilled, melting under the attention.

"Ready?" he asked.

"Definitely," I replied.

We posed as we were told to. A hug here, a fake laugh there; we were performing so that the papers would have something to spread about the soon-to-be king being in love. It was fake love, but it was the closest to the real thing that I'd ever experienced.

If it became true love . . . unfiltered, real love . . . would I realize?

I often wondered, even now, if Darla was right about me. That I was some boring, broken person that no one would want. Even after everything I'd gone through to gain my bolder persona, deep down there was a tiny voice that told me I meant nothing to anyone.

Not my parents.

Not Thorne.

No one.

"Are you okay?" he asked. His onyx eyes swarmed with concern. It froze me where I was. As much as I'd wanted to be seen, it was no small feat to be stared at so intently by Hawthorne Badd.

And he looked . . . worried. Actually concerned for me. I'd let my fake smile crumble as my mind had wandered. Gathering myself, I reached for his hand and grinned. "I'm fine. Let's keep going."

"You're sure?"

"Of course," I said, shoving him lightly. The camera flashed. "This is what we're here for."

"I just don't want your heart to explode."

I made a face. "Why would my heart . . ." He dropped to one knee. I'd expected this for the photo shoot, but knowing hadn't been enough to prepare me for the moment. My breathing became shallow—the camera was clicking, capturing the moment when Thorne slid out the red velvet box.

The ring inside was small, elegant. The diamond on top created a rainbow in the sun as he lifted it free. *This is all a show,* I reminded myself. *We're marrying for our families. This is pretend. And that's fine, totally fine.*

"Nova Valentine," he whispered.

Oh, hell. Oh no. Oh God.

My dress was too tight. There was a tiny, high-pitched noise in my ears and it was a full minute before I realized it was *me* making that sound. *Overwhelmed* wasn't the word for this. *Thorne is asking me to marry him, but there's no one recording us. The camera can't hear his voice.* So was he pretending like me? Was this part of the farce to get the perfect photograph?

He took my hand, the ring poised in front of my finger. "Will you marry me?" He asked it gently. It was a set of knuckles to my ribs. Something terrible had never felt so good. But this *was* bad, undeniably bad. No one should be swept off their feet by a proposal gained by threats.

I hoped God couldn't read my thoughts, because if so, I was going to hell.

"Yes." I swallowed the word. "Yes, I'll marry you."

The ring coasted into place. The photographer said something. I ignored him, too swept up in Thorne. He stood again, blocking out the sun with his broad shoulders. His warm palms captured my face. As he dipped to kiss me, I stood on tiptoe, calves stretching, to reach his lips as fast as I could.

Our sweet kiss became something else. His hands moved to my shoulders, to my waist, and when he grabbed my ass I became conscious once more that I was panty-less. His teeth slid over my ear as he whispered, "Did you follow my directions?"

"Yes," I said, my eyes rolling in my head. The wave of pleasure was blinding me.

"Ahem," the camera guy said.

Thorne kissed my cheek, then he stepped back. He looked extremely proud of himself. "Do you like the ring?"

Studying it again, I smiled. "Very much."

"I'm glad. I was worried you'd know what I was up to when we were shopping."

My hands fell into my lap. "You bought this?" That was why I hadn't seen him buy the bracelet for his mother. He'd gotten them both while I was buying my lingerie.

"Yeah, though I guess I didn't need to. Mom brought some spares for me to pick from." His lashes drifted low as he avoided my eyes. Leaning back, he suddenly smiled at me straight on. "I don't know. Even if the situation isn't ideal, it seemed weird to do this without choosing the ring myself."

I had no response. It was a relief when the photographer put us back through our paces, an excuse for me to keep my thoughts to myself.

"Okay, kids," the guy said. He squinted into the back screen of his camera. "I've got plenty to work with. Good luck, tell your parents to hire me for your wedding!"

I watched him go. When he reached the table in the distance where our mothers were sitting, Thorne circled my wrist with his hand. He wrapped so far around his fingers closed over his thumb; I felt so tiny. "This way," he said, hauling me into the rose maze.

Thorne led us into the greenery. The sunlight through the leaves turned us both yellow, insects creating a chorus that matched the hum of my heart. I stared at the back of his head, marveling at his speed. Desperate to keep up—to run as fast—I kicked my heels off.

He glanced at me as I appeared beside him, breathing heavily. Clinging to his hand, I accelerated even faster into the bushes. We took a corner in the maze, the sky hiding under the clustered roses above our heads.

Thorne was panting. He didn't look tired, though. Spinning me around, he wove his hands into my scalp, cupping the base of my skull. Leaves scratched at my bare back where the dress didn't protect me. His lips fastened on mine, allowing nothing to get between us. He kissed with a barely controlled energy—what had gotten into him?

Turning away, he ended the kiss. The front of his pants was bulging. "Show me," he said, his hands slipping down my arms, lifting goosebumps as they went. "Lift your dress."

I knew what he wanted to see. Trembling with anticipation, I hoisted my dress hem up my legs. It was cool where it touched, parts of it clinging from sweat after our brief sprint. My mouth hung open, breath coming in short, fierce bursts.

The front of my dress cleared my hip bones. Air caressed my pussy, my juices sticking to the insides of my thighs. "Fuck," he grunted. "That's stunning." He was transfixed on my pussy, and for a while I was free to study his face as it shifted through honest, unguarded expressions of greed. He wanted me more than anything. If I'd had something to ask for, I could have, right then, gotten it.

Except what I wanted was him.

And I already had that.

"I need to taste you." He dropped gracefully to his knees in front of me. It was a testament to his male aura that even on his knees, he radiated absolute power over me. Grabbing my hips, Thorne guided my pussy to his mouth.

"Ah!" I whined. A single lick had sent sparks up my limbs.

"You're on edge," he said, the words dancing over my clit. Another lick; another part of my brain collapsing. "You've been thinking about this all day, huh? Since you woke up?"

"Since last night," I whispered.

He stared up at me. Then he bent forward, grinding his nose on my clitoris, his tongue flat as it swept through my swollen labia. He ate me out, his strength all that kept me standing. Without his muscles clamping my thighs, I would have toppled into the grass.

His tongue wagged faster, eagerly lapping every drop of my juice. Glancing down, I saw it clinging all over his cheeks. Awestruck, I covered my mouth. The sight was so fucking filthy. It would be burned into my memory until my bones became dust.

"I can't wait," he said. "Not anymore." He scooped me up from where he was, pressing me into the cool ground. I saw the vines above—a single white rose dangling there, half-bloomed.

Kissing me, he shifted around, reaching into the back pocket of his pants. I saw the foil square; a condom. Meeting my uncertain stare, he pulled back, sitting over me. "Listen," he said, working at his tie. It fell away in a coil of silver. "I know everyone expects us to have a baby. But I'm not ready to jump into that, not yet." He faltered, trying to read my face. "Is that okay?"

Reaching out, I plucked the condom up. "They want us to give them an heir, but no one can make us do that before we're ready."

The relief that washed through his smile tugged at my heartstrings. He sat on his heels, going for his belt. "Wait," I said. "I . . . want to see you without your shirt on. Please."

His lips dipped down, then rebounded into a sharp grin. "*Please?* Oh, sugar, you don't have to beg for that." His deft fingertips cut through the buttons of his cream-colored shirt. His muscles bulged, eager to be free.

Beneath the cloth I got my first eyeful of Hawthorne's bare chest. He was a masterpiece, smoky ink covering him from his neck all the way down until it vanished into his pants. I'd never seen anything like it in my life.

My attention went to the crown on his ribs. It was the emblem of his royal heritage. That crown was embroidered on every banner, every guard uniform, and every servant's outfit. I'd seen it swinging off ships' masts since I was tiny and visiting my aunt for the first time.

But I'd never seen it on a real person.

Shaking through my fingertips, I softly brushed that tattoo among the rest. It was the only spot of color on his whole body.

Unzipping himself, he motioned for the condom. I gave it to him, fascinated—flushed—by the sight of him gliding it over his engorged cock. I'd had him bare; somehow the latex added a layer of taboo to our sex.

"Look at me," he said, laying his weight over my body. "Watch my face. I want to see every eyelash of yours sway as I fuck you into oblivion."

He pressed the head of his cock against my seam. If he wanted a response from me, he didn't wait for one. The first thrust dragged along my flexing inner walls. My nails buried in the dirt, my cheek tearing grass up from how my head tossed.

"Oh!" I moaned, a ripple running through me when Thorne slid fully into place. My ears were ringing; distantly I heard seabirds, which seemed impossible in the garden. Was I losing my mind from pleasure? Was it the weight of him on my chest, keeping my lungs from doing their job?

He leaned forward, holding my hips to move me how he wanted. Withdrawing with the patience of a saint, he lingered with just the head of his cock inside of me. He pistoned forward, his hard muscles grinding over my sensitive nipples. The sensation was maddening. I was becoming delirious, wanting nothing more than to chase the orgasm that he'd built in me while eating me out.

Reaching between us, he kissed my temple, then my mouth. Agile fingers found my clit, strumming it as he maintained his pace. "Talk to me," he demanded. "I want to know how this feels."

"Wonderful!" I cried out, rewarded by a hot tingle because I'd done as he'd commanded me to. "It's amazing, Thorne! Please, let me come, I need to come so badly!"

He chuckled darkly along my jaw. "I know you do."

He was teasing me, but with every shift of his prick inside of me, I sensed his composure slipping. It started small, a bit of yarn dangling in the air. Then it snagged on something solid—something shaped like me. I was making this man come undone.

His breath turned ragged in my ears. One hand petted my clit, the other hooked my knee, spreading me open to him, keeping nothing from his reach.

The pressure in my center expanded. I was going to be crushed by the weight of my own slick need. "Your pussy is burning up," he said. "I can't take it anymore."

Swooning, I closed my eyes—his hand spanked my hip. Shocked, I stared at his serious, thunderstorm eyes. "I said not to look away. Watch me while I make you come, Nova."

His cock jerked, I was sandwiched between pleasure and pain. Between wanting to obey, and my body desperately trying to shut down so my orgasm could consume me freely.

I was hovering on the edge. So close, right fucking there. "Come," he growled, clutching my cheeks, daring me to break our eye lock. But I didn't. I'd never let him down.

"Ah!" I squealed, my body one big knot. I milked him, tingles rocking from behind my eyes, flowing into him, both of us shuddering in bliss. He looked away before I did, teeth flashing in a snarl as he came. I was still coming as he finished, the warmth, the swell of his body making me think the condom wouldn't be enough.

Linked together, we relaxed into each other's nooks and crannies. The grass under me wasn't cool anymore. Nothing around me was.

Wincing, Thorne braced himself, pulling free so he could dispose of the used condom. He wrapped it in the foil and put it in his pocket to throw out later. Being so empty so suddenly left me carved out and wanting. I hated it; it was a relief when he returned to kiss me, his arms winding around my waist. "I have to know," he said, his fingers clinging to the hair at my nape possessively. "How do I stack up against other guys? Better or *amazingly* better?"

And here it is. Just be honest. "I wouldn't know," I whispered.

His laugh came out a bit choked. "What do you . . ."

I untangled myself from his grip. Writhing thorns of anxiousness filled me. But somehow my voice was calm. "You're my first. At everything, actually."

Thorne's jaw dropped open. His raw shock was too much; the vines inside me strangled my lungs. He ruffled his hair in dismay. "Then, the night in the cemetery, you were a virgin. And I didn't even realize. I fucked you without a hint of gentleness. If I'd been better . . . if I'd cared more . . . I should have noticed. I should have fucking realized!"

He was spiraling, flushed with shame, remembering what we'd done in a tainted light. My hands steadied on his. "Thorne, stop rewriting history. I can see it all over your face." Pulling myself into his lap, I swung my legs over his thighs. "You're worried about what you did. Don't be, okay?" Red heat swam up to my cheeks. "Thanks to you, my first time was better than I ever dreamed it could be."

I hoped he could sense how earnest I was being. "Why didn't you tell me?"

"I didn't think it mattered."

"Of course it matters!"

"Why?" I challenged. "Would you have not slept with me if you knew?"

"I—well, no. I don't think I could have walked away at that point."

"Would you have treated me like I was made of glass? Because I'm not some brittle teacup, Thorne. And if you dare to remember our first night together as something awful, I'll be really pissed off."

He went quiet. Sitting beside me, looking at the grass between his shoes, he said, "I did wonder. You come off as so confident, this youthful eagerness to do things. At the same time, I glimpsed some of your inexperience. But to imagine that you'd be a virgin . . ."

I glared at him, daring him to ruin what I'd just told him not to.

Looking me in the eye, he gripped my chin. "I'm the first man to taste your lips?" My blood raced; I nodded in answer. "Maybe my luck is finally turning around after all."

Relieved that the tension was resolved, I threw my arms around his neck. My mouth traveled his collarbone, kissing his ink, imagining that the swirls of black tasted like real smoke. When I'd made it from one side of his body to the next, I changed course. Thorne curled a fist in my hair, his tongue wrestling gently with mine.

Just like him, I was happy he was my first.

I also hoped he'd be my last.

- CHAPTER EIGHTEEN -

HAWTHORNE

Sipping my coffee, I wandered the long hallways of the castle. I'd been sleeping here for over a week, and the residents still hadn't warmed up to me, to put it politely.

For example: This morning, when I'd gone to find a cup of something hot in the kitchen, the maids were in the middle of putting away the breakfast spread. They took one look at me and frowned. "Did you want something?" one of them had asked.

I'd eyeballed the plastic-wrapped tray of scrambled eggs that a maid was shoving into the refrigerator. She gave me a wary glance. Before I could say anything, she piped up. "Everything is being put away on schedule—sir." She added the last part after a long second. "If you had been here this morning at breakfast time . . ."

Quickly I threw my hands up, giving a nervous laugh. "I get it, I get it, I'm a terrible person who doesn't follow the schedule."

The girls looked at each other, talking with their expressions. I knew they were debating whether or not they could get away without pulling the food out and serving it to me after they'd already done so much work cleaning up the kitchen. I had a feeling that if I pushed them they would do it. After all, whether they liked it or not, I was going to be their new king.

But I've never been a bully.

"I'm not hungry," I'd lied. "But I noticed that there's still coffee sitting on the counter over there. Would it be all right if I got a cup of that?" The girls deflated, relieved that I hadn't asked more of them.

Now I sipped my coffee that didn't have enough sugar or cream in it, but I'd been too eager to get out of the kitchen to ask for them to add more, and kept walking down the hall. As I passed a long section of windows that faced the outside of the house, I saw a row of men wearing the blue-and-red uniform of the royal guard. On their shoulders were small embroidered crowns that I'd missed the first time I'd seen them.

They were doing marching drills, creating stiff patterns as they walked across the gravel. Intrigued, and not knowing what else to do with myself, I walked until I found the door that led to where they were. Standing at a distance, I sipped my coffee and counted the men. They were sixteen of them, all wearing the exact same outfit, the exact same shiny boots, and the exact same rifles strapped to their backs. Each of them kept his hair cropped tight near his ears.

There was someone shouting instructions to them. Looking across the field, I recognized Glen. He was strutting back and forth with his arms folded at his lower back. Every time he yelled, the men would act. I'd never seen anything like this before. It was quite a show.

Suddenly Glen's eyes fell on me from across the distance. I remembered the conversation I'd overheard him having with my father when we'd first arrived at the castle.

Clutching my coffee cup tight, I debated turning and going back inside before he could reach me. But he was a big man who took long strides, and he was on me before the guards had pivoted to begin their next routine.

"Hawthorne," he said, lifting two fingers to his forehead in a salute.

I saluted back, but it was impossible to hide the mocking laziness of it. "You know, some people just drink coffee to wake up in the morning." I showed him my cup. "We don't all need to yell at a bunch of men to get ourselves going."

Glen laughed, looking back at the group as they marched crisscross over the gravel, their rifles switching arms. "I don't drink coffee, never liked the stuff."

"More for me," I said, shrugging.

Glen considered me with his eyebrows smoothing in a friendly way. "We haven't gotten to talk much, you and I."

"There's a lot going on," I said, deflecting. "Besides, I'm not planning to take your place at running the royal guard, *or* joining, no offense. What would we even talk about?"

"I'm not so two-dimensional that all I can talk about is being the head of the guards," he said, his laughter a low rumble. "In fact," he said, his voice going quieter, "I'm surprised you haven't asked me anything about your father."

Hairs rose on my neck. "Why would I ask you about him?"

"Because he and I were childhood friends. Because this is the first time you've been in this country, the first time meeting me. It just seemed . . . Well, I think I would ask if I were you."

"But you're not me." I regretted saying it the second it came out of my mouth.

Glen didn't look put out. Crossing his arms, he took a step closer. He was so big that my head only came up to his shoulder. He was bulkier than my father, who was the biggest man I'd known until now. What did they feed the people in this country? "Hawthorne, I know that you must be going through a lot. The pressure you're under, I can't even imagine. But there are people here who are more than happy to help. People who believe in you."

"People like my father?"

"Of course. Your father chose you to be the king."

"He didn't choose me," I said, staring at my coffee cup. "I was just the only option he had left." I poured out the last of the dregs—bitter grounds that no one would ever touch.

"Don't say that. Your father believes in you."

"That's not what he said last week," I mumbled. Glen looked surprised. "Yeah. I heard you guys talking about me in the rose garden. I wasn't trying to eavesdrop. In fact, I almost stepped out to talk to you both. It seemed a good time to get whatever information I could on this country, it felt like the right thing to do if I was going to wear the crown like everyone keeps asking me to. But then, well." I shrugged, trying to take the sting out of the memory. "Dad doesn't think I'm fit for the job. It's not really surprising. The guy never thought I was fit for much."

Glen was staring at me, thick eyebrows furrowed into tight knots. I stared back at him, noticing the thin scar on the left side of his jaw that his beard mostly hid. The massive calluses on his loosely curled fingers. This was a man who took his job seriously, and I felt the weight of his judgment as he watched me. I regretted telling him that I'd overheard their conversation. I regretted coming outside to watch the guards.

Both of his hands came down on my shoulders, holding me in place. "Your father is a hard man," he said. "But he wasn't always this way."

"What are you talking about?"

"I'm not sure if you would believe me, but it's like I said when we first met. You remind me a lot of him."

That gave me the strength to break away. I took three steps back, lifting my head high. "Now you're fucking with me. Or maybe it's been so long since you've seen my dad that you remember him differently."

He held his hands in the air, hovering where I'd been. Slowly they fell to his sides. "I have to get back to the guards. They need to be ready for the coronation." He started back, pausing to speak over his shoulder. "Your family is arriving today. You'll be too busy to speak to me like this for some time, I think—but if you ever want to, I'll be here."

I watched him go, unsure how to respond. *I forgot everyone would be landing at the airport today.* They'd have almost no time to settle in before they had to watch me marry a woman none of them knew. One I still didn't really know.

Nova and I had spent some weeks together now, but the situation was so dire that it was like a sheet of paper was constantly passing between us whenever we got too close. I could see her shadow, I could hear her voice, and sometimes I could even feel her touch. But there was something that I couldn't quite name that was keeping us from reaching forward into a real relationship.

Maybe it was the fact that this wasn't ever supposed to have happened. If my uncle hadn't died, there'd be no marriage. I might have never come to Torino at all. Ever.

At least Nova was fun to be around. She knew this country, she'd shown me many things as we wandered. She even spoke fluent French, which blew my mind.

I wondered if my siblings would like her.

And then I wondered if it mattered.

At five on the dot, my siblings arrived in two separate white Rolls-Royces. Both vehicles rolled up, bumper to bumper, stopping at the top of the long driveway. Drake and a few servants hurried over to open the doors, more men setting to the task of unloading the luggage from the trunks.

"Thorne!" Francesca squealed, leaping out the door, giving Drake a fright. She was wearing a short orange skirt and a black feathery top, her gold heels wrapping up her calves in a way that made me wonder how long it had taken her to get them off on the way through airport security.

In one arm was her huge Gucci purse. In the other was Mic, because of course she'd brought that little monster. The white dog growled, eyeing me as my sister drew close for a fierce hug. "How was the flight?" I asked.

She stuck out her tongue. "I wish we could have taken the private jet. Do you know what our plane had to watch? Gossip Girl *season two!*"

I blinked. "Do you . . . not like that show?"

"Oh, I love it. But what if someone hadn't seen the first season? Do they expect them to start in the middle? I mean, come on!"

Unsure how to respond, I waved over her head. Kain waved back, busy helping his wife, Sammy, out of the car. Her loose peasant top couldn't hide her round belly. If I remembered right, based on how my mother had screamed and cried happily for a day straight when she got the news, Sammy was six months along.

I'd teased Kain about not waiting until the ring was on her finger to knock her up. But he'd just smirked, not offended in the least.

He held her hand as they came over. Kain's hug was quick. "Brother, you look good."

"Thanks," I said, running a hand through my hair. "Speaking of." Wrapping Sammy in my arms, I carefully avoided her belly. "You look amazing, Sammy. How are you feeling?"

"Good now. I haven't had morning sickness in a month. However, the flight was awful. Hours of waddling the aisle over and over thanks to this little guy or girl smushing my bladder." She put her hands on her stomach, rubbing it fondly in spite of her disgusted face.

Costello approached our growing group. He was dressed in dark jeans and a dark blue shirt that I was sure he'd regret soon in this sunny heat. "Hawthorne," he said, giving me a partial smile. "Good to see you in one piece."

I whipped a hand over my scalp. "The country hasn't beheaded me yet. Maybe they're waiting until tomorrow night when the crown is actually on."

My older brother's smile crumpled into a hard frown.

"Thorne!" Scotch shouted, grabbing me in a hug tighter than everyone else's.

"Hey!" Laughing, I hugged her back. "Easy, you'll make your boyfriend jealous."

Costello crinkled his eyebrows, his long scar shifting with the motion. But he said nothing.

"By the way," she whispered, her mouth near my ear as we kept embracing, "I don't want you worrying about the mess with Gina. I've talked to her, and she swears she'll agree to a deal soon with her lawyers."

I stared, not comprehending. "Oh. Right, the club." I'd managed to forget entirely about the Dirty Dolls. It was off-putting to me that I'd actually let that drama slip my mind. The club had been such a huge part of my life; to simply forget about it, when just weeks ago I'd been sulking on its roped-off doorstep . . . It was like forgetting it was your own birthday until everyone jumped out and said, "Surprise!"

Looking back at the cars, I asked, "No Lula, huh?"

Frannie buried her face in Mic's fur. "I tried to talk her into it, but . . ."

"It's fine. Really." I waved it off, giving her a light push toward the castle. "Go, get inside and swoon over the crystal toilets and stuff."

"Whaaat?" she gasped. "Real crystal? Seriously?"

"Yup. Next to the diamond-crusted toothbrushes."

Fran scowled at me before she jumped up the steps. Watching her go, I tucked my thumbs in my pockets. My smile was solid, no one could have guessed I was trying to pretend that my older sister's absence had any effect on me.

Lulabelle's issues with our family were well known. Ten years ago she'd been injured in an attack orchestrated by some men working for the Valentines. They'd been trying to strong-arm Costello into giving them a huge sum of cash. Lula had tried to help him out of the situation. Instead she'd ended up as bait to lure my brother into a trap.

It had been an awful experience for everyone involved. It only got worse when, after she'd recovered from her wounds, Lula had run away in the middle of the night. She'd been seventeen—the only one of us who'd never gotten her crown tattoo. It had been intentional. Her silent rejection of our royal blood.

Her absence had hung over us. The rift between my siblings and I had only grown wider with time. Then, just last year, Lula had appeared on our doorstep out of the blue. She'd said she'd missed us.

But she didn't miss the danger associated with our family.

Ultimately, it wasn't shocking that Lula hadn't shown up here. But it still stung.

Costello grabbed my forearm, pulling me farther from the cars. When he spoke, he kept his voice low, for our ears only. "Why didn't you call me?"

I shrugged out of his grip. "I didn't call anyone. What could I even say? You, of all people, know how dire this situation is."

He didn't respond, he just surveyed me in that judgmental way he was good at.

I was compelled to keep talking, terrified of the silence creeping in. "I didn't call because there was nothing to discuss. I'm the only one who can wear the crown. The only one who can marry Nova Valentine. That's just the way it is."

Unable to handle my brother's intense blue eyes, I looked behind us. Sammy was talking with Scotch; the two of them laughed, Sammy's hands lovingly caressing her round stomach. As I watched, Scotch touched her by her navel. She was feeling the baby kick.

It's on my shoulders to keep everyone safe.

Costello's eyes burned into my skull. Meeting his stare evenly, I shrugged. "It's seriously fine. Ma's thrilled. She never expected me to get married, you know? Good ol' blackmail, making dreams happen."

His frown remained solid. Reaching out, he gripped my shoulder, fingers digging in. "You should've called me. Or messaged me. Thorne, I'm your brother. I was worried about you."

I almost pushed his hand off me. Almost. Somehow his touch was giving me strength beneath my new burst of guilt. I couldn't deflect when faced with his honesty. "Thanks. But you don't need to worry, okay? It is what it is."

He clenched my shoulder harder, then dropped his hand to his side. "How has it been living under the same roof as them?"

Them. The Valentines, people my brother hated more than even I. Last winter, when Darien had gone off the rails and attacked Gina at the club, Scotch had stepped in and saved her life. It had been a bloody mess that ended with Darien accusing Scotch of trying to kill him. The Valentines had gone on the offensive. It was a miracle no one had died.

Thinking about Darien made me think about Larchmont . . . then Kurtis . . . then Richard. Valencia and Darla swirled at the bottom of the toilet bowl in my mind. All of these people were awful in their own crazy ways.

All but Nova.

"Let me pick my words tactfully." I paused. "It's been shit." Costello cracked a half smile. "The only saving grace is how big this castle is. I don't have to see anyone if I don't want to."

He glanced at the huge structure. "It's strange to imagine Dad growing up here."

"Tell me about it."

"And Nova?" he asked, studying me with new interest.

I locked my knees. "She's . . . good. Nothing like her family. You'll understand when you meet her."

Costello scrutinized me more intently. I squirmed. "I do want to meet her. I don't think doing that will change what matters, though."

"And what's that?"

"She's a Valentine." Ducking his head, my brother walked away from me. "That makes her our enemy."

- CHAPTER NINETEEN -

HAWTHORNE

The coronation party took place in the grand ballroom of the castle. The staff had started preparing for the event two days ago. They'd done as much cooking as they could, my mother helping to organize the menu, pick colors, anything they'd let her get her hands on.

And though she'd only arrived recently—never mind being quite pregnant—Sammy jumped into the fray to show off her party-planning skills. I knew her wedding business had taken off soon after she'd helped make Francesca's dress last year. With her own marriage last winter, the honeymoon, the baby on the way . . . I didn't know how she found time to brush her damn hair. Who could manage so much? I was overwhelmed with juggling the list of things my father continued to send my way.

It had gone on that way since I'd moved into the castle. It only got worse after the engagement became official. Whenever I thought I could dodge some boring meeting with another elected official, or business mogul, or son of a son of some other son I could never keep straight . . . Dad would send a new maid darting after me to drag me where he wanted me to go.

But today? Today was different.

Instead of being called on to do things, people kept stopping me to ask how they could help. The reality of me becoming king had sunk in. The servants wanted to gain whatever favor they could, in any way they could. My shoes for the coronation had been shined by five different people already.

It was strange to be fawned over. Having my siblings around, busting my chops, helped me feel stable. Between breakfast and lunch I'd harassed them all, which was easy, since they'd been put up in my wing of the castle. I could even hear Fran while she shouted about how she'd forgotten to pack the *perfect* dress for the event tonight. It was like being back at the estate. Like being home.

Then everyone kicked me out so they could get ready for tonight. Now I studied myself in front of my floor-length mirror, adjusting my red tie, wondering what else I could do to fill the time. I was fully cleaned, shaved, changed. What was left? *Maybe I could write a speech.* Did I have to? Were they expecting that?

Fiddling with my phone, I sat on the bed.

Me: Are you getting ready?

Nova: Hour three of my hair and makeup. I might starve before they finish.

Her response made me grin.

Me: I'll mourn the loss in my speech. Do I need a speech, by the way?

Nova: No. But you can still write something about me, anyway.

Me: Shouldn't you write about me? I'm the one becoming king.

Nova: Nope. Do it to show your modesty. Make it poetic.

Me: I'll write about how pretty you sound when you come. That's poetry, for sure.

The word bubble popped up, then vanished, multiple times—she was typing, then erasing her response.

Nova: Saying bye before the makeup artist stabs my eye out because I keep giggling.

Turning my phone off, I spread out on my bed. She'd been joking . . . but I didn't think it would be hard to write poetry about Nova. The way she moved through my dreams each night was a sweet verse all its own.

I wasn't looking forward to tonight.

But I *was* looking forward to seeing her.

Even so, in the end, I waited until fifteen minutes after the party began to make my way toward the ballroom. All excitement aside, I knew any good socialite never arrived on time. Tweaking my cuff links, I rounded the hallway that spilled out by the foyer.

Nova was facing away from me by the stairs. Her dress was bronze, embroidered with silver diamonds around the shoulders and hemline. It hugged her the way a lover would in private. The way *I* wanted to.

"Boo," I said in her ear.

"Oh!" She jumped, giving me a disapproving squint. It was brief, though—I watched in wonder as she absorbed the sight of me. I did the same to her, loving how amazing she looked whether she was dressed up or lounging in a bathrobe.

"Come on," I said, leading her into the gigantic ballroom. "You can ogle me inside. They're waiting for us." I didn't need to say who; she knew I meant my family.

Silver strings of stars dangled from the arching ceiling. Along the wall were black banners with the red crown I knew so well. They were placed strategically, the majority of them clustered around an elaborately carved throne at the far wall.

It was where I would sit when I was finally crowned.

Seeing it, my blood began to race. Nova must have sensed my reaction, because she snatched two champagne flutes off the tray of a passing servant, handing me one. "Here, liquid courage."

"Thanks." I drank it down in one swallow. "Feel free to hand me those all night long."

"I'm not sure you want your first impression as king to be you stumbling around drunk."

"Why? At least these people would know what to expect going forward." Handing off the empty glass to one of the many servants crisscrossing the room, I waved at my mother. She was standing among the growing crowd, talking to every single person who would give her their time. She'd always been good at these events.

"Who *are* all these people?" I whispered into Nova's ear.

She smiled, waving at someone as she whispered back, "Every important person this country has to offer. The guards outside must be doing overtime to make sure no one sneaks into this party."

A bright flash on my left side half blinded me. "Important people includes the damn paparazzi, huh?"

"Of course. The locals are going to want to see pictures of you being crowned, Thorne."

"Everything feels like a media circus here." We'd reached my mother; I hugged her, nodding to the strangers surrounding her. "Ma, you're looking lovely as usual."

Grinning, she adjusted her peacock-green dress. "Always so kind. Thorne, this is Lane Southerbie, Earl of Ducop. Lane, this is my son Hawthorne."

Lane looked to be my father's age, his hair wheat blond and gelled until it glistened. His handshake was feeble. "Pleasure," he said. "And this must be Nova Valentine, your fiancée. Loved those engagement photos."

Nova slid her arm around mine. I thrilled at the sensation. "Thank you," she said. "We loved them as well."

"It's always nice when a photographer can get their work out so *quickly*. Do you like when things are done quick, Hawthorne?"

Nova's smile fumbled. My mother looked surprised, eyeing Lane like she'd spotted a spider in his hair. Whoever this Earl of Wherever was, he was making it known that he thought our engagement was suspiciously sudden.

"Excuse us," I said, looking Lane up and down. "I think we should go eat before we lose our appetites." With my palm on Nova's hip, I walked us away from the group.

She stared straight ahead. "You didn't need to do that."

"Yes, I did. He was an asshole," I mumbled.

Her pink lips inched higher. "Most of them will be."

Unsure who else at this party would try to figuratively spit on our feet, I headed toward the only people who, while not fans of Nova, were predictable. "Hey," I said as we drew up beside my siblings where they were standing in a circle. "Some party, huh?"

Kain smirked. "Whoever they're throwing it for must be really important."

"I heard he's a dick," I laughed. Pulling Nova closer, I gave everyone a meaningful look. "This is Nova Valentine."

My little sister lifted her nose higher. "The bride-to-be. I'm Francesca."

Nova crossed her hands at her waist, tipping her head politely to each person as she spoke. "No need for introductions. I know who you all are." Costello narrowed his eyes—Nova widened hers, knowing she'd phrased that all wrong. "I hope you're enjoying Torino."

"We are. But I wish we could stay longer and see more," Sammy said.

Kain bumped her gently with his elbow. "If you hadn't spent all morning helping Mom decorate this room, we could have."

Sammy shrugged sheepishly. "I'm a sucker when people ask for help."

"You did an amazing job," Nova said, gesturing at the decorations. "The staff were happy to have some direction that was . . . modern. There haven't been any parties here in a long time."

Leaning into Costello, Scotch gave the wide room an appreciative smile. "That's too bad. It's the kind of room that's meant for big events."

"Hopefully there will be many more in the future." Nova peered up at me as she spoke. "Torino has been in need of a fresh face leading them. Now they—we—have it."

I was frozen under her vote of confidence. Costello's blue eyes flashed, fixing on something behind me and Nova. I moved aside in time to see Valencia approaching. In her long red dress with its golden-scaled front panels, she reminded me of a cobra ready to strike.

Her hooded eyes rested on me, then my brothers, my sister, and the others. "Nova," she said, her voice bubbling in her throat in a way that some would find sexy, but I just found irritating. "There are some people who want to meet you. Come with me."

"Right, okay." Pressing her palms together to say she was sorry, she then spread her hands and waved at everyone. "Sorry! I hope I can get to know you all better before the wedding." She hesitated long enough to kiss my cheek, leaving a hot flush on my skin as she strolled across the ballroom beside her mother.

Everyone stared after them. Then they stared at me. "I hope that's the only polite exchange I have to make with her mom," Kain muttered. "Not sure I could keep from rolling my eyes."

Sammy focused on me. "Nova seems nice."

"She is," I insisted.

Fran squinted at me over a glass of champagne she'd just snagged from a passing tray that I regretted missing. "You might be marrying her, but you don't have to fall in love with her. She's a Valentine. You know how they are."

"Don't act like she's manipulating me, okay? She doesn't have any more choice about this marriage than me."

Fran pointed with her chin at Nova. The young woman was laughing at something one of the people chatting with her had just said; her head was thrown back, a hand to her chest.

"Doesn't exactly seem miserable about her situation, does she?" Fran whispered.

I didn't answer. There was nothing I could say anyway. Nova was either good at pretending to have fun, which was dangerous . . . or she was actually enjoying meeting these "important people" her mother had dragged her off to make small talk with.

Studying the pair from afar, I was able to notice the similarities between Nova and her mother. They had the same softness to the curve of their noses—a richness in their honey-golden irises. Nova only lacked her mom's height and willowy frame. Unnerved by their shared traits, I desperately searched for differences in them.

Darla sidled into the frame. At first I was bothered, but then I began to breathe easier. Darla looked so much like Valencia that, by comparison, Nova became a black sheep. The younger woman's curled hair was the same shade and exact same length as Valencia's. And when Darla laughed—louder than anyone else in the room—I saw the same wicked gleam in her face that her mom wore like perfume.

Nova didn't laugh like that. Never.

From out of nowhere, Larchmont slid into their conversation. He dipped to give his mom a kiss on the cheek. Then, after he hugged Darla, he saw me watching them. At first his smile drooped. The hatred swimming in his face was unmistakable.

With me looking on, Larch lowered to Nova's height, giving her a fierce embrace. He never tore his eyes—or his sneer—from me the whole time. Like the rest of them, Larch was dressed in a well-made outfit. Black, which he seemed to favor.

Richard broke through the crowd to join them. Larch whispered in his brother's ear; both of them surveyed me now.

Next to me Fran said, "Remember, you're not just marrying Nova. You're marrying her family, too."

Larchmont winked from across the room. Taking a glass from a tray, he held it to his shoulder. To anyone looking, he was toasting me. But I knew when he straightened his thumb on the edge of the glass, passing it in front of his neck, he wasn't wishing me well.

He was imagining he was cutting my throat.

- CHAPTER TWENTY -

HAWTHORNE

The live band in the corner played as we ate. After the food was served, the music became lighter, catchier—encouraging the attendees to dance. I jumped right into the fray, happy to have something to take my mind off things.

Each time I twirled Nova, I spotted the throne waiting for me on the other side of the room. There was a wide space around it where no one dared to draw closer. The damn thing might as well have been under a spotlight.

"Are you okay?" Nova asked.

"Better than ever," I lied, scooping her up, spinning her easily. Her dress fluttered in the chandelier lights, transparent, blurry, like a hummingbird's wings in flight. It made me think of the day she'd pleaded with me to give this a shot. To choose her.

When I set her down, she dug her fingers into my sleeves. Her heels skidded on the slippery floor. "You're nervous."

"Me? No, God. Never." I tried to make her move; she dug her shoes in harder.

"I know fear when I see it. What I'm wondering is if you're nervous about the coronation . . . or about the wedding."

I started to respond. Flicking my eyes to the throne, then back to her, I sighed instead. "Why would you ask about the wedding?"

"Because of them." She swung her hips, moving us so that I was able to see the rest of the room. Though they were dancing apart from each other, I spotted my family without much struggle. Fran was eyeballing us over the shoulder of some random guy in a tux. Costello and Scotch were more subtle, but barely.

Grabbing her hips, I pulled her against me. "You think they hate you."

"They *do* hate me."

"Well, so what? They hate a lot of people." I grinned, but Nova didn't. "Listen . . . they don't hate you. They hate your family. Give them time, they did say you were nice."

"Nice." She tasted the word, and though she didn't look comforted, she did finally smile. "You said that, too. Do you think that's all there is to me?"

Chuckling, I brushed my palms up her spine. Lowering my face to her cheek, I kissed her smooth skin. "You're more than just nice. But the things I love about you aren't exactly easy to show off to a whole room."

She shuddered, clutching me around my broad back. Her nose tickled my earlobe. "That's true. I'd rather not show my soon-to-be in-laws what you do to me when we're alone." Her fingernails scraped lightly over my suit jacket, making my cock twitch. "But . . . I have an idea for how we can make a different scene."

Baffled by her cryptic words, I let her pull me away from the dance floor, toward the live band. The grand piano was a polished chocolate brown. I saw my awed face in it as I walked closer. Most of the players had gone to take a break and eat, leaving just a violinist and some brass players to perform for the dancers. They all watched me curiously.

"Go on," Nova said, running her hand down my arm. "Sit."

Overwhelmed with disbelief, my voice cracked. "What do you expect me to do? Play it in front of everyone?"

"I told you I'd love to hear you. I meant it."

"Sure, but here? Now?" Fuck, my heart was thumping wildly. I couldn't tear my eyes away from the piano.

Gently but firmly, Nova put her hands on my shoulders. With her guidance I settled on the bench. Her fingers linked with mine, tightening pleasantly. "Do it," she whispered, "for me. Please."

Swallowing the mountain that had made a home in my throat, I reached for the white keys. There was sheet music on the piano, but I didn't need it. The thudding in my ears got louder. Through it I noticed the other players had stopped. Without their music there should have been audible chatter. There was none. The room had gone mute.

I turned my head enough to see Nova. She was smiling. Waiting. Believing in me.

I'm going to make a fool out of myself.

Well. So what? If it made her happy . . . then . . .

My fingers glided over the keys, muscle memory coercing forth music.

Without raising my head, I knew people were watching me perform. The room was transfixed. I imagined that Larchmont was hoping I'd make a mistake and embarrass myself. With Nova at my side, her presence a constant strength . . . I realized I couldn't fail.

The last note hung in the air. It went on and on, sinking into my blood, my teeth. Seconds after it ended, the applause began; soft, polite, then finally enthusiastic. Spinning on the bench, I scanned the ballroom. My siblings were cheering, my mother clapping hardest of them all.

The Valentines had grouped together. Each of them applauded, none of it genuine. But I'd expected that out of them. They didn't matter to me. I kept searching until I found who I was after.

There: my father's lips were a crooked line. He sucked away every ounce of joy in the air, replacing it with a severe heaviness I couldn't understand. Was he angry? Had I let him down somehow? I couldn't see how—the whole damn room was *exploding* for me.

Nova touched my wrist. "That was wonderful," she hushed. The centers of her eyes were expanding. I sank into them, eager for the comfort her delight brought me. Let my father sulk. He was the only one.

"I can't believe I did that," I said.

"You were amazing."

"I was only okay. No one here seems to be a music critic. Lucky me."

"Thorne!" Francesca gushed, slamming into me on the bench. "That was the coolest thing I've ever seen! Wow!"

Laughing, I scooted over so she had room to sit. From the corner of my eye, I noticed that Nova had receded into the crowd.

Kain swaggered up, his arms crossed, his smirk in full force. "I haven't heard you play in years. I'm surprised you didn't forget how to do it."

"Like riding a bike." Clapping him on the shoulder, I got up so he could sit beside Fran. "Go ahead. I can tell you're dying to show off."

He snorted, but when he whispered in Fran's ear, I knew I was right. In a synchronization born inherently to twins, the two of them began to play the piano in perfect harmony. It was a tune with lots of mistakes—a cringeworthy wrong key here and there—yet no one cared. Especially not Kain and Fran, who laughed heartily in the face of imperfection.

Backing away, I started to look for Nova. Before I could find her, someone blocked my escape. "Son," my father said, looming over me. In his pale gray suit, his eyes appeared lighter. "That was a risky stunt."

"It wasn't a stunt." I kept my eyes on his, not blinking. "It was something I'd always wanted to do. Now excuse me—but there's a prettier face I'd like to spend the evening looking at."

As I started around him, I thought he'd stop me. He didn't.

Closing in on Nova, I reached out to put my arm around her middle. She twisted into my touch, grinning up at me. The chandeliers created a thousand gold diamonds beneath the surface of her dark pools.

She looked beyond me, her smile fading. "What did your dad say to you? Was he happy with your music?"

"That man is never happy about anything." I kissed her quickly on her forehead. "Let's dance."

Nova continued to stare over my shoulder.

"Hey," I said, cupping her chin. "It's fine. Do I look like it matters to me?"

"You're right." Holding my forearms, she pulled me to the center of the room. "Who cares what he thinks?"

As I spun her around the glossy floor to the broken music my siblings created, I saw my father watching me again. He reminded me of a sponge that, long ago, had been full . . . but was now parched and waiting for more water. An empty man. Briefly I was struck by a twinge of sympathy.

Then Nova wrapped her arms around my neck, her teeth glittering as she beamed.

He told me to quit piano because it was a waste of everyone's time.

I'd thought he was right.

Now, thanks to Nova, I knew he wasn't.

The night wore on. My calves had started to ache from all the dancing, so I'd dropped down in a chair along the wall. Costello joined me, both of us looking on as Scotch, Sammy, and Fran laughed in a small circle on the dance floor. Nova was nearby, and, to my relief, Sammy waved her into their little group.

All of them smiled, plied by alcohol and good cheer. My heart swelled to see Nova looking so happy next to my family.

Costello leaned toward me. "I can tell you care for her."

I shot him a scalding look, then stared back at the dancing. "Yeah. I'm obvious, huh."

"Not at all. I just recognize it because I've been there." He wasn't watching me, he was looking at Scotch where she was spinning in a circle, her dress a whirl of green. "I won't tell you what to feel, like Fran is trying to. You can't help if you fall in love."

I sat up like there was a rod jammed in my spine. "I never said I loved her!"

He was still as a statue. "I know. You don't have to say it for me to tell." He closed his eyes, and in the ballroom lights, the long scar that crossed his face looked white as a dead fish's belly. "Love is love. It's in your heart, it holds on like a tick in your flesh. It can bring joy or ruin everything you hold dear."

My fingers dug into my thighs. "Why are you saying all this?"

He opened his eyes, the bright blues freezing me to my chair. "Because you falling in love with Nova is only a problem if she doesn't love you back."

"Hawthorne."

Twitching in surprise, I faced my father. He'd managed to sneak up on us. The creases around his mouth had deepened since I'd spoken to him half an hour ago. "It's time. They're waiting for you."

My stomach dropped off a cliff. "Oh. I hoped I'd be drunker first."

Maverick faced away, striding through the ballroom, creating a path for me to follow him through the people. Because he *did* expect me to follow him. He had every reason to; I'd gone this far.

Costello's eyebrows rose. As I stood, he gave my arm a quick grab. Then he released me. I couldn't tell if it was meant for comfort . . . or if he'd instinctively tried to stop me from going forward with this plan. If it was out of worry for me or jealousy, I wasn't sure.

What is it like for him? For my father? Both were firstborn sons. Both had been fated to sit on this throne, and now, both had been robbed of it.

This was happening to me.

Not them.

In a daze I passed through the crowd. There were angry glares, but there were also a few subtle head bows. To those people I was already king. They didn't need the next few minutes of ceremony to feel it in their guts.

On either side of the throne were two men dressed like priests. A third hovered in front, his hands holding a glass case at chest height. Inside it was a crown with dagger-sharp tips, the surface a dull bronze. The man holding it was shorter than me, thick and soft all over in a way his ceremonial robes didn't hide. His aura was one of pure seriousness— the dry crackle right after a snowstorm, where the wrong sound could bring down an avalanche on your head.

"Sit," he said solemnly.

Turning to face the ballroom, I settled on the throne. I'd expected it to be warm, but the lacquered surface was cool. Or maybe I was simply too hot, so anything would have felt cold in comparison.

"Hawthorne Luca Fredricson." His voice boomed over the crowd. "Second son of Maverick Julius Fredricson. You are hereby elected as ruler of Torino. By blood and lineage, you shall lead this country. We shall be your subjects. And we will pray for your long life, long health, and eternal protection. Long live the king!"

Glass clinked above me as the case opened. The man lowered the heavy crown onto my skull. It touched my hair; the people swayed forward in a wave as they bent their knees. I wanted to crack some joke about how this felt like prom. But my mouth was too dry. My skin too slick. This moment had gotten away from me and it was no longer something I could make light of.

There was a crown on my head.

I was the king.

- CHAPTER TWENTY-ONE -

NOVA

"That dress is beautiful," Darla said, unable to hide her wonderment. Her light amber eyes were glowing as she watched me turn slowly in place in the wedding gown. The top hugged me like a corset, strapless and tight. Ribbons even whiter than the gown itself crisscrossed my spine. The bodice vanished into the full layers of lace and tulle.

"Thanks," I said, blushing, smiling too wide. "I just hope Thorne likes it as much as you do." I sat carefully in front of the vanity, studying how my veil fit over my hair.

"I don't know why you care what he thinks," Darla said. "It's not like it matters."

"It does matter," I argued.

Her eyebrows moved up and down, her lips quirking. "Oh my. Is our frigid Nova in *love*?"

My fingers busied themselves adjusting my earrings. "No," I said, the word catching in my throat. "I'm not in love with him." It wasn't a full truth. It was the kind that, if cut into pieces, could still be identified as what it was from a single slice.

"Remember why you're doing this," my mother said, standing behind me. Her hands rested on my shoulders; her nails were bright red on my snowy-white lace.

I said nothing. Just stared into the mirror.

"Please," Darla snorted. "Knowing Little Miss Never Been Kissed here, you can expect that baby in a decade."

Neither of them had any idea what I'd been up to with Thorne. How we'd already done much more than kiss. That man had cracked me open, burying his fingers in my liquid core, and I'd healed back over with him sealed inside.

I might not love him—yet.

But he was a part of me now.

Darla smoothed her palms down the front of her lilac maid of honor dress. "This is why you should have let me marry him, Mom."

"He picked *me*, not you. Let it go." The acidic words exploded.

Darla gaped at me in the mirror. My backbone was new to her.

Our mom backed away. "Yes," she said solemnly. "He picked you, Nova." Turning, she motioned at Darla to leave the room. "Go. I'll be out in a minute."

Though I twisted my veil, pretending to be busy with it, I watched my mother approach me. I wished she'd left with my sister. The way my mother made me feel . . . it wasn't afraid. Not quite. There was a fraction of my existence that tugged sharply when she came close, a craven, awful eagerness to please her however I could.

"Nova." She breathed my name out, letting it linger. When she stood behind me, she was so tall the mirror cut her off at her chest. In the smooth reflection she was nothing but manicured hands and a disembodied torso wearing the finest silk. "I know you don't get along with your sister. But please don't fight with her. We're all in this together."

I looked down at the smear of makeup left over on the vanity. The girls who'd done my hair and painted my skin had left only half an hour ago. I wished I'd left when they had.

"Nova."

"I know," I said, still not lifting my head. "I'll try not to fight with her. I just don't like how she talks about me and Thorne."

Her grip tightened. "Is she right? Do you love him?"

Glancing at the mirror, I focused on the stitching on her dress. "Is it bad if I do? Isn't falling in love normal?"

She grabbed the chair, turning it, making the legs scrape over the floor. I had no choice but to face her now. "Loving him might make things more difficult."

My lower lip pulled between my teeth. I started to bite, but she tapped my arm, reminding me not to ruin my lipstick. "How could love do that?"

"Because no matter what, he can never do what I have for you. He can never make the sacrifice I have." My mother trapped my chin with her fingers, and something in me twinged. "Nova . . . I'm your mother. The way I love you, and the way *you* love *me*, always comes first. I'm saying this only because I care. I worry that if you do come to love this man, that you'll be confused over who you owe your allegiance to."

Unable to break her intense eye-lock, I gave a quick nod. "I'll never forget what you've done for me, Mom. I promise."

Kissing her fingers and pressing them to the bridge of my nose, she released me. "Good. Now let's hurry."

Standing up, I adjusted my gown. I could fix the way the tulle hung, but I couldn't remove the wrinkles of worry in my heart. Eyeing her, I said, "Is there something you're worried about? Something with Thorne or his family?"

Considering me as she stood by the door, she tilted her head. "Nothing more than I imagine you're worried about."

I half tripped in midstep. *She knows I'm upset about them hating me.* Her attention to detail had always been keen. It drove home the bitter reality between us and *them*. Suddenly I imagined Thorne's family teasing him the way Darla had teased me. Were they instructing him not to get too close?

Did he think that loving me would complicate things?

That sobering thought settled in my belly like a bucket of wet sand. If I wasn't already taking small steps, it would have slowed me down on the way to the aisle. My mother went ahead, servants escorting me toward the rose garden, where the ceremony was.

This whole wedding . . . all these smiling faces and flowers . . . it was all a sham. I'd known that before boarding the plane to fly to Torino.

I was here to do a job.

It was okay if what Hawthorne and I had never evolved beyond sweaty fun.

I could handle being married to someone without love.

I could have a baby with him . . . without love.

Couldn't I?

Lifting my eyes as I exited into the fresh air, I saw Thorne. He was standing at the end of the rose petals scattered along the white paper roll on the grass. The black tuxedo he wore brought out the richness of his eyes—it enhanced the hard corners of his shoulders and his slim hips.

He was unquestionably male: powerful, stylish. Ever since I'd seen him shirtless, I'd thought about the tattoos he kept secret from the world. I knew they were there, covering every inch of his body, stopping only at his wrists and throat. I hoped I was one of only a few who knew about them. It made me feel . . . special.

He hadn't blinked since our eyes had met. The sight of him washed away every doubt in my mind. I forgot what I'd been thinking about. I forgot how to breathe.

An arm wrapped around mine firmly. My father looked down on me with benevolence. But I knew he wasn't proud of me. He was happy he was getting what he wanted. That was all he'd ever cared about.

I let him walk me down the aisle. Thorne's presence was magnetic. Drawn to him, I was able to forget, for a little bit, that we'd only gotten to know each other recently. I could pretend we were old friends who had shared everything on their path to marriage.

At his side stood his older brother. Costello looked like a silver sword someone had stuck into the ground, something from a legend that couldn't be pried free no matter how hard you tried. The jagged scar across his nose enhanced the threat in his face as he observed my approach. This man loved his brother. He did not love me.

Beside him was Kain. He, too, looked handsome in his tailored suit. He'd have looked better without the distrust seething in his glare. All at once I became aware of the other eyes on me. This family who thought I was their enemy, each of them here to support Thorne—but not our marriage.

Hawthorne inhaled, the sound packed with a million things: hunger, lust, appreciation. Looking into his eyes was enough to lift away the darkness. His smile . . . the excitement and longing in his stare . . . it made me forget my fear.

My father released me. Hovering in front of Thorne, his hands curled lightly at his sides. It was customary to shake the groom's hand. I waited to see what they'd both do.

Kurtis started to sway backward. *He isn't going to do it.* But then Thorne reached out, snatching the man's hand, gripping hard. He yanked him in close for a hug so theatrical that people in the audience who didn't know them clapped. Both of them were grinning.

I was close enough to hear Thorne whisper, "The only good thing you ever did was make her."

The fireball in my chest flared hotter.

Dad let go, his grin still solid. He moved away until he was sitting beside my mother in the front row.

There were no vows. Just lots of yammering about decorum, royal history, and the expectations that came with being husband and wife. Becoming queen to the king. I tuned everything out. The priest was speaking, but I kept staring at Thorne, trying to see into his head.

He had a habit of keeping his real feelings hidden behind sarcasm. I'd seen it again and again. I wasn't used to his silence. I'd never had a more intimate chance to gaze on his face without him being able to make a joke and turn away.

"The ring," the priest said.

Darla held her hands out to me so she could take my bouquet. I passed it off, and, as I did, I spotted her envious frown. I'd never seen that pointed at *me*.

Long fingers curled around my wrist. Thorne turned me to him, a simple platinum ring in his other hand. He slid the cool metal onto my finger so that it caressed the engagement ring he'd put there only a week ago.

"Hawthorne Fredricson," the priest said, loud enough for the crowd. "Do you take this woman, with everything she brings, with everything she *will* bring, to have at your side for as long as you both shall live?"

Deep down, I was sure he'd say yes. Who could go this far and say no? Even with that certainty, my throat constricted. My heart was going to burst. It had to, this was too much for one person to bear.

In slow motion I saw him wet his lips. "I do." It was a simple statement. Only one other phrase had ever made my eyes water so much: *You're going to live.*

"And do you, Nova Valentine . . ."

Black spots flashed in my vision. I made myself breathe.

"Take this man—"

"Yes," I blurted. The crowd murmured; I caught the sounds of amusement. "I mean—yes, sorry, I do." Thorne's eyes went wide, his smile faltering. Then it came back tenfold.

Before the priest finished saying, "Then I now pronounce you husband and wife, you may kiss the bride," he'd swept me into his arms, dipping me with his hand on my neck and the other on the small of my back. His lips were hot, his kiss insistent, unending, as if he was proving to every suspicious eye that he *did* love me.

And you can call me a fool, but without him even saying it, I felt that he did.

The reception was bigger than the coronation ball had been.

Thorne and I sat at our sweetheart table, placed so we could view the gigantic dining hall from every angle. We would miss nothing. But my attention wasn't on the people laughing on the floor. I wanted to research how Thorne's lips could smile, or frown, but do very little in between. In his midnight tux he was stunning. Sometime after the ceremony, he'd dropped his jacket on a chair, letting a servant fuss over what to do with it.

He turned his head, catching me staring at him. "Hey there," he said, clutching my hand under the table. Our fingers rested on one of the many layers of my wedding gown. "You good?"

"More than I thought I could be," I whispered.

Under the table, where no one could see, he stroked over the lace. He went deeper, prying the ruffles aside until he found my bare knee. "Think anyone will see us slip away?"

"Let them." I reached for my champagne and finished the tall flute. "They won't stop us."

The heat in his hooded eyes scalded me. "They couldn't if they tried."

Together we broke away from the table, wending our way through the noise, the sparkling dresses and suits, smiling politely at anyone we bumped into. The sounds faded at our backs as we ran down the hallway.

"My room?" I asked.

"No." He pulled me by my wrist. "Mine. I've wanted you in my bed for far too long."

Flooding with anticipation, I barely kept up with him in my heels. We didn't have to go far before his door rose up in front of us. I started to follow him in; Thorne turned, hoisting me into his arms before I could react. "Oh!"

His kiss was a firm, hungry thing with a smile hiding in the shadows. "It's how they do it in the movies, right? Wife over the threshold?" He kicked the door shut behind him. The loud *bang* of it ricocheted through my bones. This was really happening.

Setting me on the edge of his bed, he tugged his bow tie free. The black silk dropped to the floor, forgotten. His cuff links went next, clinking softly to the rug. I surveyed his undressing like it was the best show in the world.

His chin motioned at me. "Stand up."

As I rose, his dress shirt fell. He was magnificent, not truly naked, the ink across his upper body like a second outfit. More elaborate than the plain white he'd had on for our wedding. This was the secret second skin that only I was allowed to see.

In just his black slacks and shiny belt, he approached me. He didn't blink, like he refused to miss a second of this. "Turn around," he said flatly.

Facing the bed, I looked across at the window. The curtains were half-closed, the sun beginning to melt into the distant line of the ocean. Waiting for him to touch me was torture. There was no sound behind me. Not even his shoes on the plush rug.

Thorne's breath trailed over the side of my vulnerable throat. Every tiny hair on my body stood at attention. Featherlight, he slid the fingertips of both hands down my shoulders. The path he took drew a heart on my skin. Stopping at my spine, he tugged at the ribbons weaving my dress together. "When I saw you in this," he said, his voice husky, "all I could think about was how much I wanted to rip it off you."

My breath quickened; the sound of the satin ribbons slithering free one by one was so *loud* to me.

He kissed my shoulder. "Now that I'm doing it, I want to go slow. Savor it."

His muscles ground into my shoulder blades. Thick arms wove around, holding me in a firm embrace. I remained still, hands at my sides, as Thorne peeled my gown away. The flowing material drifted apart, finally crumbling at my ankles, a giant bird's nest of lace and ivory tulle.

Thorne held my naked waist, turning me like I was a ballerina, performing for him in private. I knew what he'd see when I faced him. As predicted, his eyes dropped from my rounded breasts, to my belly, and then they stayed there.

"This," he said, running his thumb below my navel. He traced the contour of the long scar. "Can I ask what happened?"

My mind was assaulted by the memories of what I'd gone through. Reaching down, I touched the spot he had, brushing his fingers as he retreated. "Acute kidney failure. It's when your kidneys just . . . stop working. All at once, with pretty much no warning. I needed a transplant."

Well. There *had* been warning signs. I'd just ignored them the same way everyone else had. The pain had left me bedridden within days. Darla had called me dramatic, asking if this was my new way to get attention. She'd told me it wasn't working all the way up until I was being rolled into the ambulance.

Thorne reached out to hold my hand. "When, are you okay now?"

I looked at the floor, trying to gather my thoughts. I didn't want to reveal too much. Telling Thorne was important, but he didn't need to know everything. If he did, he'd look at me with new eyes. He'd see me as something fragile.

I wasn't.

I refused to be.

"I'm fine now. It was months ago, the recovery wasn't even bad." I put on a brave smile, but his grimace didn't budge. "Shh. Don't worry. I'm really, *really* okay."

In spite of dancing around the details, I'd failed to keep his eyes from changing. Hawthorne watched me with his smile a distant dream, his pupils wide, absorbing all that I was so he could process it anew.

Taking him by the hands, I tugged him toward the bed. He came with me, stepping around my dress as I climbed out of it. "Thorne," I said, kneeling on the mattress. He stood over me, my face level with his stomach. "All you should be thinking about right now is this moment." Linking my hand with his, I crossed our fingers; our wedding rings ground together. "I'm here. I'm healthy." *I'm alive.*

The wax-paper stare went away. He blinked, focusing on our hands and the metal bands. "You're right. This moment is what matters." Climbing onto the bed, he hooked his arm around my middle. With ease he positioned me under him in that sea of green and gold blankets.

Gazing upward, my world was nothing but his sharp features and soft mouth. I was overwhelmed by how naturally we clicked. My body resonated toward his like we were lovers reborn a thousand times.

In that state of ecstasy, I nearly said something. Words I'd never imagined would come from me, or be directed at me.

I opened my lips. My tongue started to curl into that sacred shape. At the last second, instead of speaking, I kissed him. Something inside me warned me that it wasn't time.

I couldn't tell him I loved him.

Not yet.

- CHAPTER TWENTY-TWO -

HAWTHORNE

Costello gripped my hand solidly. "I wish we could stay longer."

Everyone had left Torino soon after the wedding. Kain and Sammy had been first—something to do with the baby, no doubt. Francesca had left late last night, her luggage having expanded twice over after a few shopping trips in the city. Apparently Mom had left her in charge of the estate while she was gone. She seemed pretty pleased with that, but I expected all the German shepherds I'd suggested would eat Mic would be rehomed in a few days.

Only my older brother and his girlfriend remained. Scotch was already in the car waiting to take them to the airport. Before jumping inside she'd given me a tight hug, then a sharp knuckle-punch to the shoulder. I was sure it was meant to be endearing. Probably.

"Please," I chuckled, squeezing Costello's hand back. "You know you're already sick of this place." The papers were running multiple stories. Some loved the royal wedding. Others were focused on picking apart me, my father, and our "mysterious" family.

Someone had leaked info about our criminal history back in Rhode Island. The servants had tried to hide the morning papers, but my mother had demanded a copy with her breakfast.

Costello, who'd been sitting across from me when the paper had been returned, had tensed up. "Fredricson Family History Full of Blood," the front page had claimed. There were photos of us all inside— that was when Dad had snatched it, crumpled it up, and thrown it away.

I'd laughed it off . . . but Costello, who was dating a police officer working her way through the academy, was unable to take it lightly. I was sure he was wondering if the paparazzi here could harm her reputation before she even began on the force.

He was still clasping my hand, fingers curled over my wrist. I tugged—he released me with a long sigh. "Thorne, you must realize this situation hasn't become less dangerous just because there's a ring on your finger."

"Are we making marriage jokes now? Because I've got a few thousand. Didn't seem the right time to use them, but . . ."

"Listen to me." He eyeballed the castle windows. "The Valentines will never feel secure with us around. The marriage benefits them, not us. All we've done is agreed to keep ourselves in arm's reach of their blades."

"Well, I use a gun. And guns beat swords, or so I've heard." He dropped his serious eyes to my face. Before he could say anything else, I lowered my voice. "Chill. Does everyone think I'm oblivious? I *know* the Valentines aren't our friends. And I know they'd slice my throat if they could get away with it. But I also know what they want more than this marriage, and it's something they can't get if I don't give it to them. Something I don't *plan* to give to them."

My brother's eyebrows hitched higher. "What's that?"

Nova's face flashed through my mind. "A baby. Guess Dad didn't tell you about that."

He shook his head almost imperceptibly. "He didn't, but I figured as much. An heir would give them a blood right to the throne that they can't get by marriage alone."

Nora Flite

Costello had easily linked the dots. He'd heard again and again the way our lineage worked; Dad had drilled it into the perfect little firstborn would-be prince's skull since birth.

"Thorne," he said, pulling me back to the moment, "you say you won't give them that. Are you sure you can . . . ?"

"Resist?" I snorted. "I'm not an animal. Plus, there's this fun invention called birth control."

"Surely Nova will think it's weird you're using condoms."

"Then I'll pull out," I said, growing frustrated. "Jesus, Costello. I'll do what I have to, to keep a kid out of this."

The car honked; he glanced at it, then back. The ice blue of his eyes had warmed, disarming me. "Brother, is your plan to just draw this out as long as you can?"

"It's all I've got. Now get out of here before you miss your flight, or Scotch kills you. Or both."

Costello ducked into the car. Scotch waved at me through the gap, then she vanished behind the tinted windows. I kept waving anyway, waiting until they were far past the gates to stop.

He thought my plan was drawing this marriage out? He was wrong. It wasn't my plan . . . because I *had* no plan. But if I could keep Nova from getting pregnant, I could give myself extra time to figure one out.

On my way up the driveway toward the front doors, I spotted someone coming toward me: Drake, the young servant I'd met before. "Your Majesty," he said, bowing his head.

God, that's worse than being called sir. I missed the sharp-tongued maids who always busted my balls. "Don't do that, please."

Drake looked up at me through his fringe of hair. "Do what, Your Majesty?"

"That. I hate that." Gripping his shoulders, I forced him to stand straight. "Just call me Thorne. I prefer first names."

He sucked on his teeth loudly. "I'll try. But it's not very . . . traditional."

180

"Good. I hate traditions." Letting him go, I asked, "Did you need something?"

"Ah. I've got a package for you." He slid out an object wrapped in brown paper, about the size of a dictionary. "Mr. Finbar said to give it to you."

"This is from Glen?" Turning it, I hefted it and felt the light weight. "Did he say why?"

Drake shrugged. "He didn't. Sorry, Your Maj—Thorne—sir, ah."

I hurried into the castle. *What would Glen give me?* Driven by curiosity, I jogged down the west wing, dodging a few servants in my rush to open the package. I shut my door behind me and sat on the corner of my bed. The brown paper was rough; I got the impression Glen didn't do much gift wrapping. When I peeled it away, a small, folded piece of paper dropped onto my knee.

Turning it, I read the messy handwriting:

> *Hawthorne,*
> *Consider this a late wedding gift.*
> *I kept this in secret since the day your father went missing. No one knew I had it, I doubt even Hester knew it existed. I didn't know what to do with it, but now, I understand that I hung on to it all this time for a purpose.*
> *Maybe it will help you understand your father better.*
> *—G*

"Huh." Setting the note on the crumpled paper, I held the gift in front of me. It was a medium-size book, the outside cover thick, mustard yellow, and faded in spots. There was no title. Tipping the book open, I revealed the first page.

January 3rd, 1976

Mom gave me this journal because she thinks she's very funny. That, or her suggestion that I write my thoughts down for a year to help understand myself better was genuine. She's not much for pranks, so I guess she's serious.

I'll give it a go. What's the harm?

I'll need to hide it from Hester. He'd torment me forever if he discovered it.

My heart slammed into my ribs; I knew exactly what this was. *My father's journal?* I fanned it in my fingers. I'd never taken my dad for the type to keep notes about his life. Flipping to a random page, I read the ink scribbles with immense interest.

March 20th, 1976

I'm eighteen today. Everyone made a big deal about it, Mother hosted a HUGE party, and when it was over, she donated massive leftovers to the local food bank. I went with her. It was nice to see so many smiles. But what I was really happy about was finally being able to get the family tattoo.

I told Hester I was a real man, now, and he got that look he always gets when I have something he doesn't. What was worse was Father overheard us. He took me aside and told me that nothing would MAKE me a man. I had to earn it. What an asshole.

I sat up straight and reread the passage. I'd been forming my own idea in my head about my father's relationship with his dad. Between the fishing photos, the big painting, and the general fond memories that came up whenever a local got talking, I'd been sure they'd gotten along.

But here he was, calling the man an asshole. My face hurt; was I grinning? Fuck, this was so weird. *Thank you for this, Glen,* I thought gleefully. When my siblings saw this, they'd lose their minds.

Unable to stop now, I kept reading.

May 2nd, 1976

Hester and I slipped out of class early today. Instead of going home, we spent all day fishing in our secret spot by the ocean. It was so good. I wish I could do it more. It's been stressing me out lately just how much both Mom and Dad keep laying into me about my responsibilities. I'm only eighteen, what are they rushing me to be an adult for? It's not like I'll be king for a while. Dad didn't sit on the throne until he was thirty-six. That's way off for me.

September 10th, 1976

Got into another row with Dad. Apparently, I'm wasting my time being friends with Glen. He says I need to consider my stature and Glen's limits. What the hell? Does he expect me to fake a smile and hang out with the same money-hungry men that he pretends to like because of "politics"?

He says again and again that I'm an idiot.

Fine.

I'd rather be an idiot than a fraud.

December 23rd, 1976

Tonight, I played piano for the Winter Ball. My mother had encouraged me to do it, insisting I'd be great. I'd practiced as much as I could, even skipping out on a hunting trip with Hester to make sure I could play "Greensleeves." I was so damn nervous. Especially with Dad watching me the whole time from the corner of the room.

It didn't matter that everyone clapped politely when it was over.

I felt every wrong note like it was scratching at the back of my teeth.

Hester's smug smile stung.

But not as much as the disappointment in my father's eyes.

I guess he was right. If I'm not good enough by now, I never will be.

Clutching the journal, I started to shake. This was surreal. I'd seen the way he'd looked at me while I'd played at the coronation, and at the time I'd thought he was irritated with me. But had he actually been envious? Reliving a time forty years ago when he'd performed after so many hours of practice, only to go away with his spirits crushed?

Then I'd played . . . and no matter my flaws . . . I'd been elated.

He'd witnessed the joy he'd been denied.

Then he'd had to watch me wear the crown meant for him.

I slammed the book shut. This knowledge was too much for me, making me second-guess my own feelings for the man I'd thought of as cold. Glen had said I reminded him of Maverick . . . I'd denied it because it sounded insane.

After reading these pages, it didn't seem so far-fetched.

That terrified me.

- CHAPTER TWENTY-THREE -

HAWTHORNE

Torino was under assault by, according to the locals, the worst heat wave in decades. Everyone walked around in a dizzy haze with their hair tied up off their necks, sweat clinging to their bodies.

I wasn't bothered by it. Yes, it was fucking hot as hell, but it lacked the smothering humidity that was torturing everyone in Rhode Island at the moment. Being on the coast here alleviated the weather with the occasional cool ocean breeze.

"You're sure you're not miserable in that?" Nova asked me.

Lifting my arms, I stretched in the long sleeves of my thin Henley shirt. "Sounds like you're trying to get me naked."

She tried to hide her smile and failed spectacularly. "I'm only saying that I grew up in New England, too, and I'm dying in this weather." Nova was in a flowing cotton dress the same color as a swan's feather. Sweat made it cling to her curves.

Sliding my hand into hers, I leaned close. "Sorry you're not enjoying it. Meanwhile, *I'm* enjoying the results it's having on everything you wear. More sun, more skin, more . . . well, you."

Nova turned pink. I'd gotten very good at making her blush. She clung to my hand, the two of us strolling down the street with the ocean to our right. The water was flat today. It was easy to imagine you could hop over the stone wall and walk toward the horizon line.

"Isn't that your dad?" she asked, stopping on the sidewalk. I followed her eyes and spotted the scene in the street. A crowd had gathered, my father standing beside Glen, facing off with some men I didn't know.

The strangers were dressed in khakis and polo shirts. Each of them looked progressively older than the man beside him, like I was seeing a peek into their future and who they would become. The oldest had thinning hair but a full gray beard. The youngest was probably my age; with a smooth face below his curly blond hair, he was on the heavier side of husky, his chin merging with his neck.

Maverick was saying . . . or yelling . . . something at the men. Glen was watching with his massive arms wound tight over his guard uniform. At their feet, lying in the street, were some pieces of heavy equipment. "Come on," Nova said, pulling at me. "We should go see what's going on."

I resisted for a single second. It had been two weeks since I'd first opened my father's diary. I had yet to speak a word to him about it. What would I even say? *Your friend shared your most personal thoughts with me as a wedding gift! It was way better than the gravy boat Kain got us! Also, funny thing, but I guess you hated your dad, too?*

I really had no clue how to begin talking to him. For all I knew, he wouldn't want to discuss his childhood or his parental relationships. I certainly didn't jump at the chance to do it. So I'd zipped my lips and gone about acting like things were the same. That nothing in me was tormented by the idea that my father might *actually* have been anything like me.

"Ridiculous," Maverick said. "This food bank needs its pipes fixed so it can open again and help people! It's been closed down, waiting for months for clean water!"

Food bank? Remembering the diary entry, I focused with more interest.

"Now, now," the oldest man replied. "These things take time."

"That's what I'm saying. *More than enough* time has passed. I looked through the files, and I can't find any reason why your company hasn't fixed this yet."

"Sounds like a red tape problem," the old man said, shrugging. "We just do the jobs when we get to the jobs. If we didn't do this one yet, I guarantee you it's because someone didn't sign all their paperwork."

"You know this has nothing to do with paperwork," Glen said, cutting in.

"You trying to imply something?" asked the youngest of the bunch.

"I don't need to imply, Kinsey. I'll say it flat out." The head of the guards flexed his arms, corded muscle showing through his long sleeves. "Your palms have been greased so hard by whatever politician wants to shut this food bank down, that you couldn't hold on to your own dignity if you tried."

Kinsey leaned forward, chest puffing up. "No one calls the Larson family liars." He turned, kicking one of the shovels that was leaning against the building behind them. It clattered into the street loudly. If people hadn't been watching before, they were now.

Observing it all with a strange serenity was the man in the middle. He looked at the shovel, then back to my father. "You understand what's going on here." He reached up to smooth his thick hair. "What you got is a problem that no one is going to help you solve. You best quit wasting everyone's time. This place isn't getting its plumbing fixed. That's the end of it."

"Shameful," Maverick said, scowling. "You came out here with your tools, and you're seriously refusing to do your job?"

The oldest took a step closer to my father, considering him as the two men behind him looked on expectantly. "We happened to have another job in the area."

"Bullshit. You're taunting us, displaying your ability to perform the job, then openly choosing not to!"

Snorting, the old man scanned my father's face. "Things have changed in Torino. This isn't the place that you abandoned when things got too tough for you. Not all of us could run, we've made the best of what we could with what's left over."

My father squeezed his hands so hard that they started to shake. Wordlessly, he snatched a pickax from the pile of tools in the back of a truck parked beside them. The red paint on the side said LARSON PLUMBING.

Ripping it high over his head, he flexed his upper body. The men, all of them, jumped back in surprise. Nova clutched my sleeve, just as shocked. I realized I'd been holding my breath as I watched the scene.

Grunting wildly, Maverick slammed the pickax into the street. "What the hell are you doing?" the youngest man, Kinsey, asked as he started forward. He retreated when my father began frantically chopping at the concrete.

"I'm fixing what you won't," he answered.

The man in the middle put his arms out. "Leave him," he said, his eyebrows drawing low. "He's a sad old man making a fool of himself in the middle of the street."

The three of them watched for a few more seconds. Kinsey shook his head angrily. "Fuck him. Let's go get some lunch." Together they crossed the street, entering a café, essentially crossing my father out of their minds. His desperate show of force meant nothing to them.

But it did to me.

I was transfixed. My father was a huge man, I knew he was strong. When I was younger he would work out in the private gym on our estate. I'd seen him bench over two hundred pounds with ease. One day, when I couldn't have been more than thirteen, I'd snuck into the gym after he'd finished. He hadn't unloaded the bar yet.

Curious, and full of stupid teenage hormones that demanded I prove I was better than my father, I'd stretched out on the bench and tried to lift the weight that he'd finished with. I had to call for help when I became pinned beneath it.

It had been some time since I'd seen my father do anything so physical. Only a few minutes had passed, and while he wasn't slowing down, sweat was starting to darken parts of his black shirt.

Glen came forward, his face glistening in the raging sun. "Maverick, what the hell are you thinking?"

My father breathed heavily, sticking the pickax into the cement. He stared at his friend while catching his breath. "It's fucking obvious that those guys aren't going to help this charity, no matter what we do. The amount of corruption in the city is too much for any one of us to untangle. It will take months to figure out who to remove and who to replace just to get things on track again." He looked back at the hole he'd created. "In the meantime, I'm not about to let a bunch of locals go hungry."

His determination fueled me to step forward. "Thorne?" Nova said as I slipped past her and out of the crowd. Most of it had thinned now that the drama was over. Watching my father chop at the street was only interesting for so long.

Maverick saw me coming; Glen followed his eyes. Scooping up a shovel, I flashed a sideways grin. "This job is too big for just one person. Definitely too much for one old man." Bracing myself, I tossed a scoop of dirt out of the hole and into the truck bed. "Besides, I can't let my dad get all the good press. How embarrassing would that be for the new king?"

He stared at me. "I've never seen you doing any kind of hard labor."

Flexing my arms, I tossed more broken concrete into the bin. "That's a weird way to say, 'Thanks for helping out, son.'"

My dad chuckled, then he went back to work. Glen shook his head. "Do either of you know anything about plumbing?"

"No," Dad said. "But I think we can figure it out faster than those jackasses would change their minds and do it for us."

Laughing, Glen snatched up a pickax and joined my father in breaking up the street. Nova's eyes shone with pride as she looked on. From the truck she grabbed a stack of orange cones, placing them around us. "Using this stuff is fine, right?" she asked. "I mean, we're the royal family. Public Works like this technically belongs to us, doesn't it?"

"I'll assume yes," I said, wiping my brow.

That was how I spent the rest of my afternoon: tearing up a road, fixing something with my own two hands. It was a new thing for me. I appreciated how my muscles burned, the exertion robbing me of the unease I'd felt earlier as I approached the scene and looked at my father.

Sweltering in the growing hours, I stole glances at Maverick, wondering what was going through his head. Was this the same food bank he'd gone to with his mother all those years ago? Was he thinking about her right now?

The crowd ebbed, and it wasn't until we'd uncovered the pipes, minutes before the plumbing team returned, that people took notice again. When the Larsons came back, they were genuinely shocked to see what we'd managed to do. But they said nothing. They didn't try to take back their tools, either.

I think they were actually ashamed. Here we were, doing something good in a city that desperately needed a hint of generosity.

A news crew showed up before the sun went down, speaking to my father as he rubbed dirt from his palms. It wouldn't be the last time my father showed up in the local news.

Together he and Glen roped in volunteers, going out of their way to fix every labor-intensive project they could. It was very clear that the city needed tons of infrastructure. The number of jobs that had fallen by the wayside thanks to politicians who wanted to force buildings to foreclose so they could tear them down and replace them with things that would fatten their wallets was immense.

After only a few days of their efforts, no one heckled my father. The media attention when they reopened the food bank was especially effective for his image. My father even managed to smile in the photo.

What a world.

- CHAPTER TWENTY-FOUR -

Hawthorne

Nova and I left the castle more often than not. I didn't want to be around her family; her brothers and sister spent too much time skulking through the hallways. I could recognize the greed in their eyes whenever I caught them staring hungrily at the locked cases on display full of old jewels and other expensive bits and bobs.

As for me, I hadn't even looked in the royal vault yet. I like money, don't get me wrong. But I'd had plenty of it before I became king. What I wanted was to spend time with the woman who was curling ever closer around my heart.

Whenever I grazed my wedding ring with my thumb, I started to smile. It was an absentminded thing that I caught myself doing. But that little metal band was a constant reminder that I was connected to her.

Nova was fun. She had a drive for adventure, always taking me to some new location in the country that I *had* to see. Or so she said. She was usually right. Today it had been an old staircase cut into the cliff east of the city. There were some giant statues there, their faces eroded by years of salt and surf.

It had been a quick drive, and we'd probably spent more time kissing than looking at the stone figures. Either way, I'd worked up an appetite and was looking forward to dinner with her.

Walking hand in hand through a part of the city I hadn't explored yet, our goal was to find a restaurant with a name I couldn't pronounce. My French was getting better—or Nova had gotten better at not laughing at me when I tried my hand at it.

Her purse buzzed loudly. She reached in, checking her cell phone. "What's wrong?" I asked, reading her face as it fell.

"Nothing. Just my mom." She typed something back. We both waited for whatever the response was. When it came, Nova sighed. "She wants me to come back. There's some meeting she wants me to be there for, some dignitary Dad arranged to get together with."

"And I wasn't invited? Their brand-new son-in-law that they positively adore?" I feigned offense.

She bit her lip, holding her phone between us. "Dad never stops moving forward. Thorne . . . I can't go to dinner with you."

"Sure you can. Blow your mom off."

"I seriously can't."

Running my fingers through my hair, I groaned. "I'm pretty sure that being king and queen means we can do whatever we want. I swear I saw that in the contract."

Her lips didn't twitch upward, not even a bit. "I'm sorry. Really, I just . . . have to go."

"Why do you do what they tell you?" I asked, losing some of my cool. "I've seen how you are around them. Half the time you look ready to spit in your dad's face."

"They're family," she said, gauging me.

"That shouldn't excuse anything."

"I figured you would understand."

"Sorry, but have you paid attention to me at all?" I asked, laughing bitterly. "All I *do* is complain about my father and all the ways they've hurt me." The words came out in a long string, and when I grabbed for them, they kept unspooling.

Nova stared at me with too much interest. "How did they hurt you?"

"He. My father."

"You said they."

"I know what I said, it wasn't what I meant." The pulsing in my eye sockets was severe, like tiny fists were punching the backs of my eyeballs. I rubbed at them in a desperate attempt to relieve the discomfort.

Nova placed her hands on mine. Her presence was soothing. "Talk to me, I want to understand."

"There's not much to talk about." That was false. I could have given a daylong speech about all the tiny wounds my father had left on my psyche. She kept staring at me; I took a breath. "It's not important. Every kid thinks his dad is an asshole, right?"

"Thorne . . ."

"Don't look at me like you think I'm some sob story. I'm not, my older brother gets that trophy." I tried to chuckle and it hurt my throat. There was so much tension in my body that every part of me felt like it was straining . . . working at capacity to hold me together. "Costello's the angsty tragedy, my older sister's the wunderkind. And Kain and Francesca—who can compete with twins? Even when they grew up, they were still the spoiled stars. All of them were so perfect . . . so much more promise than me."

Standing inches from my chest, she held still, as if moving would make me realize what the hell I was saying and I'd cut off before I was finished. What she didn't know was that I *couldn't* stop. Not after going this far.

"I guess when I said 'they' hurt me, I did mean it." My voice was a wry whisper. "Nova, I never had a chance."

She'd wrapped her fingers around my wrists. "At what?"

"Being more than the forgotten middle child." Fuck, why was my mouth so dry? Was it because I was spilling everything I had, all of my essence, out onto the ground? Lifting my head, I looked down on her. "All I was ever good at was being the funny one. I'm definitely a damn joke."

"You're not. Not to me." Her fingertips braced on my cheek. "Hawthorne—I'm sorry. I didn't mean to drag this out of you and cause you pain."

"I'm not in pain," I said, trying to make myself smile.

"Don't." She tapped my jaw. "No fake smiles. Not for me, you're better than that."

My mask slid. I felt naked without it. "You're right. You deserve more than a bunch of cheap grins. I'm just not used to letting people see me like this."

Wrapping her arms around me, Nova placed her forehead on my chest. "Being vulnerable, needing people, isn't easy." She said it like she knew it personally. Maybe I should have pushed, digging out what she was keeping from me. But . . . I couldn't. Not with her pressed so warmly in my grasp.

Not when she made me feel *loved*.

I buried my nose into her scalp, breathing her in. "If I say I need you to sit with me at dinner, looking gorgeous, so no one sees the new king dining alone like some sad nobody . . ."

"Okay, okay." Laughing gently, she turned her phone off. "But when I get yelled at, I'm blaming you."

"I'll happily accept being the bad guy."

For Nova, I was starting to think I'd do anything.

The looks aimed at us when we entered the restaurant were intense. People cupped their mouths by their faces, speaking in hushed whispers.

Our host tripped over his own feet twice as he led us to our booth in the corner.

Torino had started to change some of its narrative. There were fewer rumors about me and my family. Glen had told me that the people were cautiously optimistic about having a young king and queen. And the wedding photos, especially the ones of me in my tailored suit and Nova in her stunning gown, had gained us some fans.

She'd shown me an Instagram account that posted every picture of us that it had come across. It was creepy, but also . . . sort of nice to be so adored.

I sat down, and our server beamed at me. "Let me know if I can get you anything, anything *at all*, Your Majesty."

Cringing, I waited until he was gone to say, "I can't stand everyone calling me that."

"Me either," she admitted. "My sister keeps teasing me about it. 'Oh, can I run a bath for you, *Your Royal Highness*.'"

I flashed a grin. "It's not so awful when you say it."

Nova considered me, her smirk growing. "Yeah? Want some more impressions?"

"Give me your absolute best."

She cleared her throat and let her voice fall until it was a velvety purr. "Your Majesty . . . my *king*."

My cock went rock hard in my pants. The flow of blood was so fast I was light-headed. "That's something else. When it's from your lips, I love it."

She giggled into her napkin, shutting up when the waiter returned to take our order. I didn't care what I picked. I was really just here to spend time with Nova. I was full from eating her with my eyes. I barely tasted my food when it arrived.

"Oh," she whispered, blinking rapidly. Her arm curled under the table as she bent forward.

"Are you okay?"

"Just my stomach. I think something in this risotto isn't sitting right with me." Pushing herself to her feet, she gave me a shaky smile. Her tan skin had become dull as plaster. "Be right back."

I half stood, unsure what to do. "Yeah. Okay, just . . . call me if you need help."

Nova barely acknowledged my request, too busy running toward the restroom. Every person in that place watched her go, some slyly, others blatantly. Phones clicked pictures of her fleeing.

Sinking deep in my chair, I twisted my fork in my plate. If she got food poisoning for coming out to dinner with me, I'd feel terrible. Conscious of the onlookers, I drummed my fingers on my thighs. Then the table. I checked my phone, sniffed her risotto, and checked my phone once more.

It came to life in my hands.

Nova: We need to leave.

I was already standing, throwing money onto the table—way more than our bill was. Grabbing her purse, I typed back.

Me: Got it. I'll meet you at the restroom.

The phone buzzed again; I'd packed it in my pocket, already crossing the restaurant. She was probably telling me she was fine, or to wait by the exit, but I was singularly focused on helping her.

The door with FEMMES written in curly letters swung open. I perked up, only to see someone with blonde hair exit. The stranger glanced at me, then deliberately averted her eyes. She was tapping her phone's text box before she reached her table.

The next person who came out was Nova. Her face was shining, like she'd washed it recently. Parts of her reddish hair were damp, the ends shading toward rich brown from the water. She gave me a surprised smile; it wasn't enough to light up her cheeks or hide how pale she was. "I texted you. I wanted you to wait by the front."

"I was worried about you." Sliding my arm around her shoulders, I handed her her purse, both of us walking toward the exit. I kept her close to my body the entire time.

"I'm fine, it's nothing. I just feel weird."

"I'll take you home." *Home?* Had the castle become that to me?

Outside the restaurant I gave the paper slip to the valet. He ran off, leaving me and Nova to stand there in the warm night air. She squeezed my hand where it draped over her shoulder. "Sorry for ruining dinner."

"Are you kidding?" Kissing the top of her head, I guided her toward the street. My car was pulling up. "I had a great time. Plus, I think you gave those diners something to talk about for the rest of the evening. That was nice of you."

She laughed, pushing her face into my side to muffle the sound. The vibrations spun pleasantly across my ribs, taking a straight path toward my heart.

Nova maintained that she was all right. Even after she rolled down my window and hurled out the side, she still insisted she was okay. That once the food was out of her system, she'd be one hundred percent perfect.

Ignoring her proud attempts to shake me off, I assisted her back to her room in the castle. When we got there, she cracked her door. From the way her eyes darted inside, then back to me, I guessed what she was going to ask. "No," I said, wrapping her fingers in mine. "You need to rest. And if I come inside, I don't think either of us will get any."

A pretty pink color spread over her cheeks. It was the most color she'd had in the last hour. Standing as tall as she could, Nova kissed me. Her smooth lips lingered, leaving me wanting more. My craving kept up after she pulled away. "I'll talk to you in the morning. Good night, Thorne."

"Night," I said, watching the door click into place. For a while I leaned on the wall outside her room. Her warmth was still with me, coating my skin, my mouth, my pores. I wanted to bathe in her existence.

Briefly I regretted turning her unspoken offer down. If I'd gone inside, I could be snuggling with her beneath the covers right now. Her hair would caress my face. I'd inhale her scent and lose myself, dreaming in it.

There'll be time. We've got tomorrow, the day after, and all of eternity.

What could possibly keep me away from this woman?

- CHAPTER TWENTY-FIVE -

Nova

"Are you still in there?" Darla banged on my bathroom door.

Gripping the toilet bowl for dear life, I groaned. "Right where you left me fifteen minutes ago. Haven't moved an inch." My sister had barged in just after sunrise, insisting Mom was furious at me for blowing off the dinner last night. She'd taken one look at me hunched in my bathroom and gone as green as I was.

"Is it your kidneys again?" she'd asked me. I sensed the unease in her softer volume; Darla could be terrible, but she wasn't so ghoulish as to wish me harm.

Shaking my head, I'd hurled some more. That had made her slam the door closed, insisting I needed privacy—and also that if she kept looking at me barfing, she'd barf, too. *Then* she'd fretted that I must have some weird illness that was contagious and had better not dare give it to her.

Now, listening to her outside, I put my forehead on the cool porcelain. I'd said it wasn't my kidneys, but how could I know for sure? This wasn't that far off from what I'd gone through before. *No. It's not that. It's something else, like food poisoning.* I focused on my breathing. It was all I could do as I waited out the next wave of nausea.

There was a soft *click* out in my room. Then some mumbling I recognized. "Nova?" my mother said a second later. "Your sister says you're sick."

"Since last night," I called back. Flushing the toilet, I made myself stand, holding on to things the whole time. "I barely slept. I'm so exhausted, and just—" Stepping out of the bathroom, I halted in my tracks.

My mom and sister were standing by my bed. In Darla's hands was a newspaper, her perfect nails crinkling it roughly. I read the front page—it was a gossip rag, one I didn't know—but I didn't have time to read the name. The headline had all my attention.

"New Queen Pregnant? Photos Inside!" But there was a photo right there under the bold words. It was a grainy shot of me from last night, taken from a high angle as I threw up in the restaurant's stall. Some asshole had followed me in and snapped the humiliating image.

"Is this right?" Darla asked, gawking at me. "Are you pregnant?"

"No." I said it too quickly. "Of course not." It couldn't be that. I was very aware that Thorne had been using condoms the times we'd had sex. Even on our wedding night, he'd wanted protection. I'd understood, willing to wait until we both decided when—if—to follow through and create an heir.

There was no way. It was impossible.

Wasn't it?

The cemetery, I thought, my heart squeezing. *Our first time, he didn't use anything. He just pulled out.* That had been weeks ago. I'd been so distracted I hadn't noticed until now that my period was late. *That . . . that means . . .*

My mother came toward me, grabbing me by my forearms. She was so tall; I stared up at her helplessly. "Darla, go and get a pregnancy test."

"What? Why can't you send a servant?"

"Because no one else can know about this," she snapped. "Not until we're certain."

My veins itched with how fast my blood was racing through them. "Mom . . ."

She shushed me, one hand grazing my cheek. It was a rare loving caress. "It's fine. This is what we wanted."

What you and Dad wanted, I thought, feeling sicker than ever. I didn't know what I wanted. The idea of a baby with Thorne was . . . exciting, in a way. I'd never dreamed of becoming a mother. Creating an heir had been a responsibility, something I could shrug off until we were ready.

But now I touched my belly and wondered how I'd do as a mom. Neither Thorne nor I had enjoyed a wonderful childhood. Perhaps, together, we could make up for our parents' mistakes and do something beautiful . . . something *right.*

Minutes later Darla returned with a test in hand. "Here," she said, throwing it at me. I caught it clumsily. "I had one in my purse." Mom shot a look at her, and she rolled her eyes. "What? Are you shocked I have sex?"

Ignoring them both, I turned and shut myself in the bathroom. I wasn't feeling sick anymore, like my anxiety was so powerful there was no room for anything else. I wasn't supposed to be scared of anything. That was what my damn wish had been meant to do.

I'm brave.

I'm bold.

I'm . . . I'm ready for this. Filling my lungs, I centered myself and followed the directions on the pregnancy test. The waiting was the worst part.

"Nova?" My mother knocked gently.

Holding the plastic indicator, I stared blankly at what it said. The next time she knocked, I opened the door halfway through her knuckles' tapping. She startled, eyeing my face, reading my expression.

Darla was sitting on my bed. She tilted sideways, squinting. "Well? Verdict?"

"Pregnant," my mom whispered, seeing it in my eyes.

Holding out the test to her, I angled it so she could see the two pink lines. "I guess you're going to be a grandmother."

There was a lot of action after that.

Mom forced me back into bed. Much to Darla's dismay, she was sent on errands. It was clear my parents felt this news had to be controlled.

"But what about Thorne?" I asked, sitting up on my pillows. "Shouldn't I let him know?"

My parents glanced at each other, then back to me. "Of course you should," my dad said. "In person. This news is too big for a text message."

"He's right." Mom leaned over to ease me back on the silken pillows. "It's barely breakfast time. Why don't you rest up here until you feel better?"

"I feel all right," I said, plucking at the covers. "I'm not an invalid."

"You've never been pregnant before," Mom said, some of her normal, cool tone returning. "I have. Multiple times. You need to be off your feet while Darla goes and grabs you some food—"

"Come *on*!" Darla groaned.

"Do it," Dad growled.

My sister curled her plump upper lip in my direction. "What would little Miss Queen like to eat? Will you want me to feed it to you, too?"

"Hey, come on," I said. My eyebrows lifted as I tried to appeal to her. "I'm not the one asking you to do this. And I don't have an appetite, I can barely hold down water."

"You need to eat!" Mom insisted.

"Give her air, Valencia. Darla, hurry and get some fruit and muffins from the kitchens."

"She said she doesn't want anything!" Darla shouted back.

"Everyone needs to back off while I go take a shower!" I cried, throwing the blankets off a second time. "I get that you want to be useful . . . but I just want to clean up, take something for my headache, and figure out how I'm going to break this news to Thorne." I shoved my way into the bathroom and slammed the door. I could still hear them talking outside, planning how to handle this new situation.

Palming my belly, I imagined it growing full and round. My pinkie touched my transplant scar. *I never imagined my life would ever change this much.* I'd hoped for many things. I'd just never expected them to come true.

But this was real. Thorne and I were going to have a *baby*.

I couldn't wait to tell him the news.

- CHAPTER TWENTY-SIX -

HAWTHORNE

The first thing I did when I woke up was message Nova.

Me: Hey, how are you feeling today?

Me: Better?

Sitting up in bed, I waited for the little bubble to pop up to show she was responding. When nothing came, I set my phone on my bedside table and stretched. *She's probably still sleeping.* It was a little after nine in the morning—I'd hoped to sleep later, but I'd forgotten to close my curtains, allowing the sun to stab me in the eyeballs as it rose.

Yawning so wide my jaw cracked, I placed my bare feet on the rug. *I'll shower, shave, then go check on her myself.* My stomach rumbled. *All right, all right. I'll eat first, THEN go see her.* It wasn't like Nova was going anywhere.

Standing under the hot water, I hummed gently. The sound reverberated through the black marble shower. Even though she'd gotten ill last night, Nova had assured me she'd had a great time. *Just hope her mom doesn't give her hell for skipping their dinner appointment.*

After drying myself off, I lathered on some shaving cream. A few careful scrapes with a razor turned my jawline smooth. I didn't normally care about stubble—but when I thought about kissing Nova, I wanted to do everything I could to make the experience pleasurable.

I'd never wanted to make a woman feel so *good* before.

Wiping my chin, I glanced at myself in the mirror. The last time I'd really stared at myself like this was right after I'd learned I was going to become king. My eyes had been hollow that day. Angry. Resigned. Today the onyx centers were glinting with joy. After dressing in a pair of cedar-brown pants, matching shoes, and a tight-fitting smoke-gray shirt with long sleeves, I checked my phone again. *Still no response?* Surely she was awake by now. Had her battery died or something?

Sticking my phone in my back pocket, I opened my bedroom door. Right away I saw the two maids huddled nearby; they were crouched over something in their hands, talking in wispy voices.

Their heads jerked up at the sound of my door opening. Wide-eyed with a guilt I didn't understand, they spun to face me. The girl on the left hid whatever she had behind her back. "M-morning, Your Majesty!" she squeaked.

"Morning," I said, arching an eyebrow. I closed the distance, studying them both. "What were you two talking about a second ago?"

"Nothing," the other girl blurted.

"It's hers!" said the first, simultaneously.

"Amy!" the one on the right gasped, stepping sideways. "How could you!"

"Sorry, Stasia," Amy mumbled.

Putting my fingers to my temples, I sighed. "I'm lost. What's going on?"

Hanging her head, Stasia revealed a newspaper. She offered it to me, her eyes downcast. I took it gingerly, squinting at the maids before I unfurled the wrinkled pages. *Holy shit.* The front was a photo of Nova in a toilet stall, the words stamped above claiming she was experiencing morning sickness. "Is this city obsessed with scandals?" I asked, handing the paper back.

The maids hesitated, then Stasia took the newspaper, folding it into a crisp square. "We'll throw it in the garbage right away, Your Majesty."

"Everyone *has* to stop calling me that," I groaned. Fuck, my head was throbbing. The headline kept rolling through my mind. *Nova can't be pregnant. I've been cautious . . . haven't I?* The first time in the cemetery pricked at my recollection. I pushed it down with a huge inhalation. *Calm your fucking self. Just go talk to her, she's probably laughing about this photo of her in the toilet right now.*

"Um," Amy said, biting her lip. "Can we go now, Your Maj—sir?"

"Fine, sure. Go." I didn't care what they did. I was having trouble thinking of anything but Nova, and the acute memory of my come sliding down her legs on the night I'd taken her virginity.

Jesus.

This could really be happening. I could actually be a dad. *One step at a time,* I told myself, running a palm down my face. I shut my eyes, breathed in, then began taking long steps down the hall.

I didn't see anyone as I headed toward the main foyer. My best guess was they were busy with their duties—probably still handling breakfast in the kitchens. At the point where the hall curved, my vision partially blocked, I didn't see the guard until he was on me.

He stopped himself just before we ran into each other. "Your Majesty," the guard said stiffly. "I need you to come with me."

"To where, and why?" I asked, narrowing my eyes.

The young man gave me a conspiratorial look, his voice dropping low. "Please, Your Majesty. It's about the queen."

My headache vanished, replaced by my abrupt terror. "What's wrong with Nova?"

"I can't say here. Follow me, we'll go quickly." His furtive behavior clinched it for me; Nova was pregnant, and this guard couldn't say it out loud in case someone else heard and confirmed the rumor. He was taking me to her.

When I nodded, he spun so fast that his short cape swirled. On the back of it was the red-and-black crown that matched the one inked into my own skin. I followed the guard down the hall, and when we reached a passage that split off, he turned down it. I was relieved he walked so quickly. My anxiety demanded I nearly jog—I'd have sprinted if it would give me answers faster. Instead I trailed behind the young man, obsessively checking my phone again, like Nova might respond to my text now that I knew something was wrong.

A short set of stairs led us deeper into the castle. I hadn't been this way before. A cold tingle rocked up my spine when I spotted three more fully dressed guards standing along a wall. They looked at me, their frowns obvious.

"Where is this?" I asked, staring at the low ceiling, the bare walls. This part of the castle was much less adorned than the rest.

The guard stopped in front of a door, moving aside, waving me through. "This," he said as I passed, letting me see inside the room for the first time, "is the royal family's personal holding area."

The small room held a flat bed in one corner, a rusted chamber pot in the other, and literally nothing else. I knew what this was: a prison.

"Hey there, Funny Man."

Whirling, I spotted Larchmont where he stood just behind the door. Another figure blocked the light from the hallway as he sealed off the only exit: Richard Valentine. "What the hell is this?" I asked, backing up.

The guard who'd led me here said nothing. He shut the door, a metallic *click* echoing through the room.

We three were locked inside.

Larchmont smiled, swinging a long leg forward until he was shoulder to shoulder with his brother. The room felt smaller with them looming in front of me. "Relax," he chuckled. "You're acting like we're going to kill you."

"How do I know you aren't?" I asked. *Fuck fuck fuck.* I didn't have a weapon—could I call for help?

"Huh. I guess you're right." Shrugging, he flipped his hands palms up. His grin turned my stomach. "There's no way to know *what* we'll do to you."

I flicked my attention to Richard, then to the speck of light beneath the door.

"No," Larch said, reading my mind. "The guards won't step in to assist you. I gave them some cash to turn their heads. It took less than I thought, once they learned what you'd done."

Breathe. Think. You can get out of this. "I've done a lot of things that could make people turn away while I got a kick or two to the ribs. What exactly are you referring to?"

Richard slid a hand into his jeans pocket. I tensed up, fight or flight making me hyperaware. I expected him to reveal a weapon; he offered me a shiny photo instead. My relief didn't last long once I saw what this was.

The photograph had been taken from the street just outside the church's cemetery. It was mildly out of focus, but not so much that I couldn't recognize my own face. Whoever had taken this had captured me as I screwed Nova from behind.

Stunned, I looked at Larchmont's smug smile. "Thanks for the memento, I guess. But why would anyone care about this?" I asked.

"It's a picture of our *wonderful* new king getting his rocks off with a prostitute in the sacred royal cemetery where his uncle had just been buried." He tapped his chin. "Yeah, why would anyone in this monarchy care about that? What a damn mystery."

Blood started to pump through me at max capacity. *Prostitute?* I looked at the photo again. From that angle, you couldn't tell the auburn-haired woman was Nova.

"I was trailing you that night," he said. "I saw you go to the red-light district. You threw me a curveball when you left and ended up at that old-ass ship, but when I spotted you again in the cemetery, I realized you must have asked that hooker to meet you there to throw me off your scent."

My head was spinning. I heard something crackle; I was squeezing the photo so hard it had started to crease in two. "You took this photo, then hung on to it for weeks?" I asked in disbelief.

"Well. What good is ruining someone before you have everything you need from them?" He took a single step, bringing him chest to chest. "The real task was finding that woman you spoke to. When I told her that all she had to do was confirm what she'd done with the king, and we'd pay her handsomely and press no charges, she sang loud and pretty. Ten years is a long time to spend locked up. Can't blame her for helping us out."

That woman I spoke to by the club . . . she lied for some money? Fear, too. She probably thought it didn't matter if it wasn't her in the picture, who'd believe her?

With my eyes straining, I stared him in the face. Nova's words entered my brain hard enough to make my skull ache. *She warned me that what we were doing was illegal.* I'd sworn I didn't care. And at the time I hadn't. I'd felt invincible.

Now I was paying for it.

But they don't know that the woman who was with me was Nova. "Ten years," I said, watching him closely. He was still wearing his sick-ass grin. "You're saying I'll have to serve a sentence that long? In *here?*"

"Not in here." He waved around at the room. "This is just where you'll stay until you're formally charged. *Then,* when you're stripped of your crown, you'll rot for ten years in the Maurine prison. Of course, it'll take around a year of back-and-forth to make your fall from grace official. By then . . . we won't need you around." He winked. "We'll have someone else who can sit on the throne. Someone easier to control."

Something whiplike bloomed up in me. It was too big, too hot, ready to burst out of my body. I knew, *knew* what he was implying, but

I had to hear it from his smirking lips. Distantly I heard myself ask, "Who?"

Larchmont's mouth opened wide as he laughed. I saw down to the back of his throat. "Didn't you hear? Nova's *pregnant*."

His confirmation was like a tornado to my guts.

"All we needed from you was your genetics, Funny Man. I didn't think this would happen so fast. I thought I'd have to hang on to these photos for months, if I'd known my little sister was such a slut, I could've—"

Thrusting forward, with just inches to prepare, I grabbed him by the throat and slammed him into the wall. Then I spun, throwing him into the bed chained to the other side. Richard shouted—I ignored him, my thumbs pressing into Larch's windpipe. "Don't you ever call her that!" I roared. "You piece of garbage! Fuck you, how can you, her own brother, be so cruel?"

I whipped my elbow back. Larch flinched, knowing I was about to hit him with all the rage that had coiled in my tendons. Before I could sock him in the mouth, a steel grip closed on my forearm. Richard yanked me back, hooking his arms around mine, restraining me with my spine against his massive chest. Fuck, he was big enough that my toes barely brushed the floor.

Straightening up slowly, Larch rubbed at his neck. It was red where I'd been choking him. His eyes were the same shade as Nova's, but they were nothing like his kind sister's. He trailed a glance at the door. I followed, noting what he was confirming: that no one had come to check out the noise. The guards outside really wouldn't step in to stop them.

No one was going to help me.

"This," Larch said, stretching his arms, swinging them lazily as he warmed himself up, "is something I've been itching to do for way too long." He looked past my ear to his brother. "Hold him steady."

Richard dug in harder—I expected my shoulders to pop from their sockets. "Ready," he grunted.

The first punch skated off my cheekbone. Crimson splotches swam in my vision, my head twisting to the side. It was a solid hit. So was the second, then the third. My world became a mushy ball of pain, everything in my skull weighted down by a sensation of saturated cotton stuffed inside the creases of my brain.

After every punch, I lifted my eyes so I could watch him.

Larchmont shook his hand, flexing his fingers. "What," he asked, breathing hard, "not going to beg me to stop?"

A tiny laugh bubbled from my bloody lips. I grinned, even though it sent jagged pain through my face. "Nah. You look like you could use the workout."

His scowl contorted his angular features, made him more animal than human. "How the hell are you so cocky?"

It took all the effort I had to swing my head up higher. My hair stuck to my forehead, my neck struggling to keep me stable enough to smile serenely at the man who'd done all he could to break me down. "I guess . . . I was just born this way. Something in my blood."

That did it. His eyes flew wide, his knuckles connecting with my jaw. "Fuck you!" he growled, spittle flying on me and his brother both. Richard struggled to hold me still, not because I was fighting, but because Larch was hitting me so violently.

A solid knee to my guts made me cough. Blood spattered on the floor, some of it onto Larch's shirt. He scowled, stepping back, eyeing the red stains with disgust. "I'll need to clean up before anyone sees me. Great."

Richard adjusted his grip under my armpits. "I think we should stop."

"Don't you want a turn?" his brother asked coolly.

I was broken on the outside. I still managed to skip my glare upward, through my sweat-stained hair, to survey Larchmont. All I tasted was my own blood as I gave a shaky smile. "Yeah, let him go for it. You look tired. Catch your breath, Larch."

He grabbed me by my hair, wrenching my head back. "I wish I could fucking kill you. It would feel so *good* to be the one to end your waste of a life."

"Larch," Richard said, and I sensed hesitation from the man holding me. "That's enough. Think about Nova."

"I *am* thinking about her!" Larchmont snarled, releasing me. "She'd want us to get revenge for how he humiliated her in front of the whole world."

His words gave me enough strength to lift my head and glare at him. "She would never want that."

"Don't kid yourself. Nova was always one of us." He straightened his cuffs. "Put him down. Get his phone."

Richard dropped me to the concrete. It didn't even hurt, not compared to everything else. It was actually nice to lie down. I was so damn tired. I felt him search my pockets, taking my phone.

The door creaked open. I could see the light shining inside from the hall, their shadows as the two of them walked over the threshold. Larchmont paused, his heels holding still in the doorway.

He watched me closely. "Remember what I said. Don't waste an iota of energy worrying about her. I'm telling you this for your own good, it's my one act of kindness. Never say I did nothing for you, Funny Man." Grabbing the door, he shut it behind him.

I was alone.

- CHAPTER TWENTY-SEVEN -

Nova

My phone buzzed. Looking at it, I read Thorne's message. Hey, how are you feeling today? Better?

My thumb skimmed over the keyboard. "Don't," Mom said. She fixed me with an intense look. "It's best not to speak to anyone yet."

"But it's Thorne," I said, showing her the screen. "My *husband*. The king."

"Even more reason to stay silent."

"I don't understand. I cleaned up, I ate some food, I feel fine. I don't want to sit in bed all day, I want to see Thorne." *I need to tell him what we've done.* I cupped my stomach and my mother watched me.

Darla kept typing into her phone as she sat in the corner of my room. "Who are you talking to?" I asked.

She looked up at me, her face going pale. Then she shifted, showing me her back. "Nobody. Why don't you worry about your own stuff, you've got a lot going on right now."

Frowning, I turned toward my mother. "Can I please just get up and walk around a bit?"

Darla shot me a look and said, "I think Mom's right. You should stay in bed. You know, for your health and all. And the baby."

She didn't sound sincere to my ears. My mom sighed, coming to sit beside me on the bed. "Nova, if you really, really want to walk around, you can. But think about this. Everyone in this city saw the newspapers this morning. It's only been a few hours, do you really think it's good for you to go on a stroll while everybody stares at you, wondering if the rumors are true? We need to keep this on the down low until we know how to present the news to everyone. You're not the greatest liar, I'm afraid if some servant girl looks at you the wrong way you'll spill the beans."

Twisting my fingers in my blankets, I glanced out the window. "I'll stay here until the evening, but after that I'm getting up and meeting with Thorne." I checked my phone again, wondering if I should reply to his messages, even if my mother had told me no.

"This evening will be fine," my mom said, giving me a benevolent smile. "Maybe you should try to get some sleep until then." She got up and closed the curtains, darkening the room before I could respond. "You had a rough night from all this nausea, I'll bring you some soda water to help your stomach. Close your eyes and get some rest. You and the new baby both need it."

"I'll come with you," Darla said, hopping up onto her pink heels. Both of them shot me one more quick look, then they exited into the hall. Puffing air through my tight lips in frustration, I flopped back on the pillows and shut my eyes. I *was* a little tired, a nap wouldn't hurt.

Shifting onto my side, I laid my cheek on the silky pillow. *Later,* I thought to myself, tucking my phone to my side protectively, *I'll tell Thorne the news in person.* Thinking of how he would react, imagining the delight and excitement in his wide eyes and wider smile, I drifted off to sleep.

When I woke up later, no one was in the room with me.

On my bedside table I found a bottle of soda water and some slices of fresh bread. Stretching, I went over to the window to move the curtains and bring more light into my dark room. The sight of the setting sun made my breath catch. *How did it get so late?*

I went to the bathroom to clean up a bit and straighten my hair. I wasn't feeling sick anymore; on the way back by the bed, I grabbed a piece of bread and took a bite. Gripping my phone, I checked for new messages from Thorne, but didn't find any.

I imagined that he'd probably come by my room, and someone—either my sister or mother—had told him that I was resting and that he should leave me alone. Why else hadn't I heard from him?

Looking around, as if there was someone in the room with me who'd interfere, I sat back down on the mattress. My mother had told me not to message Thorne about the pregnancy, but I wanted to let him know that I was awake now. I wanted to see him. I was ready to give him the news in person.

Me: Hey there. I know I should say good evening, but it still feels like good afternoon to me. Did you have dinner already?

Holding my phone, I watched the screen eagerly. I sat like that for five minutes, and when no replies came, I frowned. Looking over at my door, I made a quick decision. I changed into some clothes that were not rumpled from sleep, slid on some comfortable flats, then opened my door to the hallway. There was a guard standing outside. He perked up at the sight of me. "Your Highness," he said, bowing his head. "Your parents asked me to stay here in case you woke up and to make sure that nobody bothered you."

Curiosity pricked at my veins. "Did anyone try to?"

"No, Your Highness."

Dejected, I asked, "Did my parents mention why I needed to rest?"

He cast a shifty look to the floor. I was sure he'd heard the rumors, the whole castle must have by now. "They just said that you were a bit ill."

"Well, I'm feeling better now. So I think I'll go find some dinner."

His face went ruby red. "Your Highness," he sputtered, "they insisted I not let you go wandering off. Why don't you go back into your room and I'll have dinner brought up to you?"

"I'm quite capable of going to find something on my own, thank you." I walked down the hallway and the guard followed me, still speaking.

"Really, Your Highness, please. I don't want to get into any trouble."

"I'm the queen, I say you're free from your post."

That made him stumble. I wondered if everyone had forgotten that I was the one who'd married Thorne. I was in charge, not my parents. Their commanding presence and my passivity in the castle affairs had made me look weak. I'd been so busy enjoying my time getting to know Thorne, I hadn't noticed until now.

Thinking of him again, I hurried down the hallway toward the main foyer. When I started past the kitchen, on my way to the west wing, the guard jogged to my side. "I thought you were getting something to eat?"

"Yes," I said with a scowl. "But I want to eat with the king. I'm going to his room to get him."

"He isn't in his room."

"Then where is he?" I asked, slowing down to stand next to the staircase. There were multiple servants bustling around, the castle full of movement in the early evening.

The guard rocked from to side to side. "I'm not entirely sure. I believe he went off to do something with his father."

That struck me as strange. Just then my stomach rumbled. I clutched it. "All right. If he isn't in his room then I guess I'll get some food and wait until he returns." The guard slumped, as if he was relieved. "But please stop following me. I don't need a chaperone in my own castle."

With some chagrin the guard remained there in the foyer as I walked into the kitchens. Three young women and two older ones were busy at the stoves, cooking whatever was going to be for dinner. They looked up when they saw me, and just like with the guard, I sensed an unspoken suspicion in their nervous smiles. I had the idea they'd been talking about me before I'd even entered the room. "Your Highness," said a young girl with red braids. "What can we get for you?"

"Anything, I'm starving."

They bustled around, one of them giving me a chair to sit in at the marble island in the middle of the room. "We can bring a plate out to you in the dining room," a girl offered.

"No, this is fine."

They all shared a glance. The red-braided girl brought me a plate covered in way too much food: piles of potatoes, two biscuits, a huge chunk of pork loin, and a mound of green peas. Then she stood back with the other women, all of them watching me intently. I couldn't eat all this food, but it told me what I had been wondering: they definitely assumed I was pregnant. It was sweet. And wasteful.

Setting my fork down, I hopped off the chair. "I don't want to eat with you staring at me like that. I'll just take this up to my room."

"Yes, Your Highness, of course."

I was so disoriented by the way everybody was treating me. Was it just because I was pregnant? *No,* I realized with amazement. *It's because I'm the first queen to give them an heir in almost sixty years.* None of the staff in this castle could remember taking care of a new baby. Certainly not these young girls, anyway. But all of them were excited by the prospect of a little prince or princess brightening their lives.

A new weight pressed on my shoulders. It dampened my excitement about the budding life. This pregnancy was so early. So many things could happen at this stage. *I could slip and fall,* and when I thought that, I instantly became wary of the staircases. I took a wide berth around them as I entered through the main foyer. The guard wasn't there; I breathed a little easier for that.

Heading back to my room, I walked in and nearly slammed into Darla. "Oh!" she barked, clutching her chest. Her thin eyebrows hunkered down, and even in anger, she managed to look beautiful. "Where the hell did you go?"

I lifted the plate up. "To get something to eat, why are you so upset?"

"Because you . . ." She shook herself. "Never mind, just sit down and stuff your face, I guess."

Eyeballing her, I sat at the vanity, putting my plate down beside the vase in front of the mirror. Shoveling potatoes in my mouth, I waited for her to speak.

She stood there with her arms folded, tapping her foot. Finally she dropped onto the bed and said, "Did you go look for Thorne?"

I sat up a little straighter. "I did. Some guard told me that he wasn't in the castle."

"Did he tell you why?"

"No, just that he thought maybe he was with his dad. Which seemed weird to me. Those two don't spend a lot of time together. What would they be doing at this hour?"

Darla stuck her pinkie in her ear, wiggling around. "Hm."

"What, what are you humming for?"

"Well, I have a theory, but you're not going to like it."

I'd taken too big a bite; when I swallowed, it hurt. "Just say it."

Darla crossed her legs, her pink shoe bouncing up and down. "I haven't seen that guy all day long. And I've been in the castle all day myself." She stared me in the eye and shook her head. "Oh, Nova, I really don't want to say this out loud. But I'm thinking he saw the newspapers this morning, the stuff about you being pregnant, and—"

I dropped my fork onto my plate loudly. "If you're trying to say that he got scared and ran, there's no way."

"I don't know. Like I said, I really hate even thinking this, but that guy, I mean, come on. It's not like he's father material. And he didn't want to be king, he doesn't like responsibility, right? Being a dad is about as responsible as you can get."

I stood up suddenly, the chair rocking from how quickly I'd done it. "Get out."

"Excuse me?"

"I said get out. I'm not going to sit here and listen to you badmouth the man that I married. Thorne is going to be a dad. We're going to raise this kid." I loomed over her. The surprise in her eyes was satisfying; I pointed at the door. "Leave, and the next time you talk about Thorne, you better watch what you say."

Darla considered me for a minute before she rose from the bed. Dusting herself off, she lifted her hands and sighed. "Fine, whatever. You don't have to believe me. But if I'm right . . ." She didn't finish, just opened the door, and as she did, I saw that the guard was standing outside again. He glanced at us, then fixated on the far wall. Darla shut the door behind her and left me alone.

I didn't eat any more of my food. My appetite was gone again, but at least it wasn't replaced by nausea. I was just too angry to think about eating. Sliding back under the covers, I checked my phone and felt a stab of pain when Thorne still hadn't replied.

I sent him one more text, saying that he should come see me when he was free.

And then I sent another text two hours later, wishing him a good night.

He didn't respond to any of them before I fell asleep again.

- CHAPTER TWENTY-EIGHT -

Nova

A new day.

No news from Thorne.

I'd woken up feeling a rising unease. It had sunk its claws into my belly, holding tight and giving me no relief. When my mother came looking for me, it took her a bit to find me, because I'd slipped out of my room and down to the garden.

The sun wasn't high enough yet to burn off all the dew. Crouching by the vibrant plants, I gently cupped a white rose. It was open to its full extent, eagerly awaiting to soak up the sunlight. It reminded me of how open I'd been the day Thorne had made love to me in the hedge maze.

I heard my mother's steps when she was a long way off. I didn't look up, I just sniffed the flower and closed my eyes. "Nova?" she said, then, more firmly, "What are you doing out here alone?"

"I don't need someone with me at all times. I'm pregnant, not an inmate trying to bolt."

"The way you keep running off, I wouldn't know." She blew out some air in exasperation. "Come inside and eat breakfast."

I opened my eyes, studying the layers of petals on the rose. "He still hasn't spoken to me. I haven't seen him in two days, Mom."

Going silent, she wrapped her woven cover-up around her thin body. "Did you consider that he might be hiding?"

That got my attention; I stared up at her. "From what? Me?"

She held my gaze calmly. "Or from something he's ashamed of. Come inside. There's hot tea and pastries waiting in your room."

"I don't want to sit in my room any longer."

"Then my room. Or Darla's. Just come into the castle, please."

Unfolding from the grass, I dusted off the knees of my soft pink pants. My mother judged me with her eyes—seeing my messy hair, my lazy outfit. But I didn't care what she thought. Not about that, anyway. What she'd said about Thorne was burning in my mind, refusing to be put out.

What would he be ashamed of? I knew him as a brave man. Embarrassing him was as likely as knocking down a building with a baseball bat; he turned every insult around on his attackers. But her suggestion bothered me deeply.

We ended up sitting in my mother's room. Darla, Richard, and Larchmont joined us to eat. My father came, too, all of us gathering in a way we hadn't in some time. I listened to them talk, my mind wandering. The food didn't register on my taste buds.

From a distance I watched my family. My siblings were sitting across from me, their heads together, voices low. Their discussion was intense, and it drew a severe glare from my father. "Shh," he finally said to them. "Not now. Nova." I slid my eyes to him. "Are you feeling better today?"

Putting on a mild smile, I sipped from my cup of tea. "I guess. Less sick." *Just as confused.*

He looked satisfied, edging his chair back from the table we'd arranged in the huge room. "I should get going. Lots to do today."

"Like what?" I asked, stirring my cup.

"Boring, but necessary, business." Rebuttoning his jacket, he moved to the exit. My mother followed him, speaking in his ear as he opened the door. I was watching, but even if I wasn't I would have heard the ruckus outside. Something was stomping, drawing closer, multiple voices talking at once.

My parents, standing in the doorway, froze where they were. Shoving out of my seat, I hurried toward them, leaning around to see what they were seeing. Nearly upon us, rolling like a train, were Maverick and Carmina, and at their heels was Glen with two other men I didn't know following closely.

"Kurtis!" Maverick roared, his voice echoing in the hallway. A few servants slid closer to the walls, heads down, listening as they tried to become invisible. The huge man pulled up short in front of my father, who, as usual, kept his face serene. "Where is he? Where's my son?"

I inhaled sharply. *They don't know where he is, either?*

My father held his head as high as possible. He and Maverick were identical in height, but where one was lean, the other was all bulky power. If Maverick swung, I predicted my dad's head would fly right off. "Why do you sound like you're accusing us?"

"Because I *am*," he snapped. "Two days and no word from him! No response to our calls, no one has seen him on the castle grounds, nothing!"

"What makes you think we'd be involved?" Mom asked, standing loyally at Dad's side.

"When are you ever not?" Carmina had stepped forward, the four of them squaring off in the long hallway.

I'd been blocking the doorway into the room behind me. A hand pressed on my arm; Larchmont maneuvered me aside so he could leap into the mess. His hands were folded behind his back, where I knew he kept his gun. I had a sudden, awful premonition that he was going to use it.

His hand moved; he was not grabbing his weapon but coming forward, covering his mouth as he cleared his throat politely. "This is getting really tense out here. You even brought your personal guards, did you really expect a fight?"

Maverick twisted, eyeing my brother like he was a dirt speck on the rug. "That depends on how you answer our questions."

"Ask away," Kurtis said.

Holding out an arm to encourage some space, Glen stood between my family and the others. His green eyes rested on us one by one. When it was my turn, I shivered. "All we're looking for is a lead. The king has gone missing, that's a problem for everyone. When did you last see him?"

No one spoke. They were all looking at me. *If they saw the papers, they know I was with him the other night.* "Don't dodge around it. You all read the rumors about the pregnancy. Thorne was with me at that restaurant, he took me back here, said good night, then that was it." Fumbling for my phone, I showed it to them. "He texted me, but never responded."

Carmina went pale. "He sent these messages yesterday morning? That's really the last time you spoke?"

Her worry mirrored my own. But when I tried to reach out for her, she closed off, not willing to completely let go of her suspicion about me. I didn't blame her, but her silent accusation ripped my heart into tiny pieces.

There was motion beside me in the room; Darla had drawn close, her sweet perfume clogging my nose. "You guys have some balls, blaming us for your failing-upward son. He probably ran off when he saw the same rumors splashed across the papers that you all have."

Maverick breathed in until his chest rose. He eyeballed me, searching my face. "Is it true, then? Are you . . ."

"Now isn't the time," Kurtis cut him off. "Not when you've come to our doorstep with violence on your minds."

Larch crossed his arms, shrugging. "I don't know why everyone is stressed. I'm sure Thorne will show up. A guy like him is too annoyingly loud to stay missing for long."

Maverick turned away, lowering into a huddle to speak with his wife and Glen. With one more glance at us, they retreated down the hallway. "Good riddance," Larch mumbled.

Our father hooked an arm around Larchmont's shoulders, leading him down the opposite hall. "Come with me."

"Wait," I said, following them, shutting Darla and Richard in my mother's room as I went. "Isn't this something we should be discussing? Even Thorne's parents don't know what's happened to him."

"Nova." My mom patted my shoulder. The other two hadn't slowed down, ignoring me as they walked off to talk on their own. "Go to my room. Eat. Rest. Your job is to take care of growing this baby."

Cradling my flat tummy, I gritted my teeth. "This baby? It's Thorne's baby. And he should know about it. He should *be* here!"

"But he isn't." Her words were clipped. The discussion was over. I watched her as she swayed after my father and brother. If I was familiar with any part of my mother, it was the back of her smooth head. I'd seen it numerous times.

I feel like I'm losing my mind. How could Hawthorne go missing? This wasn't something small. He was the king! He was my husband. He was . . . he was going to be a father. I had to find him.

Unsure what to do next, I wandered back to my mother's room. I had it partially open when I heard my siblings squabbling inside.

"Just let me—come on!" Darla grunted, yanking something out of Richard's hands. She leaned whatever it was—a phone?—over the bed. She was taking a photo of something there. With a proud grin, she winked at Richard and typed something. "Aaaand . . . send. There. Now the madness can happen."

"What madness?" I asked, entering fully into the room. Darla and Richard both stared at me. His expression was flat, but hers was wild. I knew that face; it was the one she made whenever she got caught doing something bad. "Darla . . . what are you . . . ?" She was paralyzed. I glanced at the phone in her hand. I recognized it, but that was impossible. "Why do you have Thorne's phone?" I asked with mounting distrust.

My nerves went haywire. In slow motion my sister hid the phone behind her back, her attention darting to the bed. I was moving faster than she was. On another level, fueled by a rising paranoia. Before she could stop me, I'd snatched the photo off the blanket.

It was a shiny picture. In it, plain as day, was Thorne with his pants low around his hips from behind, his tattoos peeking between the material and his shirt. He was standing in the cemetery, and I knew what—and who—he was doing.

"Nova, wait," Darla said, lifting her hands in front of her. I glanced at the phone again—so did she. "This isn't . . . I was only trying to save your dignity!"

"My dignity?" I repeated, so lost I was feeling ill. Or maybe that was from the pregnancy. "What the hell is going on in here? Someone explain. *Now.*"

Sputtering, my sister twirled a hand by her head, searching for words that she could scoop up and use. Her own were failing her. "Don't get so pissy at me! I'm the only one who wanted you to know the truth about Thorne." Snatching the photo from me, she stuck it in my face. "It's hard to look at, I'm sure, but this is the real him! The kind of guy who'd bang a streetwalker in the royal cemetery isn't good enough to be a dad *or* your husband."

Lifting my eyes from the photo, I glared at Darla, then Richard. He shrank under my furious stare. "This *streetwalker* is *me.*"

"Oh shit," she whispered. "Well . . . it's fine. No one I sent it to can recognize you if we didn't."

"*Who* did you send this photo to?"

"Just a few contacts I've made at the local papers." She shrugged casually. "This city is obsessed with scandal. It'd be sad if it wasn't so fun."

A horrific block clogged my esophagus, then moved to my throat before coming out as a shuddering gasp. "How could you hurt me like this?"

"Hurt you? I was trying to help you." She wrinkled her nose. "I didn't know it was you in the photo with him. Larchmont thought it was a prostitute—which Thorne *did* meet with, by the way—and she apparently lied to get some money out of this. My point is, only Thorne gets in trouble for breaking the law."

Grabbing Thorne's phone, I shook it at her. "Him being in trouble hurts *me!*"

She blinked owlishly. "Huh? I don't get it."

"Of course you don't," I snapped. "You've got no idea what it means to feel the way I do about someone. I don't know if you're even capable of it. You're selfish and empty inside."

Lost for a response, Darla gaped at me. Then she eyeballed Richard, but he offered no help. In front of my eyes I watched her mind working. Darla could never take, had never taken responsibility for her actions. But she was good at deflecting. "If you want to be angry, aim it at Larch and Rich. They did way worse to Thorne than I did."

As I watched him, Richard's face crumpled. He avoided my eyes, staring out the window. "Richard," I said, drawing out his name. He still didn't look at me. "What did you do to Thorne? Where is he?"

"Nova," he whispered, like my name caused him pain. "I didn't know it was you. I thought he'd . . . Larch made it so easy to believe that guy was scum."

"*Where is he?*"

"The private holding quarters. It's a small room downstairs, only the royal guards use it."

My sister reached out for me. "Wait—Oh, my phone." She slid out the black-and-pink mobile, checking it instead of grabbing me. "Fuck! Wow! That picture I sent is blowing up all over. It's been shared two thousand times online already!"

Her glee disgusted me. But I didn't have time to waste on calling her out.

I had someone to find.

Someone who needed to know he hadn't been forgotten.

- CHAPTER TWENTY-NINE -

HAWTHORNE

Lying on that stiff bed, barely able to move without pain shooting through my face, I stared at the plain gray ceiling. No one had spoken to me since I'd been left here. A guard had opened the door a crack late last night to shove a cup of water and some bread inside, but he had avoided looking at me during the exchange.

I wondered if those men who'd stood by, listening to me get pummeled, regretted any of it. Did they really hate me because I'd fucked someone in their sacred graveyard? I didn't think the ghosts gave a shit. I should have worried more about real flesh-and-blood people, apparently.

Lifting my hands, I gazed at my fingers as I spread them. It was hard to imagine the sky was somewhere through that thick ceiling. That a place so magical still existed. A sky full of stars that I'd gazed upon with Nova in my arms. I hummed softly, and my fingers moved, playing an invisible piano. In my head I heard the song clearly; it was the same one Nova had encouraged me to perform at the coronation. Her belief in my ability had driven me to do something I never would have. To a passion I'd long abandoned.

Larchmont's last words haunted me mercilessly: *Nova was always one of us.*

I hadn't believed him. But the longer I lay here, throbbing in pain, my hurt growing beyond my earthly bruises until it coiled in my soul, the more I began to wonder. To think that everything between Nova and me had been fake . . . it was too much.

But was it worse if it had been real?

I was going to be stripped of my crown. The Valentines didn't need me. They had what they'd been after—what I'd promised Costello I was smart enough to prevent: a growing baby.

My baby.

Fuck. Fuck fuck fuck. Squeezing my eyes shut, I clenched my hands and dropped them to my sides. Ten years in prison? All that time without being with the woman I loved. A decade where I wouldn't get to know my own child. There was some irony in ending up a worse father than my own, even before I'd gotten to try my hand at it.

Noise clanked outside my door. Shifting, I looked over at the single foggy panel of glass. A figure was there—another guard? The door burst open, shining light into the room. It lit her up from behind, her hair a crimson halo. My angel had come for me.

"I'm so sorry!" Nova cried, dropping to her knees beside my bed. Her hands reached for my shoulders, cradled my bruised and swollen jaw. "Oh, are you all right? You look awful."

Gently, like she'd turn into dust if I pressed too hard, I touched her cheek. "I knew Larch got some solid hits in, but I didn't think he gave me a concussion. Am I hallucinating, or are you really here?"

"Of course I'm here!" Nova grasped my wrist, kissing my palm. "I didn't know they did this, Thorne. When I got your messages, I wanted to respond, but I couldn't."

I stiffened, midway to pulling her in for a taste of her lips. "You . . . got my messages? When?"

"Yesterday. As you sent them." She studied my injuries, frowning in sympathy. I must have looked like death warmed over. I sure felt like it.

"You mean to tell me you saw my texts asking if you were okay, and you just didn't answer me?" That cut me to my core. Nova looked into my eyes, sensing my growing despair. "I came down here, got ambushed by your brothers, because I thought something had happened to *you*."

She withdrew, covering her mouth. "Oh no. Thorne, I—I was in the dark about their plan! I swear it!"

Nova was always one of us. He'd said it. He'd warned me. Yet she denied being involved. Who was lying? *Why* come down here to get me now? My skull was ready to split from my confusion.

"You said you couldn't respond, what does that mean?" I asked, feeling like I was having the shit kicked out of me all over again.

Drawing herself up, Nova stood a foot away. "I wasn't allowed. My mother—"

"Right," I said, cutting her off. "I forgot. You do anything she tells you, huh?" *Of course she does,* I thought bitterly. *She was always working with her family. She was always on their side.*

She was always my enemy, and I was too blind to realize it.

I'd been so sure I was nothing like my brothers. No woman, no matter how beautiful or kind or compassionate or *everything* that Nova is, could make me so naive that I'd ignore every warning sign. But I had. I'd fallen for every trick in the book, and some I hadn't known existed.

I turned my back on her, facing the cell wall. A malaise unlike any other was choking away the energy in me. I'd felt so relieved to see her, but now I was swimming in despair.

"Please," she said, the word squeezing from between her teeth. She was barely holding herself together. "I'm so sorry, but please, let me help you."

"You've helped me plenty," I said sadly, pressing my hand to my eyelids. "Even if you could take back everything about me breaking the law, keep me out of jail . . . it's not enough. Don't you get it?" I couldn't look at her. I wanted to, but my body wouldn't let me. "Your brothers did their best to hurt me. They didn't realize the damage beneath my skin was worse than anything they could inflict."

The worst part was knowing I had some power here. An awful, terrible ability to bring her down with me. I *knew* it was her in the photo; so did she. If I could prove it, she'd suffer the same sentence as me, and then . . . and then . . .

And then nothing.

Because even though she'd burned my world to ashes, crushed my heart, she was still curled so firmly around my soul that I'd never hurt her.

"I get that you're angry. You probably even hate me." Her voice cracked on that last part, but she pressed forward. "I don't blame you. You're right about everything, I'm pathetic for listening to my mother. I should have told you I was okay . . . If I had, you wouldn't be down here."

The pain in her voice pulled at my protective side. But the way she'd ignored me yesterday had left me feeling so betrayed . . . so *unimportant*. It was the exact way my father had made me feel while I was growing up.

Nova breathed in through her nose. It was a desperate breath that went on for some time. I wondered if she'd ever release it. I wondered if she even could. "It's okay if you think I'm awful. I think I am, too. Please let me fix this. Let me *try* to make you understand why this all happened, and why . . . why I'm the way I am."

The part of her still living in my chest curled ever tighter. It choked some of my resentment away, encouraging me to listen to her confession. Turning on the bed, I focused on the bottomless sorrow in her beautiful face. It was a challenge not to tell her everything was fine. To please not cry, especially not because of me.

But I couldn't.

Not until I heard what she had to say.

"Around six months ago . . . about a week after meeting you . . . I got very ill."

"The kidney failure," I whispered, remembering how she'd brushed it off on our wedding night.

She nodded frantically. Tears streamed down her cheeks in infinite lines. "I was sick, and in so much damn pain. I kept it to myself because I never told anyone what was going on in my life. Every time I'd tried before, they never cared. Not really."

Wringing her hands, she shuddered. "I went downhill quickly. I remember being alone in my bed, and my sister came in to stand over me. I couldn't focus on her face. The world was just wobbly, all curves, no edges. She called me pathetic." Nova looked at me straight on. "She was right. My heat was rubbed out of me, just stripped until I was cold and going blind. I remember lying there, looking at the ceiling and thinking . . . *This is what I get.* I wished for more, for better, and this is the result of my selfishness. Thorne, six months ago, my kidneys didn't just fail."

She kept staring at me. A wild plea to get her meaning without her having to say it. I felt as frail as she must have months ago, lying in her bed.

Her lips parted ever so slightly. "I died."

Though she was standing right in front of me, I had an irresistible urge to grab her up and make certain she was still there. Stumbling forward, forgetting my pride, my anger, I swept Nova against my chest and *squeezed.* "You didn't die," I growled. "You're too warm to be a fucking ghost."

Her arms didn't wrap around me. She was stiff as a cord of wood. "The paramedics told me later that my body shut down from the toxins I couldn't filter. They restarted my heart in the ambulance, kept me alive long enough for the surgery that would be my new beginning."

New beginning? I wondered.

Nova was vibrating so hard I expected her joints to detach. "When I finally woke up, there was a hospital ceiling above me. My father was sitting nearby in a chair." She looked up at me, unflinching, as she relived that day. "He told me Mom had given me a kidney. She'd saved my life, but doing so had ruined hers. She would struggle now, he said. She'd never be whole. Her life would be less vibrant. And it was my fault."

Her eyelids pinched together. No matter how I wiped at her cheeks, the tears kept coming. "Nova, that's not your fault at all."

"It is. I *wished* for something to happen that would make me brave enough to live fearlessly! I got that when I nearly died. Because of her sacrifice, I'm alive. You're able to do *this*," she said, grabbing my wrists, driving my palms into her cheeks harder, "because of her! That day, I promised myself three things: I'd never forget the sacrifice she made for me. I'd make sure my wish wasn't wasted. And I swore to live my life without fear . . . like you do."

Tension dug its claws into my neck. *She told me that before. That after meeting me she'd wanted to BE me.* I'd thought it was odd. I had no idea how much impact I'd had on her life. Knowing the depth of it all, hearing how she'd suffered . . . I found my heart splitting down the middle.

"You think I'm fearless?" I growled. There was pressure behind my eyes, building to the point where I expected my forehead to tear apart. "Haven't you been listening to me? I was *terrified* something had happened to you! I was so, so afraid, Nova." I hugged her all over again.

Nova snaked her arms under mine. The tension she created with her embrace stole some of the pressure from my head. "I wanted to tell you this," she said, softly enough that I had to strain, "because I hoped you'd forgive me. But that wasn't the only reason." Nova curled her hands against her own chest between us. Her lower lids were swollen. "Until you knew what had changed my life . . . I could never tell you what I've known for some time. Thorne, I love you. I loved you weeks ago at our fake wedding, when I said 'I do.' That moment was real for me."

The leftover bitterness that had been clinging to my heart fell away. *She loves me.* This amazing woman who had been through so much and thought she had to live life at full speed because she owed it to her second chance . . .

Someone so pure loved *me?*

I didn't deserve this happiness. That didn't stop me from crushing her in my arms, my forehead resting on hers. The bridge of my nose was damp from her tears—my chin was wet from my own. When was the last time I'd wept?

"I love you," I said, each word thick and heavy. "I love you so much, Nova." I kept saying it, afraid she wouldn't hear me, that my declaration wouldn't reach the parts of her that it had to for this to be meaningful. My palm skated over her belly. Both of us went still. "Is it real, are you pregnant?"

Sniffling, she flashed a helpless smile. "Yes. You're going to be a dad." Her eyes traveled the gray room with its stripped bed and blood-spattered floor. "This wasn't how I hoped to tell you the news."

Through my fingertips, I imagined the life growing inside her womb. *I'm going to be a father. It's really happening.* My face twisted up, everything in me bunching as I hugged her anew. "I'm so sorry."

"For what?" she whispered.

"Not remembering who you were. I don't know how it's possible to forget the face of the woman who'd own my heart someday." Tilting her chin up, I kissed away the tears at the corners of her eyes. "Maybe I should be locked up, because what crime is worse than that?"

- CHAPTER THIRTY -

HAWTHORNE

Glen was waiting for us just outside my cell. His face was slightly red—I suspected he'd heard what Nova and I had spoken about. But that was all right. The world had seen our fake love; I wouldn't be ashamed about the real thing.

"Did you help her break me out?" I asked as we approached.

"She ran into me on the way here. When she said she was looking for some royal holding cell, I knew exactly the place. Wasn't much of a breakout, though."

The three of us hurried up the stairs. I realized he was right; there was no one guarding this section. "Where did they all run off to?"

He didn't look at me, he just hurried faster. "There's a problem. Every able body is in the middle of handling it."

Nova glanced at me, her hand wrapping around mine. "It's all thanks to Darla. Just . . . look!"

We'd made it into the west wing of the castle. On my left, through the huge windows that allowed sunlight to stream onto the red rugs, I glimpsed the front gates. There I saw something that blew my mind. A mob had gathered on the front lawn. Media vehicles with satellites served as backdrops for multiple people speaking to camera crews.

"What the hell?" I asked, running faster down the hall. There was a dull roar now, the cacophony of hundreds of voices all talking at once. Through the opening ahead I saw the main staircases at the entrance. Much of the crowd had poured through the front doors, swamping the foyer. At the base of the stairs on either side of the upper level, the royal guards—as well as some of my men and the Valentines' men—had blocked off access. Against the banister, staring down at us all, were Kurtis and Valencia. Over their shoulders I saw their other children; those three were huddling by the wall.

"What *is* all this?" I asked Glen when we pulled up behind the first row of shouting bodies.

"Those bastards up there have started quite the riot," he said, his hand hovering at his hip. I saw his holster and wished for a gun of my own. "Your parents gave up on trying to talk to the guards or the Valentines and went into town to get help from the police. They were sure something had happened to you, your mother insisted you'd never send a photo like *that* from your own phone."

"Photo?" Glen wouldn't look me in the eye. My stomach ate itself—I knew what the photo was.

"Yeah," Nova said. "My sister handed it to the world this morning. Then my father made an official statement that they planned to begin the process of stripping you of the crown for your crime. This is the result."

I recognized some of the castle staff among the faces. Everyone was screaming; I caught bits of sentences.

"Pure bullshit! I never . . ."

"Why are his parents speaking to the cops? Is the king really missing?"

"He deserves a fair trial! Don't judge him guilty before that!"

"It's fake! The photo is fake! Give us the king, let him answer himself!"

Kurtis slapped his hands down on the banister. "None of you have permission to march in here!" Amazingly, his voice carried over the crowd. He scanned everyone—then he saw me. Fury blackened his features. Valencia followed his eyes. Leaning close, she spoke in his ear, though the noise would have made it impossible for anyone to hear.

I hated how his smile lit up.

"Hawthorne Fredricson!" he shouted. Every set of eyes, one by one, turned to me where I was standing in the hallway. Glen tensed at my side, as did Nova. "Everyone is here to cry havoc at me and my family. They think I've done something wrong by requesting the crown stay with my daughter, with or without your support. These people have grown fond of you quickly. They're suspicious that what was emailed to them this morning was a lie. But I think, if they knew your true nature, that would change."

"Shit," Glen said under his breath.

Everyone was silent. Larchmont drew closer to the banister, more eager to see me put on the spot than he was afraid of being injured by the mob.

"Do you deny you had sex in the royal, sacred cemetery?" Kurtis asked me.

The crowd gasped collectively. Standing there with their mix of disgust and disappointment raining on me, I found my eyes moving upward. I saw the large painting on the wall. The one of my father and his family.

I'd rather be an idiot than a fraud. I held my head high. "I don't deny it."

That made him hesitate—he'd expected me to argue. "Well, good," he said, "because we have proof beyond a photo. The prostitute confirmed that you took her to the cemetery, wanting to have sex on the former king's grave."

I grimaced violently. "I didn't want . . . That's not . . ." How could I explain? Denying the accusation involved chancing that Nova would get caught. All those faces were shooting disappointment, disbelief, and defeat on me simultaneously.

"It wasn't her that was with him!" Nova stepped forward. Her hand was tangled with mine, warmly glued into place. Her eyes fixed firmly, without fear, on her father. "It was me."

Her bravery gave me strength. Kurtis had gone white—in contrast, his wife was glowing red. "Nova, stop this. Do you understand what you're saying?" he sputtered.

"I do." She made us face the crowd. Camera flashes popped off like fireworks as we stood there. "Your queen *and* your king have broken the law. If Thorne doesn't deserve to sit on the throne, let alone rule this country, neither do I."

"*Nova!*" Valencia hissed.

"Fine," Larchmont scoffed, his hands flying over his head dismissively. "*I'll* sit on the damn throne if neither of them plan to."

"That's treasonous!" Glen shouted. "Only those from the Fredricson bloodline can wear the crown."

Larch stared at the head of the royal guard. The madness in the whites of his eyes made the writhing red veins even bolder. "You think you can tell me what to do? Fuck, I'm so tired of people doing that." From his lower back he revealed a silvery pistol. The crowd gasped, seeing the gun, starting to panic.

Glen, however, didn't look nervous. "Step down, boy."

"I'm no *boy*." He aimed the weapon upward, and, to my shock, he fired once. The whip-crack of the bullet flying free sent a ripple through the foyer. People shouted, some running away, others ducking down with their hands over their heads.

On the stairs, the royal guards reached for their own weapons, looking to Glen for guidance. The few men in my family's pay stared at me. This was pandemonium. I clutched Nova's wrist, my mind racing as I searched for a plan.

I didn't know what to do.

I just knew I had to keep the woman I loved safe.

"Larchmont," Valencia said, drawing his name out. She was frozen where she stood. "There's no need to do this. We've already won, we're in control."

"You call this control?" he spit, gesturing with the pistol out over the foyer. The remaining bystanders dropped down, covering their heads. Only I, Nova, and Glen still stood. "These people are so set on making sure their rulers were born with the 'right' blood. They don't care if their king is lazy or selfish. They don't care if he knows the first thing about the country he's supposed to run!"

Glen's fingers slid closer to his gun. I watched him communicating with his men to stay where they were, all without making a sound.

"Son," Kurtis hissed, "you're making a scene."

"No, I'm not. But I will." The tip of Larch's pistol swung. I held my breath as it hovered, aiming between me and Nova. "These people don't know what they need. Let's just kill the last of this toxic bloodline off, force them to crown someone who *knows* about ruling. We've been coming to Torino for years. Any one of us would know how to run this country better than Thorne." He fingered the trigger, aiming at my forehead. "I'm thinking . . . me."

"Larch, *no!*" Nova screamed.

Everything happened at once. I saw the gun's flash—felt hands on my shoulder, shoving me down toward the floor. More bangs; more gunshots. I curled my body around Nova on the cold marble. Shoes stampeded around us, someone stepping on my legs as they tripped over me.

I didn't care about the pain. *Protect her! Save her!* I sheltered Nova beneath me. Noise continued to storm around us. But all I saw . . . all I heard . . . was Nova. Her breathing was ragged—as if she was sucking in air with all her might. *Oh God, the baby.* The burst of primal rage shocked me. I was consumed by the possibility that Larchmont had managed to put not just Nova in danger, but my unborn child.

Sitting up, I cupped her face, searching her eyes for information. "Are you okay?" I hushed, knowing she'd hear me over the ruckus around us.

Her whiskey eyes were pulled wide. For a terrible second she said nothing, did nothing. Then she nodded. "I'm fine. The bullet missed."

Fuck. It was a miracle. Kissing her, I squeezed my eyes shut. I'd thought I'd known what regret was. I hadn't until I'd nearly lost not just the woman I loved . . . but someone I hadn't even met yet.

"Let us through, let us pass!"

I knew my father's voice anywhere. Lifting my head, I spotted him marching through the open front doors. At his side was my mother, and sandwiching them both were Rush and Donnie with their weapons drawn.

At their backs, pouring into the room and up both sides of the stairs, came multiple police in riot gear. "Freeze!" one of them commanded.

My eyes flew to the banister. I'd thought I'd see Larchmont there, ready to fire more bullets. Instead I saw Richard holding his brother in a bear hug from behind. His massive arms kept Larchmont still, even though he was throwing his legs around wildly, eyes furious.

The police and the guards worked efficiently. In seconds they had Larchmont in cuffs. Most of the mob had fled out the front door during the shooting. The people left were guided out onto the front lawn.

My mother caught my eye. She sprinted at me and hugged me hard. "Thorne! Your face, are you hurt?"

"I'm fine," I said, unable to keep from wincing when she touched my bruised cheek.

"Lord, I was so worried! No one would tell us where you were! We confronted the Valentines and they played dumb!" Her eyes narrowed on Nova.

"She wasn't behind this." I looped my arm around Nova's waist possessively. My mother stared harder, looking uncertain. "She found out where I was and rescued me."

"I'm so sorry this all happened," Nova said. She clasped her hands in front of her in a tight ball. "My parents didn't tell me they were going to do all this once I had a baby on the way. I was a pawn. Really, I'm sorry."

My mother covered her mouth with both hands. "Did you say baby? Then the rumor . . . Oh—oh, I'm going to be a grandma! A ma-maw! *Me!*"

I debated pointing out that she'd forgotten *Sammy*, Kain's wife, was due in three months. But Mom looked so relieved I let it go. My soft spot for seeing her happy was always getting bigger.

"Son," Maverick said, coming beside us. "The police are going to need to talk to you."

Helping Nova to her feet, I nodded. "I've got a lot to say." I paused. "To everyone, actually."

All of us walked through the front doors together. Larchmont was thrashing and yelling as the police shoved him into the back of a car. The rest of the Valentines stood in a circle as the police spoke to them. The tension was different, now, but it was still there. "I don't know why you're talking to me," Kurtis said. He spotted me and pointed. "If you're looking for someone who's committed a crime, arrest him."

"Arrest who, the king?" the police officer scoffed.

"Yes!" Kurtis shouted. "Didn't you see the photo? That man had sex in the royal graveyard. He broke the law, there need to be consequences. Punishments!"

I thought about what Nova had said to me the first day I'd arrived in this country. She asked me what kind of king I would be if I were in charge. At the time, I hadn't considered that ruling was a possibility for me. Now here I was, listening to someone else decide what should happen to me for breaking the law.

The police and the royal guards stood there, looking unsure. I didn't see the ones who had allowed me to be led to the small room and beaten bloody yesterday. I wondered if they'd sensed that things had gone out of control and it was best to hide out until they saw where the chips were going to fall.

"If you're going to arrest Thorne," Nova said, stepping forward, "then you have to arrest me, too. Remember? It was me that was breaking the same law as the king was."

Valencia narrowed her eyes. "You're seriously going to do this, you'd sacrifice everything we've worked so hard for just to defy us? After all that I did for you?"

"I'll forever be thankful that you saved my life, Mom," Nova said, striding closer to the group, as if she was trying to make her mother understand . . . like she thought it was possible to appeal to her. "But I'm not going to let you control me with that anymore." Holding herself to her full height, she took a solid breath. In that instant she transformed into a natural queen. "Guards, arrest my family. They're enemies of the crown, their goal was always to steal the throne."

"Ungrateful," Valencia spit. She was bristling with so much anger that the cops looked ready to handcuff her next. "You're ungrateful! Why did I ever think we could rely on you to do what's best for this family? I wish I'd never saved your life!"

Nova didn't even flinch. She was rooted to the earth, looking like a calm statue of a regal knight on his way into battle. But even if she was steady, I was flooding with sorrow for her. I had issues with my family, but I never once thought they'd be happy if I was dead.

Curling my arm around her hip, I held her against me. She flashed me an appreciative smile.

My father scanned the Valentines, his tone as cold as a melting icicle. "Did you seriously try to overthrow the king?"

"Earlier," I said, finally speaking up, "Larch shouted as much from the balcony. He wasn't afraid to try and murder me with everyone watching. From the beginning, the Valentines have wanted us gone. When they heard that their daughter was pregnant with my child, they realized they had an opportunity to ensure the crown would stay in their control without us around to interfere."

"It's true," Richard agreed, drawing some surprised glances from his own family. Larch, sequestered in the cop car, had his face pressed to the window.

"Richard!" Kurtis gasped, reaching for his son with a vein in his neck bulging. The officer nearest him grabbed him before he could get there. Two other cops handcuffed Kurtis's hands as he struggled. "How could you say that? What's wrong with you? Treason in this country— they kill you for that!"

Richard looked toward me, then settled his stare on Nova. "It's one thing to make a power grab. It's another to willingly risk your sister's life. When Larch pulled that gun, he didn't care if he hit her accidentally. I couldn't stand by and watch that happen. Sorry, Nova. Sorry this went so far."

She held my arm with both of hers, squeezing, talking to her brother. "It's okay. I get it. Thank you, Richard. I mean it."

Glen cleared his throat. Every one of the guards and officers looked at him with a respect that had no doubt grown firmly over the years of his service. "You heard the king, these people worked together to commit conspiracy against the crown. Arrest them all."

"And what about what he did?" Kurtis yelled, fighting the officers who shoved him into the back of a different car.

"He's the king," Glen said, shrugging. "No one here is going to arrest him for using his own land however he wants. Especially not when he's given the monarchy its first child in decades."

The paparazzi from earlier surrounded us, snapping photos as the Valentines were driven off the property. There was a constant buzz of talking now. Every microphone was shoved in our faces.

My father and mother stood to my right, and Glen was on my left, opposite Nova. I maintained my grip on her hand like I would never be able to let her go. I didn't want to. So I wouldn't.

Questions swarmed us with the cops now gone:

"Your Majesty, is it true that you broke the law?"

"Yes," I said gravely. "I did."

"Do you think it's appropriate for a king to be caught with his literal pants down?"

I knew it was wrong to laugh, but I couldn't help it; all the stress inside me melted away in that split second. "Oh no, it's definitely not appropriate. No king worth his salt would do something as stupid as what I did. Getting caught, I mean," I said, amending my statement as I pulled Nova closer to me. "I don't want anyone to think I meant that I regret having sex with my wife."

There were a few chuckles from the crowd.

"Is the queen really pregnant?" another reporter asked, mic halfway to banging my nose.

"Yes," I started to say, glancing at Nova. "The queen is pregnant, but I—"

"Who attacked you, leaving that black eye?"

Touching my temple, I flinched. "Larchmont Valentine. He coordinated with some guards in the castle to arrest me in secret."

"Do you think the guards can be trusted?"

"Can anyone be bribed these days?"

"Has this country gotten better or worse since you came into power?"

The questions started coming faster and faster. I wasn't able to keep up, I was getting dizzy. The camera lights were bright and blinding. Whatever relief I felt now that the Valentines had been taken away evaporated under this new assault. That last question hit me particularly hard.

My father stepped forward, standing to his full height. "Of course this country has gotten better since my son arrived." His voice boomed over the camera shutters. "Look at the productivity over the past month alone, at the amount of construction that's being caught up on and even

245

started anew. The corruption left behind by the influence of the former queen's family is being extracted day by day. How could anyone ask if this country is better off?"

I stared at him in amazement. The words coming from his mouth were defensive, like he couldn't handle the idea of people slandering me in front of him. I didn't know what to do. He'd never been so openly kind, not that I could remember, anyway.

He thinks Torino's better with me here? I wondered to myself. Nova laid her head on my shoulder. She said softly, just so I could hear, "Everything your father says is true. I haven't seen this city flourishing for a long time. Every summer when I visited it seemed to get worse. But not now."

My flutter of pride was brief. *Both of them are right, but for the wrong reason.*

This country *was* doing better. But it had nothing to do with me.

Maverick was the one attending all the meetings with the politicians I loathed.

He was the one working on the backed-up contracts.

The physical work being done that no one else could get to fast enough for his satisfaction? All him. My father had worked both mentally and physically to begin the long process of healing his home country.

The paparazzi were still yelling questions, but I wasn't listening to them anymore. Lifting my head, I said, "I have an announcement to make." People went quiet, the microphones edging ever closer. I could've taken a bite out of one of them if I wanted to. "I, Hawthorne Luca Fredricson, the king of this country, have decided to step down."

The roar of disbelief was deafening. My father stared at me with his lips going thin and white. My mother clutched at the shawl around her throat.

Nova lifted her head, her eyes not shocked—they were simply curious.

"Everything that's happened, everything you all have said, it's made me realize something." Shrugging, I clasped Nova's hand with both of mine, staring at her, speaking to her. "I love this woman. I love that she's carrying our child. I want to be at her side for every last breath we both ever take. But I don't need to be king, and she doesn't need to be queen, for me to do those things."

"Thorne," she whispered.

Smiling, I scanned the crowd; they were a wall of camera lenses. "I created nothing but scandals. I'm not entirely sure that me being here has actually been good for any of you. Yet the country *is* better on the whole . . . you just don't have me to thank for it." I turned to lock eyes with Maverick. "You have him. My father."

"Hawthorne," he said, "you can't do this. If you step down, there is no one—"

"There is," I said, catching my mother's startled smile. She'd guessed what I was about to say. "Dad, from the beginning this crown belonged to you. It was never meant for me."

Maverick's hands went slack at his sides. He was at a loss for words, something that was very rare. As he stood there watching me, reading me, trying to decide what to do next, a new voice spoke out from the crowd. "Your son is right."

I recognized the man as the one who'd slung slurs at my mother the day we'd left our hotel on the way to meet with the Valentines. He said, "You're the first person in a long time to give a shit about this country. I don't know why you ran away years ago, and as much as it pisses me off that you did, it doesn't matter now. You're here. You're the one who should sit on the throne, because you're the only one who seems to know what the hell needs to be done anymore. I don't know about everybody else, but I'd celebrate you being king."

More flashes of cameras, more whispers that rose into excited cheering and exuberant nods of affirmation. These people knew a real king when they saw one. The newscasters moved away, surrounding my father and abandoning me to the side.

I'd spent years sitting to the side like this. The sensation of impotence had driven me forward without any purpose. It had left me hollow and hurt and angry. Right then, standing in my father's shadow, watching him be praised . . . watching his smile grow . . . it was the first time that being ignored didn't hurt.

- EPILOGUE -

HAWTHORNE

The news article on my phone showed a photo of a solemn Kurtis Valentine in front of a white wall, his mug shot. "What will happen to them?" I asked, showing it to my father.

He leaned over, eyeing the screen. "Treason is a serious crime. I told you before."

"I know. But death?" I flicked my cell phone off. "They're Nova's family, awful or not. And Richard . . . he did try to help at the end."

My father inhaled gently, huffing the air out after a second. "The sad thing about this country is that it's changed." He glanced my way. "The happy thing is that . . . well, it's changed. When I was younger, I couldn't picture a time when the crimes they pulled could be handled with anything but brutal death. Now? It's my decision. I make the law. Let Nova know her family won't be killed for this, but they won't be leaving our prison anytime soon, either."

Smiling in relief, I looked back out over the huge castle yard. "She'll feel better hearing that."

"Good." Clearing his throat, my dad studied the same part of the garden I was. "Hester and I used to play out here." He pointed with a thick finger. There was an ivory-colored statue of an angel, its base tinted with green ivy. "We climbed that one a lot. Even after we were too big, and the gardeners would shake their fists at us, swearing we'd snap it in two."

"Did you?" I asked, chuckling at the image.

"Hester chipped the tip of the right wing off. We both pretended it had always been missing that piece."

From our distance, I could almost spot the broken feather. As we stood there, the light wind playing through our hair, we forgot how to force a conversation. This was how we were. How we'd learned to interact.

Any other time, I'd have walked off. His silence was a cue to leave. Instead I stayed there with my hands in my jacket pockets. I didn't know the next time I'd be around my father. Or even in this country.

"You don't think I believe in you," he said abruptly, still looking out over the roses.

I gave him a wary side-eye. "Did Glen tell you I overheard you out here weeks ago, talking about me?"

My father scrutinized me with a bittersweet smile. "Son, I don't need anyone to tell me how you perceive me. It's in your face, in how you speak to me. In the brittle jokes you make to keep us from ever having a serious conversation."

"You've got me pegged," I admitted, feeling uncomfortable. "I've known for years that you never wanted to have to rely on me. I guess I didn't need to hear it out loud, was all."

"Hawthorne, what I said to Glen was the truth."

"Jesus, if this is supposed to be you apologizing, you're shit at it."

He shook his head briskly. "Listen to me. It was the truth at that time. You weren't meant to rule this place any more than I was when Hester threatened my life. My brother pulled open my eyes and showed me what a damn coward I was."

My mouth went slack. "You weren't a coward. You told me you didn't stand up to him because you knew he'd be put to death for trying to overthrow you."

"That's what I convinced myself of." Shrugging his massive shoulders, my father looked to the sky. "It helped me sleep at night. Then something happened that forced me to admit my own failure at being a leader."

"What was that?"

He closed his eyes. "I became a father."

I couldn't speak, afraid that if I did, it would close up the hole that had opened, allowing me to glimpse his heart.

"When I was younger," he said, "I rebelled against everything my old man was. I didn't want to play the same political games he did. I believed he hated that I wasn't as good as him, and that I never would be. I've always seen myself in you, Thorne." He breathed in slowly, gathering himself, before facing me again. "We're the same. Your flaws are mine. I wanted more from you, and when I feared it would never come, I shied away. Watching you grow up to be exactly like me . . . always running away from your problems . . . it scraped my soul raw."

My voice was more broken than I wanted it to be. "Glen said I reminded him of you. I hated that."

"I don't blame you. *I* hated realizing what I'd done by abandoning my country. It wasn't until we came here, and I saw how this place had fallen apart, that I grasped it was my only chance to make amends." His arm came up, and he clutched my shoulder. In spite of his grim expression, I believe he was just as surprised as I was. "Hawthorne, I'm sorry. I tried to push you to be like me. No, better than me. But you saw through those desires even as a small child. You were never meant to succeed where I had failed, and putting that pressure on you when I'd run from it myself was unfair."

I held his steady gaze. The lines in his skin, which I had associated with rage, now reminded me of all the suffering he'd gone through. All the pain that he'd lived with, the pressure to be a perfect son, brother, king . . . and father.

He thought he'd failed at them all.

I grabbed his forearm and pulled him in for a solid hug. "It's okay," I said, my brain getting smothered by nostalgia thanks to his warmth and heavy scent—memories of being knee-high, of when he would spin me through the air, sit me on his lap, read to me by the roaring fire in his study. I'd buried the good to more easily live through the bad. "You messed up. So did I. We've still got plenty of time to do it right."

My father clutched me hard enough that the last air in my lungs came out in a wheeze. His beard scratched my cheek, he hung on so tight, like it was possible to make up for years of negligence with one hug. It wasn't. And we both knew it. But this was a start.

Letting me go, he stepped back. His smile was weary, the corners of his eyes red and damp. "You're right. We've got time to make it right." He paused. "The years do fly by, though. It's amazing to think that I'll have two grandchildren soon."

"Yeah. I know." Palming the side of my neck, I laughed. "Hope Kain doesn't get too upset that we'll be stealing his spotlight. Speaking of . . . you might consider talking to him and the others. I get the feeling I'm the first to have a deep talk like this with you."

He nodded gravely. "You're right. All of you deserve better than what I've managed. It will be hard, though, with me being in Torino now."

"I don't know," I said, grinning sideways. "You being king here has given us all an excuse to come around and enjoy the beautiful weather. This place really is gorgeous, you know."

My father inhaled the sweet garden air. "Yes. It is. I missed it a lot."

"Listen," I said, kicking at the ground. "Nova and I are flying back to the States in a few days. Before we leave, do you want to . . . go . . . fishing?"

The bridge of his nose crinkled. "Fishing?"

"Yeah. I might have heard a story about you, a giant swordfish, and the *Sandpiper*." As I spoke, my father's expression smoothed. His blue eyes lightened, his head lifting. "Of course, the old sailor was *probably* senile. But I'd concede if I saw you in action."

The understanding in his smile made him look younger. "I can't believe they kept that damn fish." Shaking himself, he focused on me. His joy became slyer, a strong arm circling my shoulder, pulling me in for a brief, forceful hug. "Son, nothing would make me prouder than taking you out on the water and kicking your ass."

- EPILOGUE -

Nova

All I wanted to do was sit outside in the gardens.

I remembered the first time I'd seen this place—the Badds' estate. I'd been severely jealous of the green grass, the trees, the roses and horses both. It had made my concrete home feel more barren. Lifeless.

Lately, nothing about me was lifeless.

Though I was outside, I could hear the voices through the open windows of the mansion. The March weather was leaning toward the cooler side of spring. That was fine; at eight months pregnant, I was constantly overheating.

My phone buzzed in my pocket. Without glancing at it, I knew everyone was looking for me. Sending a final look out at the gardens, I filled my lungs with the fresh air, then waddled into the back door of the house. The smell of sugar made my stomach growl. I followed it into the dining room. Pink and blue balloons were taped to every surface, some stuck to the ceiling next to giant Mylar baby heads. Groaning, I pressed my palm to the front of my loose shirt, enduring as my hunger made the baby thrash. "I'm starting to think this isn't a baby in here. I might be the first woman to give birth to a typhoon."

"Uh-huh. Sit down, and we can find out in a few minutes if that typhoon is a boy or a girl," Carmina said, waving a napkin at me. I followed her instructions, settling into the cushion-covered dining room chair with relief. One of the maids poured me a glass of lemonade, then rushed off to refill the other guests before I could say thanks.

I could understand her hurry, though. Carmina had invited every single person even somewhat related to them for the gender reveal of Thorne's baby. In a way I was thankful. I certainly had no one to invite.

After being charged with conspiracy against the crown, my parents and brother had been sentenced to fifteen years in the Maurine prison system. Larchmont had an extra twenty years added for attempted murder. Darla and Richard would be out the quickest, both of them having taken plea deals, revealing anything asked of them about my family's plot.

That still left them serving five years each, minimum.

If someone asked me how I felt about it all, I'd have struggled to answer. Luckily, no one asked. They were always too excited to gab about the coming baby. The gender reveal party was almost pointless—I was due in a month, I'd gone this long without knowing. I could wait until the moment the baby was born.

Carmina, though . . .

Well.

After Sammy gave birth to her little girl, Carmina became obsessed. She'd dropped a thousand not-so-subtle hints about needing to know if she was getting another granddaughter, or her first grandson. Thorne had finally taken me aside, begging me to let his mom throw a party for us.

I'd never been good at saying no to him. The bastard.

"Nova," Sammy said, swaying into the room and looking unfairly gorgeous for someone who'd had a baby five months ago. "Should we put the gifts in here with you, or in the living room?"

"I don't need gifts." I sipped the lemonade, worried I'd be hobbling to the restroom no matter how slowly I drank it. "I need someone to fast-forward me so this baby isn't sitting on my bladder anymore."

She laughed, pulling her sleeves up, bracing herself for some hard work. "Okay. I'll put them by the toilet for you."

"Sammy! No!" Carmina gasped, chasing after her out of the room.

Giggles exploded from my lips. I covered my mouth, then winced, a pair of tiny elbows . . . or feet . . . or both stabbing inside my belly.

"Later," Thorne said, entering the room with Kain at his side. "I don't want to talk about it now."

Kain, cradling his five-month-old daughter, pursued his brother. "Someone has to take the job! I just assumed you'd go back to it, and—"

"Here she is," Thorne said, cutting Kain off, crossing toward me. "I was worried someone had let you wither away without food, and I was right." Leaning in, Thorne gave me a warm kiss—one a bit too passionate for company, but he'd never cared—and then handed me a cupcake. Half of the frosting was blue, the other half pink.

My stomach rumbled again. "Thank you." I took a bite and wiped at my mouth with a napkin from the stack on the table. "What were you two talking about?"

Thorne shared a look with Kain. "Nothing that matters."

"Tell her, man."

Sighing, Thorne leaned against the back of my chair with his hip. "The Dirty Dolls is officially opening next week. The lawsuit was settled, all parties are satisfied, I guess."

"Oh." Blinking, I tried to read his face. "Are you worried I'll be upset because you want to go back and work there?"

His forehead crinkled tightly. Bending low, Thorne kissed my temple, then my mouth—I knew he'd taste the sugary cupcake, but he licked his lips afterward as if he were enjoying it way too much. Like he was tasting me, too. "I'm not going back."

"You're not?" I asked, stunned . . . and secretly relieved.

"Of course. I've got more important things to put my energy into." Reaching down, he palmed my belly possessively. My entire body thrilled, my scalp tingling.

"How nice of you to leave it to me to find a replacement," Kain said, coming closer. He lightly jostled the baby, her eyes bright as ocean jewels when they moved to me. Her mouth was a pink dollop of jam. "You feeling okay these days, Nova?"

Leaning forward, I cooed. "I'm fine. Oh, but Kain, Julie's more beautiful each time I see her."

"Takes after her mother," he said, winking. Then he paused, considering me. "Want to hold her?"

"Always." Each time Kain and Sammy stopped by the estate since having the baby, I'd been taken with Julie. I couldn't get enough of snuggling the little girl. It helped remind me that my swollen feet and late-night insomnia were worth it.

He passed me his daughter, helping settle her in my arms. At five months old she was a wonderfully chunky child, her round cheeks and arm rolls delighting me. When she reached up, chewing her fingers and smiling, my ovaries exploded. "Seriously. So cute." I noticed Thorne was watching closely, his arm on the back of my chair. "You want a turn?"

"What, me?" Laughing, he held up his hands in defense. "She'll have time to get sick of me. Let's not rush it before she can walk."

"Come on," I said, kissing Julie's forehead. "You're her uncle. Use this as experience."

Kain crossed his arms, his dark eyebrows furrowing. "If you drop her, you're dead."

"I won't drop her," Thorne scoffed. He became focused, taking the baby from me extra carefully. I wasn't used to seeing him so nervous. In my husband's strong arms, Julie looked tiny. He cradled her head, even though she didn't need it. He treated her like she was a newborn. If my heart wasn't already full of this man, I'd have made room for him.

"It's time!" Carmina said, sweeping back into the room, a box in her hands. She led a train of people behind her. Several faces I knew: Francesca, Sammy, Scotch, Costello, Lulabelle—whom I'd met when Julie was born, and who clearly didn't know how to talk to me. The older sister had said maybe five words to me directly.

Costello placed an iPad on the table, near the edge so it could get everyone in the frame. A few clicks, and he had a video call going.

Maverick's wide jaw filled the screen. His face seemed bigger thanks to his huge grin. "I'm here!" he crowed. "I'm ready to know what my next grandchild is going to be!"

Carmina put the box on the table in front of me. Then she pantomimed kissing the iPad. "Honey," she said sweetly, "you seem very excited. You didn't put a bet on this, did you?"

"Of course not," Maverick said, scowling. "What an awful thing to gamble on."

"Well, I don't know what you're up to when I'm not there!"

"Nothing but work, darling. I promise."

"When I come back there next weekend, I'll know, so don't lie."

I giggled at their banter. It was obvious that, even with the distance, these two adored each other. Carmina made trips to Torino every month, staying for two weeks at a time. The rest of the days she lived at the estate with Thorne and me.

Francesca was here as well, but I sensed she was trying to figure out what to do with herself now that her other siblings had their lives getting off the ground. Lately, she'd dropped hints she might move to Torino to live in the castle with her dad as a *real* princess.

Maverick's attention moved to me. Under his rich blue eyes, I shifted in place. "I'm thrilled to find out what Thorne and Nova are having. Let's do this, the whole family is here."

Family. My pleased smile hurt my cheeks.

"Here you go," Sammy said, handing me a knife. The box was removed, leaving a round white cake on a plate. It had nothing to identify what color the batter was inside. But once I sliced through the frosting, revealing blue or pink, everyone would know what the baby in my belly was.

Our OB had sent the information to the bakery, ensuring no one but those bakers knew what I was having. That struck me as weird, suddenly—some strangers in a store, mixing batter, knowing what I was having before I did.

"Nova?" Thorne said my name gently. He'd returned Julie to Kain, and now he sat beside me, his hand in mine. "Having second thoughts?"

Looking at his worried mouth, at his tilted eyebrows and warm eyes, and feeling his concern in every molecule in the air . . . I wanted to say that second thoughts had gone out the window months ago. We were *here*, this baby was real and it was coming whether this cake was pink or blue or green.

Firmly I wrapped his fingers in mine, then around the knife. "Together," I said. "Let's see if we're having a prince or a princess."

Our rings touched, pressed tight as we cut into the cake. The room began clapping, squealing the second the blue-crumb center peeked through. At the same time, the little boy in my womb kicked me harder than ever. He was rolling, as if he was celebrating his own coming debut. Hearing all the people excitedly cheering for him before they'd met him.

And as I kissed Thorne, I knew our child had every reason to celebrate.

ABOUT THE AUTHOR

Photo © 2016 Kristen Carter

USA Today bestselling author Nora Flite firmly believes that the very best heroes are passionate, filthy, and slightly obsessive—which is why she features them in *all* her romances. Nora's always been a writer, which means that you'll have to pry her keyboard, pen, or some kind of magical future writing device out of her cold, dead fingers before she'll ever stop writing.

Nora lives in Southern California, where the weather is warm and she doesn't have to shovel snow—something she never loved in her tiny home state of Rhode Island. Nora loves to hear from her fans, so email her at noraflite@gmail.com, and visit her online at www.NoraFlite.com.